NEW EMBRACE

CINDY ERVIN HUFF

For my wonderful soulmate Charles Huff.
Fifty years in love with you is the greatest gift God has given me.

1

BITTERNESS AND GUILT

Isabella Melinda Marklin scurried ahead of her husband Ron. She reached the driver's side door of the red Dodge Durango first. Ron closed the gap between. His breath brushing across the top of her head. "I'm driving."

She faced him feeling for the handle and pulling the door open.

Anger flashed in his dark brown eyes. Melinda stood her ground.

"You have one of your migraines. "I'll drive." She climbed in before he could grab her arm.

"Fine." Ron moved to the passenger's side, slammed the door, and leaned back on the gray leather head rest. "It's so bright." His forearm covered his face.

"Here's your sunglasses." Melinda took them from the visor before gazing into the rearview mirror. The gravel driveway flowed beneath the tires. Her chest tightened with the gears shift into drive.

Ron adjusted the sunglasses. "Can you drive a little faster?"

"No." A tremble escaped her lips. White knuckles gripped the steering wheel. Fear wrestled her confident tone. "We've got time."

"You'd better be right." Ron massaged his temples with his index fingers. "If we're late it's all on you."

Typical.

Everything always seemed on her lately. Always her fault, always her problem. Blame had been the morning focus.

"What'd you do with my socks?"

"Why haven't you folded the laundry?"

"Did you break the iron? I wouldn't hand off this shirt to the homeless"

"You forgot to charge my phone again."

His harsh words produced her own headache which found solace in a bottle of pain reliever.

The silent treatment a welcome change. Sweet worship music streamed into the car comforting her soul relaxing her thoughts. Peace flowed from the melody. She turned the wheel and panic assailed her. Her wrist was bare. *I left my witnessing bracelet on the bathroom sink.* The colorful beads used to share the gospel. Oh, how she hated it. *He gets so mad when I forget it. Please, please don't notice.* Another reminder of her failure in the ministry.

"Turn off the radio. The music's killing my head."

"Maybe we should return home and you can rest."

Ron raised his head, lifted his sunglasses, and glared. "And give you another excuse. Six Sundays, Melinda, six times sitting in the pews and not helping with worship. Well, my migraine will not be your seventh excuse."

Melinda's knuckles ached on the steering wheel. Tight lips held back tears. Arriving at church in the middle of an argument would make things worse later. God forbid anyone would see them arguing. *That would be my fault too.* She hated being in ministry, on the worship team and under a magnifying glass in this congregation. *If I don't get away soon, I'll go insane. God forgive me.*

Ron made no mention of the headache once they arrived at the church. His spotless dress shirt and neat pressed Dockers (no thanks to her imperfect ironing ability) added to his confident air. His look had changed over the past few years from casual jeans and collar-length hair to short moussed hair and black dress shoes.

Ron wanted her to get a make-over. The CDs sales had switched her husband's focus. When they first married, Ron asked her to grow her hair out. "Sweetheart, the Scripture says long hair is a woman's glory." Now a file folder of acceptable hairstyles created by the church secretary lay in the bottom of her underwear drawer.

Maybe I should bleach my hair and spike it, wear my bra outside my blouse if he is so interested in a professional image. The bitter taste of her thoughts convicted her. *Father, I seek your peace again. Please be with Ron when he shares his new song and don't let my attitude hamper what you're going to do here today.*

"Blessing." Ron hugged each member of the worship team in turn. "How's the new baby, Mark." Ron's smile never giving time for a response before he continued.

"Angelina, nice dress."

He seemed to have pushed through the headache, making Melinda wonder if it was all an act to keep her in line.

"Melinda, sweetheart, go tell Graham to watch for my cues."

Mister sweetie pie is back. I swear... Every Sunday Ron used the same syrupy tone to issue the same instructions.

"Graham, you know." Melinda tried on a sincere smile.

The sound tech took a sip of his coffee and grinned. "Yeah, yeah."

Melinda headed back to the front of the auditorium muttering. "The mics worked. Why doesn't he tell Graham himself? Another irritating thing to add to my I-Hate-My-Life List." Her face warmed as people filled the pews. Fake smile in place. Wave at a few friends. Don't dare stop during the warm up to chat.

Once the worship team prayed together she gained composure. Ron was presenting his newest song, "I Am Your Bond Servant". The worship team had worked hard to get it right. Graham was recording it to add to Ron's growing collection of songs for his latest CD. Next month would be his first live concert.

She'd told Ron she was done. He'd laughed. "Sugar, you know you love it as much as I do." Then he'd squeezed her arm. The bruise covered by her sleeve.

Today would be her last performance. His last critique of her performance, her last time to pretend she cared.

Melinda took her place left of Trevor, the bass player with Angelina and Griffin the other backup singers. She preferred not being center stage. The service started with announcements and prayer. God's presence filled the stage when worship began. "I Am Your Bond Servant" was the last song in the set before the pastor's sermon. Ron, for once had given equal parts to all three singers as well as special orchestration for all the instruments. Her husband, in great form. He seemed connected with the Lord in a way Melinda hadn't seen in years. The crescendo before the last line seemed to lift everyone's hearts to God.

Ron finished the song, lifted his hand in praise and crumbled to the floor, knocking music stands and microphones in all directions. The clatter echoed through the sound system reverberating off the walls.

Melinda stood dazed, hands shook at her side, and legs rooted in place.

Trevor started CPR. Andrew, the guitarist, called 911.

Ron's vacant eyes stared heavenward.

Clamminess covered her skin.

The congregation erupted in screams, weeping, and concerts of prayer all over the sanctuary.

Her heart reached out to Ron, but her body betrayed her.

The paramedics entered the sanctuary in a slow-motion run. Before they reached the stage, blackness enveloped her.

THE COOLNESS of the stage floor greeted dulled senses. Muffled words. Gentle arms held her.

"Melinda." Maureen, her mother-in-law, hovered. "He's dead, dear. What are we going to do?"

Her blunt announcement rambled through Melinda's numb brain. He's dead. Who's dead? Ron's dead.

"Oh God! Oh God!" Her shrieks joined the congregation's. Guilt shrouded her. Relief mixed with guilt ate at her, and the packed suitcase in the trunk of her car.

2

BURYING THE PAST AND ESCAPING TO THE FUTURE

Four hours of being hugged and patted.

Four hours of "I'm sorry for your loss."

Four hours of "He was so gifted."

The track of instrumental music became a monotonous drone as it cycled through the funeral home sound system for the fifth time. Melinda's bun now a scraggly mess. The weight of her waist length hair causing a headache. Curses rolled in her head in response to the constant clichés spoken with every sympathetic pat. Colorful metaphors never thought of in the light of happier times.

She chewed on her lower lip to keep from vocalizing her bitter thoughts and draw more unwanted attention to herself.

"You OK, Isabella?" Her older sister's use of her first name a peaceful caress. Ron had insisted on calling her by her middle name, Melinda. The lines of mourners calling her Melinda reminder her how much she hated it. "Isabella, honey." Carla held a glass of water and a box of tissues. Her tender ministrations welcomed. *Just like Mom making sure I'm all safe and secure.* She missed her parents. Dad's ALS made it impossible for her mother to leave his side.

"Let's sit down." Carla placed her items on an end table. Then cloaked her younger sister in her arms and guided her to an overstuffed chair.

My Guardian Angel. Don't leave me. Isabella searched the compassionate face, a young version of their mother.

Long, gentle fingers pressed Isabella's stray locks back in place. "How you holding up?" The same comforting hand placed the water glass to her lips.

Isabella took a sip. Carla squeezed her shoulder before taking the neighboring seat. Ten years her senior, Carla's ever-present touches transferred comfort and hope, easing the burden. Unlike the thousands of unwanted pats from strangers that rubbed her grieving guilt-ridden soul even rawer. The line of mourners grew with each passing hour.

Her mother-in-law appeared tireless standing to receive and speak to each mourner. Maureen reveled in the attention, while Isabella wanted to find a closet and crawl into the dark recesses.

She sat facing forward, staring at the little box of Ron's ashes, hoping to be mistaken for a visitor and not be sought out for mumbled condolences. Two more hours of visitation then the funeral tomorrow.

"Ma'am." A gentle baritone caused her head to turn.

His army dress uniform decorated with ribbons contrasted with the wheelchair he maneuvered. Their eyes met, his presence drew her pain into the peace of those azure blues. They told her he understood.

Bawling on the shoulder of a total stranger seemed tempting but she held back. The tears fell. This soldier's unspoken sympathy brought more solace than the attempts of all those who had loved and admired her husband. The man's vulnerability matched her own, his silence soothed her ragged soul. After she composed herself, he handed her a tissue. Isabella blew her nose and wiped her tears.

"We grew up together. I know there are no words of comfort I can give when a guy like J-Boy leaves this world before his time." He extended his left hand again and nodded before releasing her hand.

Don't go. Stay. She watched a woman push his wheelchair toward the door.

"Who was that?" The question reminded her of Ming's presence. Her younger sister's sunny disposition and confident heart a contrast to her present melancholy. Ming hugged and rocked her back and forth. Their special hug full of love and comfort. "Sis, who was the guy?"

"He knew Ron as J-Boy." She tried to remember if he had mentioned an old friend in the army. Her husband never talked about the past. Instead taking the Scriptural reminder, Christ made all things new to his usual extreme. Severing ties with anyone outside his immediate sphere of influence.

Ming stared in the direction the wheelchair had been. "Really, he knew Ron when he preferred being Jeff back in his wild days. I didn't think any of his rapper buddies still kept in touch."

Isabella followed her sister's gaze. The hallway, clogged with mourners, blocked their view of anyone exiting the funeral home.

"There's food in the other room." Carla said. "You need to keep up your strength."

She nodded and stood. Ming took her hand and leaned on her shoulder. Her sisters' nearness, the one thing keeping her together.

ONE YEAR *later*

Maureen's shrill voice raised an octave. "What a terrible excuse. Ron continued to minister with migraines. So stubborn. At least come and ask for prayer."

While her mother-in-law lectured a reel of all the horrible things the woman had said in the past year played in Isabella's head.

"Melinda, why red? It's so street-walker." The dress had disappeared from her closet. Donated to Goodwill before she even had a chance to wear it.

"A widow must be careful." Maureen often shamed her when she wore modest capris. "Men assume you want *it* and need *it* because you've been with a man."

Isabella pushed the revue from her mind. The present tirade was tiring enough.

"I'd rather rest and wait for my migraine medicine to work." She kept her back to Maureen. A blush formed with the lie. "Please, go without me."

"Let me fix you some tea."

"No." Her voice sharper than she intended. "What time is it?"

"My, my, I mustn't be late. I swear, Melinda, you have an arsenal of excuses not to attend. This is the third Bible study you've weaseled out of. And when has anyone seen you at church? I suggest you pray for forgiveness while you hide under those covers."

Maureen slammed the door. Isabella waited. Heels scraped the stairs. The front door slammed. She went into action.

Two hours: her window of opportunity.

Maureen didn't care to socialize after the weekly women's Bible study. "One should go home and reflect on the truth one has learned from the Bible, rather than stand around chit chatting about unimportant things." *Get out of my head.*

"I've hidden away long enough."

Guilt heavy on her heart, she'd moved in with her mother-in-law after the funeral. Grief muddled her mind. A penance for her bad behavior toward her late husband. Isabella allowed Maureen to handle everything while she grieved. Reality bloomed, awakening her to her mother-in-law's controlling techniques. She needed to escape this self-imposed prison. When Isabella mentioned getting her own place, her cell phone had disappeared and her car sent out for repairs.

Peering in the closet, it took less than a minute to decide to leave all the church lady dresses with matching accessories. "No more Maureen's mini-me."

She filled her large gym bag with undergarments, jeans, tops, sneakers, flats and toiletries. Things her mother-in-law would never notice. Her backpack contained her laptop and a folder with all her personal documents for starting a new life. Sweaty-palm fear mixed with excited heart-flutters fueled her resolve.

She changed from her pajamas into her favorite jeans, the ones Maureen thought inappropriate for a widow. Then added a pink blouse and a black blazer. The mirror's reflection startling. Dark circles under her eyes made her soft brown skin appear worn. Isabella plaited her waist-long hair into a braid. One last appraisal of her appearance. "It'll do."

Adjusting her backpack on her shoulders with a cleansing sigh, she reached for the gym bag.

The new revelations concerning Ron's death had turned her guilt into anger. Freedom loomed on the horizon and she would grab it.

She'd prearranged a taxi pick-up through the Internet the previous night. Isabella watched the car arrive from her perch on the front step. Once it pulled away from the curb, her body relaxed. The cab stopped at First United Savings and Loan.

"Can you wait while I take care of some bank business?" The kind eyes of the cabby peered at her from the rearview mirror. "Then drop me at the airport."

"Sure, as long you aren't planning on robbing it." The large black man's deep laugh made her smile.

Maureen will feel robbed. "It shouldn't be long. Go ahead and keep the meter running." Isabella hung her purse over her shoulder and headed for the entrance.

The huge bank foyer reflected its 1920s design. Her shoes echoed on the marble floor. She tucked her purse close under her arm and surveyed the room. Isabella relaxed when she realized Henry Jackson, Maureen's favorite banker, wasn't there.

A tall dark-haired man rose from his desk and greeted her. "I'm Ryan. How may I help you today?"

"I'm moving away and want to close my accounts."

"Sure thing." He indicated the chair in front of his desk. "If I can have your account information, please." He pushed a small pad of paper across the desk for her to write her information on. "How would you like your money?"

"I'd like most of it wire transferred to this account." Isabella wrote a series of numbers on the pad. "The account is in my maiden name." Her father's suggestion of leaving her account open when she married had seemed ridiculous at the time. Dad thought they were rushing things. So, to appease him Isabella had agreed. *Thank you, Daddy.*

The bank clock showed the whole thing had taken less than fifteen minutes. A quarter hour of heart-racing anxiety. Shoving the pre-paid debit card and a few thousand in cash in her purse, she thanked Ryan. "I assume this transaction will be kept private."

"Of course, Does the other signatory know you left her the one checking account?"

"My mother-in-law will be in sometime this week." *And have one big hissy-fit when she finds the golden goose has run away and taken her eggs with her.* Ron obsessed about life insurance. The premiums became a financial strain. A source of arguments. His mother was the beneficiary on one policy. After his death, she'd burned through the money like tissue on fire.

Maureen, you're going to have to learn to budget....

"Melinda, dearest, Jeffrey told me to take a vacation, so I bought tickets for Reno."

"You can't just write checks without asking me."

"But he insisted."

"Maureen, Ron is dead and whatever he insisted on still needs to be discussed with me."

"But, Melinda, it's my money."

Isabella recalled her haughty look. It reminded her of a scene from an old movie where the matriarch dismisses her servant. This scenario, the beginning of the end of their less than loving relationship. The bank, the first step to reclaiming her life from everything turned ugly in it. Heaviness left her as she stepped through the exit, warm sunshine washed her face. She opened the back door to the cab.

"Airport, please."

~

TICKET IN HAND she approached the Gate B42. The first-class ticket, a whim purchase, to check something off her personal bucket list. The middle age clerk at the counter repeated the same question he'd asked every passenger ahead of her. "Window or aisle seat."

Her mouth curved up as she made another decision on her own.

"Window."

The clerk printed the boarding pass and with a practiced smile added. "Enjoy your flight."

She'd be airborne by the time Maureen pulled into her driveway. She imagined Maureen not bothering to check on her until she didn't appear for lunch. Then she'd find the note on the bed. Tomorrow she'd visit the bank and attempt to retrieve the lost money. *Oh, the scene she would make.*

The view from the plane window change from miniature plats of land to tall skyscrapers as the jet touched down in Chicago.

O'Hare Airport's sprawling walkway provided a nice hike to the baggage claim. Wearing her backpack reminded Isabella of the time spent in Greece with a few college friends viewing the ancient architecture. That summer she'd almost changed majors. Architecture a better career choice in many minds. But would it have matter? Ron had insisted she stay home hinting art wasn't a career. Would he have rejected architecture as well? Arguing it wasn't a feminine pursuit or... *Stop it! The might have beens left with my choice to marry Ron. There is no going back only forward.*

She joined the mass of departing passengers gathered at the luggage carousel, and people watched. During her before-Ron years, a sketch pad captured these moments. Now, the muse was locked in a cage, it took too much effort too free.

A boy three or four rolled his ninja turtle suitcase alongside his parents. Isabella clutched her chest. *Ronny would have been three last month.* A child's squeal of delight accompanied his run toward an older couple. He dropped his bag and jumped into the man's arms. The hugging scene dug up a deep sadness. Tears glistened. She spotted her gym bag on the carousel, grabbed it and headed toward the cab stand.

3

STRUGGLING FOR INDEPENDENCE

Aurora, Illinois

Dan Sweeney slummed on the floor of his utility room trapped behind his new water heater. The old water heater tilted against the new one. His wheel chair out of reach. The whole leg wedged between the new water heater and the wall. While his stump throbbed from his attempts to rise. His struggles to free his belt loop from the piping forced him to call for help. The one thing he hated.

Dan had bought the house with a VA loan and partially finished the rehab before his accident. Eighteen months and three surgeries later he could get back on target even if his progress was as slow as an old lady with arthritis.

"Finally." The sound of car tires on the gravel drive caused Brutus, his service dog, to rise from his place beside him. The canine had kept the panic attacks away while they waited. Brutus barked, the front door opened, and a slow growl turned to a whine, then a happy bark of recognition.

"Down, down, you're killin' me here." Steve's voice grew louder as he came closer to the utility room.

"Brutus, down." Dan's German Shepherd Pit mix jumped and tried to lick his friend's face. "Brutus, to your bed."

The dog obeyed walking a snail's pace toward his bed—a rug on the floor in the living room.

Steve grabbed several paper towels from the roll near the sink and wiped slobber off his hands. His tall frame blocking the light from the kitchen window creating an angelic silhouette from Dan's perspective on the floor. *Note to self, get blinds for the windows.* He crossed his arms.

"Can you be any slower?"

Steve turned toward the utility room and shook his head with a smirk. Then dried his fingers one at a time with paper towel. "Can you be any dumber?"

Throwing the toweling in the trash, he strode toward Dan and stared down at him. Humiliation warmed Dan's face as he looked up at his friend.

"Ok. You're right. Now that I've admitted I'm an idiot, can you help a guy out here?"

"How'd you get stuck?"

"My belt loop caught on the piping after I fell."

"Well, super dude, I guess a one-legged man can't do everything by himself."

"Shut up and help me."

Steve righted the water heaters, locked the wheels on Dan's wheelchair and assisted Dan into the seat. "Geesh, Bro, couldn't even wait for your prosthetic leg to be repaired before you tried this on your own. Least ways your balance would be better."

"The VA Hospital takes forever to make repairs. Might have it next week." Dan folded his arms across his chest. "Got tired of cold showers."

Steve surveyed the home repair mess. He grabbed a mop to sop up the water puddling near the old heater. "How'd you empty this old tank?"

"One bucket at a time." Dan lifted the bucket still upright near his chair and placed it on his lap.

Then he released the locks on his wheels and rolled toward the kitchen. "Want coffee?"

"Sure." Steve took a seat at the kitchen table.

Dan emptied the bucket in the sink before he took two mugs from hooks under the counter and poured coffee.

He pulled up the tray attachment on the side of his wheelchair. Placed the mugs on the tray and rolled up to the table. Steve grabbed the mugs and Dan flipped the tray back out of the way and rolled his wheelchair under the table.

"Called Allen," Steve said adding sugar to his coffee. "He's taking over his dad's plumbing business."

"I didn't ask you to." The coffee soured in his stomach.

"Well, I hate messing with plumbing. It always takes ten times longer when you don't have a clue what you're doing."

"I read this article." Dan tamped down his frustration at Steve's eye roll. He gripped the cup handle, "I lost my leg not my brain."

The clink of the stirring spoon signaled Steve was holding back.

"Come on. It can't be that hard." Dan said.

"If you know what you're doing." Steve pointed at his friend and took a sip of coffee. "I watched my dad try to stop the pipes from leaking after he installed a new water heater. Five hours later and a lot of cursing under his breath, he got the leaks sealed."

"I'm not your dad."

"True, but you have zero patience when these projects don't come together." Steve look through cabinets.

"There are no cookies." It galled Dan to admit his friend was right. "How much does Allen charge?"

"He's reasonable and he can knock this out in under two hours. And..." Steve waggled a bag of cookies he found in the back of a cupboard. "He owes me, so it's free."

"I don't want charity." Dan rubbed his stump. A phantom Charlie horse ached in his non-existent calf.

"This isn't charity. I did some free legal work for him. He fixes your water heater, and you share those awesome steaks you've been talking about with me, a finder's fee." Steve grinned opening the bag of cookies.

"I'll light up the grill." Dan conceded, snagging a cookie before Steve ate them all. "Hey, thanks for coming to my rescue, Bro." Dan grabbed a couple more cookies. "I can't help pushing myself to do more."

"I get that. But, that old water heater has a brass tank and that's down right heavy. Even Allen may need a little help." Steve started on his sixth cookie. Dan envied the guy's metabolism. Dan keep his weight in check. If he gained weight, his new prosthetic would be too tight. Lose weight the artificial leg chaffed against the stump. Until the loss of his leg, weight was never an issue. He'd enjoyed working toward a six pack just because. Now he worked out to stay fit enough to deal with his loss. "Hold up there. I promised you steak not my last bag of chocolate chips."

"Sorry" Steve secured the bag. "I was thinking."

"Yeah, my food always disappears when you're thinking."

A wrinkled-brow formed on Steve. Never good.

"I've been giving some serious thought to your social life."

Coffee spewed out Dan's lips. "What? Since when is my social life your responsibility, man."

"You're my best friend. I'm concerned about you. Your whole life revolves around work, school and vegging here."

"Not true. I... I go to church. I visit with my uncle every week."

"Your uncle is your pastor so that's doesn't count as two."

"Okay. I play video games."

"Alone." Steve drove his point home.

"I walk my dog." Dan said.

"Even he's male." Steve laughed.

Irritation caused Dan's jaw to tighten. "Your hinting my social life is lame."

"And so's your kitchen wallpaper."

"Yeah, well, rooster wallpaper came with the house. Removal is on my to-do-list."

"Hey, me a a and a few friends can strip it in a few hours."

"I'll get to it when I get to it."

"Dan, we'd help—not take over the job."

This investment turned into a remodel for his needs now that the Army didn't want him. The missing leg drained away the satisfaction of doing the repairs himself. *Quite the pity party, Sweeney.*

"Would I have to grill again?"

"Nah, cook your world-famous beef stew, and invite us over to watch the Bulls on your awesome big screen, and we'd be good."

"I thought only the homeless worked for food."

Steve's snorting laugh brought a chuckle from Dan.

"Bro, you sound like a pig stuck under a freight train."

"Enough." Steve held his side, while he wrestled his laugh into submission. Once he gained his composure he swatted Dan's arm.

"Let me see your list."

Dan pointed to the refrigerator. Steve retrieved it from under a Go Army magnet without leaving his seat. He grabbed a pen from the table and added to Dan's list.

Steve held the list just close enough for Dan to read his giant script but out of his reach.

"Get a life. Get a girl. Get a haircut." Dan reached for the list, but Steve stepped away hiding it behind his back.

"You need to put yourself out there."

"And you sound like a commercial for one of those dating sites." Dan said.

"Well, maybe you should try one."

"I will if you do."

"Not going to happen."

"Ha!"

The men's stare down brought silence. Steve opened the cookie bag, retrieved one and pointed it at his friend. "I'm worried about you, Dan. Major worried." He popped the cookie in his mouth before continuing. "You've never been the lady's man. But since the accident. Your free time is divided between vegging here in the house or trying to do insane things like change out a water heater all by yourself."

"Yeah, so, your point?"

"Trade this solitary life for a new one."

Dan rolled his chair to the kitchen window. He noticed the spring flowers were starting to bloom under the carpet of leaves that never got raked. "You're right. But I'm not ready to trade yet." *Maybe never.*

"There are some wonderful godly women at my church's singles group. "I'm sure any of them would go out with you."

"So, your singles group is a dating service."

"No. Come on Dan. It's not like that. Make a few friends—and you know." Steve's crooked smile followed by a wink. "Might find your soul mate." Before Dan shared a rebuttal, Steve rambled on. "At least you'd be part of a great Bible study and others to talk to besides Brutus."

"I'll think about it." *But there is no way.*

The doorbell ended the uncomfortable conversation. Brutus dashed to the door wiggling and barking.

"I'll get the door. You find those steaks." Steve said.

"Hey, wait until I put Brutus in my bedroom. Thanks for calling Allen for me."

"No problem."

Dan closed the protesting Brutus into his room. "Better not be any girls with Allen."

"Never thought of that." Steve chuckled. He opened the door for the plumber.

4

A NEW PLACE

Isabella traced the path of long sloping driveway to the garage. Where a steep outside staircase lead to an apartment. Her heart quickened, doubt pierced through resolve.

"Why hadn't I called ahead? Maybe we'll catch up then I'll find my own place." A lame plan seemed better than assuming her sister would receive her with open arms. The shame of failing as pastor's wife kept her from visiting. Her mother's need to know every detail of her life contrasted Ron's insistence of the perfect façade. It had been easier to avoid her family.

Isabella hoisted her bags from the curb. Taking a deep breath, she headed toward the apartment.

A two-tone Toyota Camry sat parked before of the garage. The front doors were beige while the rest of the vehicle red. A smile formed at the familiar. Same car her sister bought before college. "Can't believe she's hung on to Ol' Bernie." Isabella strode up the stairs.

She rang the doorbell, stepped further back on the landing and watched her sister through the half-closed blinds on the door window. Ming put her laptop aside and rose from the couch. Her brows formed a W. Irritation filled her face. A knot stuck in Isabella's throat. Maybe coming had been a mistake.

Ming jerked open the door. "What now!" Her hand went to her chest and her lips formed a perfect O. Then a huge smile took its place.

Isabella drank in the sight. Ming's coal-black chin-length hair had white highlights. The joyful grin caused her almond eyes to sparkle.

"Issy." She hugged her with the intensity of a mother finding her lost child. Tears trailed her face. "I can't believe you're here." Ming released her. "Sorry, for yelling. I thought you were Maggie, my ex-roommate's cousin. She always drops by unannounced." Ming pressed a hand to her sister's cheek, a gesture reminiscent of their first meeting on Isabella's adoption day. Warm. Inviting. Home.

Isabella picked up her bags and entered the apartment. Tears brimmed her eyes. "Can I stay?"

"Can you stay?" Ming's tiny frame quivered with delight. "You're an answer to my prayer." After hugging her again she stepped back to gaze at her sister.

"Wow! You look…"

"Old, haggard, long in the tooth." Isabella said. Shame crept up her neck.

"No, tired. You look very tired." Ming gave her another hug. "I missed you, so much."

"Me too. You, on the other hand look fantastic."

"Always the flatterer." Ming smiled. "I just lost my room-mate last month. The truth, I asked her to leave. Too much of a party girl." Ming grabbed Isabella's gym bag with one hand and pulled her toward the center of the living room with the other.

"So, I can stay?" Isabella said.

"Forever." Ming dragged the heavy bag to the empty bedroom. "You'll have to sleep on the couch until we get a bed in here."

Isabella surveyed the room. Smaller than her room at Maureen's. *I can see so much potential. Bare walls to decorate as I please. My taste not Maureen's.* Hope trickled through her heart at the prospect of a new beginning. She walked to the closet and set her bags in it.

"Look, Gracie left hangers." Ming flipped them, the rattling sound echoed in the empty room.

"Tea?"

Isabella nodded and went to the couch. "That sounds perfect." Looking with unseeing eyes as she tamped back another urge to cry. "Your apartment is adorable."

"I moved here three years ago."

The gentle barb reminded Isabella how much she'd neglected her sister. Unlike her mom, Ming never pried or criticize.

"And it's only half adorable." Ming's voice carried from the tiny kitchen. "Gracie took her half of adorable." Returning with a cup of Chai tea and a plate of cookies, she placed them on the Rattan coffee table. Ming sat with her leg tucked underneath her on the other end of the French provincial couch. "It's been weird living alone. Gracie was bratty and overbearing, and our last argument was a doozy. I'll admit, at times though, being alone is worse."

Isabella nodded, accepted the cup.

They sat in comfortable silence. Ten years since they'd shared a room and the quiet, still golden. Their adoptions had been a month apart. Neither knowing English, they had their own language—a mixture of Chinese and Spanish for the first year. "Ming, I want to apologize for ..."

"For getting married, moving away and having a life." Ming smile, her hand dismissing any further explanation.

Isabella swallowed the lump in her throat. "Catch me up on everything."

"Well, for one, my friends call me Mindy. I opened my own salon a few months back, and have three other women renting chairs from me." Sipping her tea before continuing, "And before you ask. None of them are Asian."

Isabella chuckled, her body relaxing more with the effort. Ming got so frustrated with ethnic stereotypes. Being raised with siblings of other races gave the girls a unique take on life. "What's the name?"

"International Beauty. When I advertised for renters, I was fortunate to get three women of varied ethnicity. Meghan is Irish, Jaton is African-American, and Consuelo is Latina. I own the salon. Well, the bank and me. When I can afford to remodel the upstairs, I want to offer other salon services. Right now, we do hair." Ming scooted closer to her sister placing her head on Isabella's shoulder. "So, tell me why you are here."

"I ran away."

"It's about time."

Another chuckle from Isabella broke the tension she brought to the silence. "You've always been on my side."

"Always."

"You're so good to me. I don't deserve it."

"Why say that?" Ming's voice sharp as her brows collided. "Still putting yourself down."

"I...can't."

"More like you won't."

Isabella's vision blurred. "Sorry."

"Shh, stop it." Ming scooted across the couch and clutched her sister's hand. "I wanted you here. I've been asking God to bring you here. I need my sister."

"You have? You do?"

Deep sobs shook her body. Ming rocked and cooed. Waves of cleansing tears joined the rhythm of her sister's caress. "Issy, it's okay to cry. Get it all out."

Her words helped wash away another layer of guilty grief. Opening flood gates stopped up since her baby died and the whole world tilted out of control. Ming pulled her in a firm embrace and stroked her hair. "Your free now."

"Maureen didn't know I was leaving. I packed up this morning and left her a note."

"Any plans?"

"Find myself again—whatever that means." Isabella took the offered tissue. How she missed her family. "How are the folks?"

"Dad's got a special thingy to help him talk. The ALS has taken his speech" Ming's voice was laced with sadness for a moment. In a cheerier tone, she added. "He can even access Facebook with a blink of his eye. He loves keeping in touch."

"I'll have to get a page." Ron never allowed her to post on their joint account. A fresh Facebook profile for a new beginning. "How's Dad coping?"

"Mom says she is amazed how optimistic Dad is about life. He gets bummed, but more often he battles on trusting God day by day."

Isabella recalled Googling ALS, an autoimmune disease that robbed all body function over time ending in death. She'd wept at the prognosis. The last Thanksgiving with Ron they spent with her parents. Tears had battled for a place on her cheek when her once active father had to be spoon-feed. Ron refused to hug her Dad afraid he'd dislodge the breathing tube in his throat. She'd stayed by his side searching for one-side conversation that might interest him. Ron had gotten out his guitar, together they sang. She remembered his joyful smile.

"I need a bit of Dad's soaring spirit."

"So, how come you're not at the folks?"

"Thought about it. Mom has her hands full. She might appreciate the help, but Maureen has their address. You on the other hand are—a mystery." Isabella felt foolish admitting it.

"Ah, I love a good mystery." Ming laughed. "You know Mom has lots of help. Carla's daughter, Beth, is an in-home care nurse. She loves caring for Grandpa. Ken's son, Jason, lives there, so if Mom has a need at night he's available. Their church family brings in food a few days a week. Her ladies Bible study group cleans her house once a month."

Ming snagged a cookie before heading to the kitchen with their empty cups. She took a bite, her face expressing appreciation before she continued. "When you're up to it, go visit. But living there would add more on Mom's plate. She's told me a hundred times when I've offered."

Isabella reached for her parent's portrait on the end table. The selfish-daughter guilt melted, but the longing to see her dad before the ALS took him remained.

"I plan to pay rent and pull my own weight around here." She raised her voice to be heard in the kitchen. "I came to start over."

"Wonderful." Ming handed her a fresh drink. "We can go shopping for new furniture for your room tomorrow, unless you have a U-Haul parked out front."

"No, all my worldly possessions are here. At least the ones I care to have."

"Tomorrow we shop and get a make-over for you."

"Sounds wonderful." Isabella peered over her cup. "Your idea of a make-over is quite different from mine, I'm sure." She pulled her braid across her shoulder fingering it.

"Hey, I'm a professional." Ming gave a mocked scowl then smiled. "I promise you'll look fantastic. I picture shoulder-length with a few highlights."

Isabella threw her braid back over her shoulder breathing in the jasmine scent from the diffuser on the coffee table. The fragrance produced a calm. A small measure of hope rose in her chest.

"Maybe we can squeeze clothes shopping in."

"You are speaking my language." Ming said.

Isabella's breath came easier now, the tension left her shoulders. Ming's very presence made her life better.

"You have no idea how much I need to be here."

"Well, I am so glad you are." Ming rose from her chair. "Let's go to Bally Doyle for an early dinner."

"My treat." Isabella smiled with the proclamation. Money wasn't a barrier anymore. What a delicious thought.

"Hey, I never turn down a chance for a free meal."

They drove to downtown Aurora. Leaving Bernie in the parking garage, they walked a few blocks to the Irish Pub and Restaurant.

Ming opened the door for her sister. "Don't you just love the ambiance? It's a converted dress factory."

Isabella admired the tall ceilings, wood trim and unique décor.

"Before we're seated you have to look around." Ming grabbed her hand. "Each room is decorated with pieces rescued from demolished churches or renovations"

"Wow. Look at the artwork." The portraits from yesteryear filled a beauty starved void in her soul. "Hey, is that a confessional?"

"Yeah." Ming pointed to her left. See the organ, it's a door to a private dining room."

Isabella drank in the creative ambiance. "It's got a wonderful old world feel to it."

"Even the restrooms are artsy. The stalls are made of antique doors."

The two sat at a table near an old safe used to store table settings and extra linens. Irish music filled the restaurant pub.

A short-skirted waitress brought their menus. Ming took charge. "We'll have water."

"Hey sis, we're ordering boxties. An Irish version of a tortilla. They're delicious." She folded the menu with the declaration.

Isabella's neck ached from trying to see every corner of the room without leaving her chair. She envisioned Maureen's shocked expression if she saw them eating in a bar. The thought made Isabella smile. Not one muscle tightened into a cower. No careful worded reply to the picture of Maureen's scowl came to mind. Ming's joyful presence a buffer for her thoughts.

The Irish fare was delicious. The boxties had a variety of fillings. Hers a flat bread filled with potatoes, peas and beef. The home-made chips crisp and salted to perfection were addictive. The girls ate two basketsful as they caught up. Laughter sprinkled throughout the childhood reminiscing. Isabella's sides ached from her sister's stories. When the bar began to fill, Ming look at her cell phone.

"Hey it's six o'clock. No wonder its getting crowded. Time to take a quick tour of downtown before we go home. Isabella reached for the check. Ming gave her a mischievous grin. "Guess what's downstairs below this very restaurant." She leaned forward, grinning, "The Basement of the Dead."

"What?"

"A laser tag game where you get to shoot Zombies. On Halloween, it has a pretty impressive haunted house." She laughed and pointed. "That look is priceless. All shock and awe."

Isabella schooled her expression, embarrassed. "I'm sorry, the church Ron and I attended might have boycotted it."

"Well, my church chooses to be proactive. Living River created a Haunted House a few years back. We designed it to show the consequences of sin. You know dead, bloody gangbangers, a wrecked car from a drunk driver, scenes of misplaced faith and hidden abuses. It was wonderfully dramatic. The last scene, Jesus on the cross. When he said, 'It is finished' and bowed his head some visitors cried."

"Creative, wow."

"We offered hot dogs and burgers to those waiting to enter. People came for the food, went through the house and left challenged."

Isabella paid their tab and they walked hand in hand along New York Street. The architecture caught Isabella's eye. Ming pointed out buildings, sharing bits of their history. "Ahead of us is the Hollywood Casino."

"Not my thing." Maureen found gambling was acceptable. *There is something so thrilling about watching that little ball spin on the roulette wheel."* Stop it. Stop it. Who cares what Maureen thinks?

Ming headed them in the other direction. "It looks like rain, maybe." The clouds menaced in the distance. "I want to show you the Paramount. A theatre built in the early 1900s. First air conditioned theater outside of Chicago. And the acoustics are awesome. There are no bad seats."

Walking through the parking garage they shaved several minutes off their walk. They emerged on Galena Boulevard headed uptown toward the Paramount. Its vintage marquee called to them from blocks away.

"Since when did you become the theater buildings history expert?"

"Steve worked there as an usher during high school."

"Who is this Steve?"

Ming's cheeks pinked.

"A friend from church. He helped me get settled here."

She pointed at the Paramount, changing the subject.

"Did you know Johnny Depp filmed the theater scene for the *Scarface* movie here? Aurora has lots of historical homes. "According to Steve, filmmakers find Aurora a great location for period movies."

Isabella nodded, a knot forming in her throat. Her sister appeared happy with her new life. *Oh, Ming it used to be us against the world. You have friends, a church family and I have... a lot of baggage to get out of my life. Like these old buildings, I need a new purpose.*

Before they could reach the theater, the clouds darkened and the wind picked up adding to her growing melancholy.

Ming grabbed her sister's hand. "It's up to you. But I think we should head for the car."

"Fine by me."

The two ran back to the parking garage, purses covered their heads against the impending rain. They slid to a stop in the entrance while rain pelted the sidewalk. Laughing they walked toward ol' Bernie.

"You're not embarrassed to be seen in this thing?" Isabella waited for Ming to unlock the car.

Ming wiggled her key for several seconds. Then she pressed her tongue in her cheek, her deal with the car ritual.

"Ah, there we go." Ming smiled and pumped her arm in the air. After sliding behind the wheel, she unjammed the passenger door with a sharp kick.

"Yes." She said. "Get in. You've insulted Bernie. He might not let you out again if you don't keep your thoughts to yourself."

"Yes, ma'am." Isabella jerked the stuck seatbelt free, releasing a giggle in the process.

Ming's antics were reminiscent of happier times. Isabella closed her eyes and savored the laughter. The piney smell of the air freshener tickled her nose. Her mind took snapshots of the sensations. Capturing the moment. Adding it to other pleasant moments. Memories from far in the past.

Before the loss of RJ.

Before Ron changed.

Before his death.

And before her self-imposed imprisonment.

5

A MAKEOVER

Ming unlocked the door to her salon, stepped in and flicked on the overhead light.

"What do you think?"

Isabella scanned the old Victorian repurposed into a salon. Stunning. Classic lines painted in neutral shades. A chic appeal. Ten foot ceilings created an open floor plan. Pillars placed around the room divided cosmetologist's areas. Each space had a cabinet with drawers, a large mirror and a black stylist chair. Decorated to suit the taste of its occupant. Photos of international beauties sporting the latest hair styles covered the walls.

"This is gorgeous. I am so proud of you."

Ming's smile reflected her pride. "Together we tried to bring as many of our regular clients from our former jobs." She directed Isabella to her chair. "For me that was sixty percent."

Tying a red plastic cape around Isabella neck, Ming didn't miss a beat in her conversation. "Jaton has a cousin who works at Print Magic, he gave us a great deal on coupons. We spent last Sunday afternoon finding places to put them. We've advertised in a mailer and mailing lists that target 300,000 homes in Aurora and the surrounding areas. Print Magic did the bulk mailing for us."

"Wow! Sounds like overkill." Isabella watched Ming undo her braid. Maybe cutting her hair was overkill too. She pressed her lips, her reflection pensive in the mirror.

"The statistics are one new customer for every 10,000 flyers or mailers. So, we hope for a boost in new clients. We're offering a discount on their first visit."

She brushed out Isabella's hair and pulled it back in a low pony tail, scissors poised. Isabella resisted the urge to close her eyes.

"Locks of Love will use your hair in a wig for a cancer patient."

Ming snipped her hair just above the rubber band.

"That's nice." She blinked away tears, staring at the length of hair on the counter.

"Now for the transformation." Ming turned her chair away from the mirror.

Isabella took a cleansing breath. "Not going to let me watch?"

"Not on your life. Your pained expressions are too much." She laughed while mixing the highlight color.

"I am so impressed with your business and decorating sense." Envy raised its grotesque head in her heart. *Look how much my baby sister has accomplished sense college. Her dreams a reality. Mine...* she slapped the villain in her into silence. Then she smiled at Ming.

"If my hair transformation is as stunning as this shop, I will look awesome."

"Prepare for awesome."

Isabella listened to her sister's chatter while she added highlights.

"I want to see what you're doing."

"No way. If you see it halfway done, you'll freak. Now be still while I finish the highlight foils. No wiggling."

"Slave driver."

"Isn't she ever." The cheerful voice belonged to a slender black woman with a blond weave. "Mindy keeps us on our toes."

"Jaton, meet my sister Issy."

"Hey, girl, your sister says nothing but wonderful things about you. Are you here for a visit?"

"I moved here." Isabella liked this woman's genuine smile.

"She's staying with me forever." Ming patted Isabella's shoulder before adding the last foil. "Under the dryer you go, so I can gossip about you to Jaton."

ISABELLA EXAMINED her hairstyle in the mirror turning her head from side to side. Deep red highlights in her now shoulder-length dark brown hair, a new beginning. "I look ten years younger."

"That's disappointing. I was going for twenty." Ming placed the pony tail she'd snipped off into a bag.

The heaviness of loss now gone as she watched her sister place the bag in a drawer. Something from Isabella's past giving value to another. She tossed her head, the shorter hair settled back into place. Ming removed the cape and swept the floor of the shorn hair. The broom gathered each strain and pushed it to an auto vacuum that suck the hair into a bin. *God, is it possible to remove my brokenness so easily?*

Ming grabbed her purse. "Time for some serious shopping."

THE FOX VALLEY MALL, a labyrinth of specialty shops and traditional anchor stores, greeted the women as Ming pulled Bernie into the first available parking spot. They entered near J.C. Penney and headed toward Macy's.

"First stop, the cell phone kiosk." Ming grabbed her arm.

"Other than you, who'd call me?"

"Well, with a new life comes new friends." Ming's giggle caused passersby to stare. She bent over the counter to peruse the merchandise. "Besides, job hunting requires a cell phone."

Isabella never cared if she had a phone or not. Ron was the one who insisted on the fancy apps. Half the time she forgot to charge hers. She looked up at the acne-faced teenage boy. "I want a simple phone."

"You'll need texting and a camera." Ming added.

"Why do I need a camera?"

"When your artistic muse returns—and it will—you may want to capture an image to paint later."

"Always the optimist."

The phone Isabella settled on still had too many apps. But it made Ming happy.

"Are you planning on tutoring me?"

Her sister 's excitement over the purchase overshadowed her doubts.

"I'll get you up to speed. You'll be walking into walls texting like the rest of the world."

Isabella pushed a sigh though her lips. Ming grabbed her hand and headed through the crowd.

They found a bedroom set at a consignment shop. The manager promised next-day delivery. Isabella bought a few new outfits and continued her makeover at the Este Lauder counter at Carson's. The bags of make-up and cleansers rested in her new purse. After the spree, they plopped on a bench in the commons of the mall, arranging their purchases on the bench between them.

"Now, you look twenty years younger." Ming squeezed Isabella's hand.

"If you say so."

"Concealer worked wonders on those black rings under your eyes."

"They were pretty bad." Isabella pulled a small mirror from her purse. "I don't know this person."

"Don't worry, you'll enjoy getting acquainted." Ming stood gathering her bags. "Where to next?"

"Home. I'm exhausted."

"I agree. Want to catch a bite first. I'm starving."

Let's grab soup and a sandwich from Panera's to-go."

"Let's order from the one closer to my apartment.

"But I saw one here."

"Did you see the line? We could order online and pick it up than eat in our new fuzzy slippers."

"Sounds good."

"Ok. I'll do the ordering because your new cell phone isn't charged yet."

"Fine, here's my debit card."

She found it with ease in her new wallet. It had been freeing to shred the numerous credit cards her mother-in-law insisted she carry. Maureen's credit reflected her unstable emotional state. At first, she thought her mother-in-law's spending was temporary—a way to grieve her loss. But the pile of credit card statements each month proved otherwise.

"Done and done." Ming's voice broke through her musings. "By the time we cross town our order will be ready."

"This has been so much fun. I haven't enjoyed shopping in a long time. Five new outfits."

"And the new shoes." Ming added.

Isabella looked forward to getting to know her new self.

6

NEW BEGINNING

Isabella blow-dried her new style. Ming had worked wonders. The long hair had added years to her age and amplified her grieving features. One more glance in the mirror confirmed her make-up was perfect. Isabella now applied it daily. Something her mother-in-law and late husband had discouraged. Ron said she was a natural beauty, yet he often paid compliments to the overly made-up women of the congregation. The hypocrisy hurts.

"Well, Isabella Melinda Wilson keep your mind in the present." Her reflection straightened at her rebuke. "Focus on dressing for success and the interview."

She had an hour before her meeting with the manager at Hobby Life. A closet full of new clothes made it hard to choose her attire for the day. After several tries she'd decided on black slacks, a turquoise blouse and her favorite black jacket. The ankle length black boots with two inch heels gave her confidence. Isabella fumbled at first with the clasp on her three-chain silver necklace—remembering how much she'd relied on her husband to help with clasps and troublesome zippers. This memory warmed her. Her shoulder's quivered as she recalled his kisses on her neck. At the beginning of their marriage he'd look for opportunities to be with her. These were the memories she tried to replay.

Isabella reached for the jacket lying on her four-poster bed. A smile played on her lips. She adjusted her jacket collar and grabbed her purse from the floor near the foot board. Isabella ran her hand over the rich wood finish. It belonged to her. She chose the style. No one to dismiss her taste.

"Thank you, Ming, for this new start." Tears glistened in her eyes, her lashes batted them away. *Like when we were kids, except... it's not.*

She headed to her car. She'd splurged and bought new. Her Prius was silver with a leather interior. Forty-five miles a gallon was impressive. The car's key fob enabled her to start it from anywhere. No shivering in the winter until the car warmed.

Hobby Life's parking lot was full. The warehouse store had a large lot. Ming had told her their prices brought people from as far away as Chicago. Her sweaty palm gripped the door handle. The main aisle lead to the back of store and the employee entrance. Classical music played overhead. She fisted her hand and gathered her wits before knocking on the door marked office.

"Isabella." The stocky, balding manager offered her a seat across from his desk. His office cluttered with open boxes of inventory. "I'm Kevin Clayton." He perused her resume. "You have little work experience."

"I married right out of college. My husband was in the ministry. Since his death..."

"No need to explain. I wish I could say this job requires artistic flair and creativity. But if you can learn to run a cash register, stock shelves and smile at difficult customers you're our girl."

"My experience serving with my late husband helped me smile at disagreeable people." No need to explain Ron was the disagreeable one.

"We pay minimum wage with opportunity for advancement. This is part-time."

"I understand." She didn't need the money, instead something to fill her days while she discovered herself.

She left the store with her employee packet and her training schedule. Now maybe her life could begin. Hunger nagged, so she grabbed sandwiches and soup to-go from Panera and text her sister she was bringing lunch.

~

"MY LIFESAVER HAS ARRIVED." Ming sprayed hair spray on a gray-haired customer. "This is my sister. Issy?"

"Your sister?" The lady's confused expression made Isabella smile.

"Yes I am."

"We're twins, you know." Ming held a mirror for the woman to see the back of her head.

"You two look nothing alike." Her eyes fixed on Isabella. "Why, you're not even the same race."

"We aren't?" Ming feigned shock. Isabella felt sorry for the woman and rescued her.

"Our parents adopted us at the same time and we shared a room. Ming always tells everyone we are twins."

"Who is Ming?"

"That's me." Ming smiled. "But my friends, like you, Clare, call me Mindy."

"For a minute, there I thought my old age was effecting my eyesight." The senior citizen reached into her purse and handed Ming cash.

"There's a generous tip. You always do a wonderful job. The girls in my senior ladies group are so jealous."

Ming retrieved Clare's cane from its place leaning against the wall.

"Thank you, dearie." Clare patted her hand. "I tell the girls the Japanese are the best hairstylists." The bell over the door rang. "There's my ride. I'll see you next week, hun."

Once the door closes behind Clare, Isabella smiled. "Japanese?"

"Well, you know all Asians look alike." They giggled in unison.

The girls took their lunches to the break room behind the styling area. Water stained paint and peeling wallpaper graced the walls. A small refrigerator, microwave and sink on the left. The washer and dryer hummed on the right. And a round table with mismatched kitchen chairs filled the center of the room.

"Want coffee, tea or cocoa? We have one of those one cup thingies." Ming reached for a pre-measured pod, inserted it into the machine and push the start button. "I love strong coffee in the afternoon. An energy jolt to get me through until six."

"I'll take decaf coffee. No jolt needed. I thought you were coming home at 4:30?" Isabella set out the soup and sandwiches.

"Got a last-minute appointment. Add extra appointments when I can because other days are super slow. Like two appointments spaced hours apart slow."

"You're brave working for yourself. I'd be too afraid of coming up short."

"Dad hammered budgets into our heads. I took a class from the small business association on finances. Then another on business plans before I opened International Beauties." The washer dinged and Mindy rose to transfer towels to the dryer. "Dad had promised to give me the rest of my college funds as seed money for a business whenever I was ready."

"They made me the same offer but art school depleted my resources."

Mindy took her place again. "I think they were disappointed you didn't pursue your passion."

Her words stung.

"Ron was my passion." *Until he wasn't.*

Awkward silenced reined. The washer changed cycles while they tackled their soup.

"Hey, I got that job."

"At Hobby Life?" Mindy's spoon finished its journey to her mouth.

Isabella nodded while she chewed her tuna salad sandwich.

"All right. So, proud of you. One small step toward a new life."

Her declaration resonated with Isabella. Perhaps surrounded by art supplies would bring inspiration. Ron had drowned her desire to create with his own dream of making it big on the Christian music scene. Wrapped her in his world as worship leader of a mega-church. Shaped her into one of his backup singers. A role she never wanted.

"I start tomorrow and work a few days a week. It's a start. Thanks for not laughing at my job choice."

"Take your time. Find yourself." Ming took a sip of her coffee before continuing. "I have to ask. How are you doing—really?"

"Really...one hundred percent better now. You have been a blessing. I appreciate you not asking me questions. Mom nags and badges until you confess everything."

"Because she loves you."

"Well, I don't need that right now." Isabella recalled the myriad of ways Maureen had nagged her.

"I get it, Still I'm dying to find out what happened. Every tidbit and morsel of what has changed my fun-loving, adventure-seeking sister into a couch potato."

"Gee, thanks." Isabella popped the last of her sandwich into her mouth giving her time to weigh her words.

"Ron... had secrets. His mom helped him keep them. If he'd been honest...."

"I'm sorry." Ming squeezed her hand then gathered the empty lunch containers taking them to the trash. "Maybe some evening we can discuss those secrets. We used to share everything. No judgment."

Isabella placed her empty mug in the sink then collected her purse. "I'll let you get back to work." The women embraced before Isabella added. "Want me to cook?"

"Tonight's singles Bible study. It starts at 6:30, I'll just have time to change clothes. This lunch should last me a while. A group of us catch a bite after. You should come."

"Ah no... just no." Isabella slid through the door not wanting to explain what she didn't understand herself.

~

ISABELLA FASTENED her seatbelt and breathed in the new car smell. If not for Ron's preoccupation with having enough insurance, she'd never have been able to buy it. His obsession had kept her on a tight budget. And the pay out from the four policies had taken her breath away and caused her mother-in-law to ratchet up her control mode.

Don't go there, Issy. Leave it alone. No negative thoughts.

And her brand-new car was just the ticket to keep joy in the forefront of her mind.

Patting the steering wheel, she giggled. "It's my car. Not Mom's or Dad's or Ron's. It's mine alone."

The motor came to life and the radio morphed her happy thoughts into panic. The familiar worship song caused her heart to race. Tears streamed as she punched buttons. The quiet interior allowed her time to calm her mind. Then she remembered the radio was voice activated. "Play classical music." A piano concerto played through the surround sound. Resting her head on the steering wheel she let thoughts click through her happy list for the next stop. Art to sooth the soul.

She pulled out of the parking lot signaling for a left turn. She took Galena Blvd into the downtown district of Aurora. Ming had mentioned some art galleries and a dancing fountain downtown. At Stolp Ave she turned right. As she waited at the light of Benton and Stolp she noticed the fountain to her right. The two simple pillars moved in rhythm to the water pulsating through them. Each block sliding in sync with the next. Isabella took out her cell phone and pressed the camera icon. After some failed attempts, she managed a few decent pictures of the fountain.

Wish I brought my camera. The resolution is so much better.

Another thing she'd left behind when she'd fled Indiana. It wasn't her camera, anyway. Ron forbade her to use it without his supervision. Translation: only when there were others present.

"I forgive you. Ron." The camera thing, one tiny item on the wrecked our marriage list. Forgiving tiny things chipped away at the hardness in her heart.

If These Walls, an art store specializing in custom framing, was her next stop. The auto park feature on her new car made parallel parking in front of the store a breeze.

She clicked the lock button on her key fob while taking a few cleansing breaths.

The gallery was in a renovated factory building. Ming told her the owners supported the arts by offering local artist display space.

"Hello, Can I help you." The clerk's eyes sparkled with her smile.

"I came to soak in the beauty."

"Wonderful. Take your time. I'm finishing up an order in the back. Holler if you need anything."

She spent a delicious hour perusing the framed creations. A placard listed the artisans as wounded warriors or their family members.

An oil of a young boy hugging his soldier father intrigued her. The man minus his limbs sat propped in a hospital bed. Joy spilled from the boy's eyes as tears streamed the soldier's face. The intense emotions captured on canvas. Awe and envy filled her. *If I pick up a brush again... It's been too long. I think I've forgotten more than I remember.*

She moved on to other paintings and photographs looking for possible inspiration. But skipped depictions of battle scenes not wanting to dwell on the sadness.

The last wall held portraits of wounded soldiers. A soldier in his dress uniform, chest full of medals, and seated in a wheelchair drew her. The right pant leg of his uniform folded with a sharp crease emphasized his missing limb. Both hands gripped the wheels. It appeared he couldn't wait to get away from the camera. A red scar glared from his right cheek but his intense blue eyes contrasted the ugliness.

He reminded her of someone. She pressed her hand over her heart. The soldier at the funeral. Her comforting angel. Tears dampened her cheek. Peace from that moment rested in her heart.

"Thank you, Lord."

She hadn't thanked God for anything in a while. It felt right. If this man.... She searched for a name. The name plate blank.

"Excuse me." Her simple petition carried to the back room.

"How can I help you?"

"Why is there no name?" Isabella pointed at the plate and the woman shrugged.

"The soldier insisted on anonymity." She perused the portrait for a moment. "Do you have any other questions?"

"No, thank you. This is a wonderful place."

"Displays change monthly. Come again."

A phone rang. "Excuse me."

Isabella gazed at the photo a while longer. If this soldier could exude peace with his visible wounds. She could seek that same peace with her internal ones. *Father, I want to try.* Confidence rested on her shoulders for the first time. She strolled to her Prius with a lighter step.

7

BAD DREAMS AND CLUTTER

"Ouch!" Isabella stumbled toward the wall switch. The call of nature had battled her desire to stay in bed. Her hands protected her eyes against the glaring light. She gazed at the floor until her vision cleared. Isabella stepped over the offending object, Ming's spiky heels. Strewn beside it was her outfit from the singles meeting. Once her eyes adjusted to the light, she surveyed the rest of the living room. Issy had gone to bed long before Ming had come home, and it was amazing how her return had transformed the room.

Isabella headed to the bathroom, scowling at the visage before her. "What is wrong with that girl?"

Once the light was on in the bathroom, her jaw twitched from a suppressed scream. Disarray greeted her need for order.

"Ming can't put the lid on the toothpaste."

Her muttering continued while she did her business then fished tin the cabinet for cleaning products. Dried toothpaste and lotion speckled the sink. The moisture from the damp towels which graced the corner behind the door assailed her nose. She shook her head at a purple bra hung on the edge of the laundry basket.

Sweat formed on her brow as a panic attack fought to the surface. She grabbed the spray bottle, and wrestled the attack into submission with every wipe of her rag. Her breathing had slowed and memories of the scowling faces of Maureen and Ron left her mind.

By the time, she returned to bed an hour had elapsed. Oh, how she wished she could have ignored the mess until morning. No natures call, pure clueless blissful sleep.

Each quarter hour announced by the clock chime from the living room. Shifting first left and then right in her new queen-size bed for the perfect slumber position.

When sleep took her, so did visions of Ron. He stood in a stadium with one of those T-shirt cannons. He searched for her in the bleachers. Strangers stared. She sat alone in her section. Ron aimed the cannon. Wrinkled clothes came catapulting toward her. Ron shouted, his voice filling the stadium.

"Where did you learn to iron? Sloth school? You're killing me here." Cheers of agreement reverberated from the crowd.

Next spaghetti splatted on the seat beside her. "Carbs, Melinda, Carbs. You're trying to make me fat." Another round of cheers. Isabella covered her ears and raced toward the exit.

Maureen appeared with an old fashion sling shot delivering hideous garments and granny underwear at her feet.

"This is how a chaste widow dresses, Melinda." Maureen's scowl woke Isabella. She reached for the bottle of water on her night stand and took a few gulps. Her heart calmed.

"Get a grip, girl." Her words filled the silence. Shadows from the past faded into the darkness of her new room.

After fluffing her pillow, she lay on her side. Shaking hand found her cell. She opened her Pandora app and set the time for 20 minutes. The soothing music brought a quieter, dreamless sleep.

FROM THE KITCHEN, an off-key singer and the blaring radio crashed into her blissful rest. Wrapping her pillow around her head did nothing to mask the noise. A frustrated moan escaped her lips. She threw on her robe and stomped toward the sound.

"What's the matter with you?"

Her angry question drowned by the soloist. Ming's foot tapped and hips swayed. The spatula conducted the music from the radio. Smells of sautéed peppers and onions filled the room.

Isabella softened her foot falls as she moved toward the offender. Her fingers trekked up the back of her sister's neck. Ming's singing morphed into a yowl. Her shoulders jerked as she stepped sideways to avoid further torment.

"That wasn't nice." Ming shrieked at her sister.

"Neither is the noise." Isabella crossed her arms matching her sister's volume.

"Hey, it's 7:30. Most working girls are awake." Ming returned to her sautéing. "Want an omelet?"

"No, have you ever seen me eat eggs for breakfast? What I want is another hour of sleep."

Ming poured eggs from a bowl into her pan and added her filling. "What time did you go to bed? When I came home at ten, you were asleep."

"I got up somewhere around midnight to use the bathroom, tripped over your six-inch heels, and slammed my toe into the end table. I took time from sleep cleaning the bathroom and the living room. After which, I listened to clock chimes for three hours before I fell asleep." She didn't care to mention the bizarre dream.

"Sorry about the shoes. I plead exhaustion. No more carpooling to Bible study. Sally never wants to go home early." Plating her eggs, she sat at the tiny kitchen table. "Why on earth didn't you leave that mess until morning?"

Isabella jerked open the cabinet and grabbed a mug. The door slammed closed. "Because I couldn't. Besides you'd leave it until next Tuesday."

"True." Ming shrugged. "Now you're here and things don't stay dirty long." Her lips extracted egg from her fork, a small smile formed. "Perfection."

"Are you going to clean your pan? Or that plate before the egg hardens on it?" Isabella set the empty mug on the table. "Are you?"

"Sure, sure. Don't get your panties in a wad."

"My panties aren't the ones in a wad. When did you become such a slob? I wonder if it was your former roommate. Or is it the roommate job cleaning up after you?"

"Aren't you ornery in the morning." Ming glared back, took a sip of her coffee and sighed. "I'm sorry, Issy. Believe me when I say I don't think of you as my personal maid. I do recall when we shared a room, clutter bred on your side."

"It's just... I like things in order." *I need things in order.* "We grow up, become more responsible." Isabella reached in the cabinet for a bowl.

"I'm an adult. I like order, too. But, this is my busy season. I have to choose what's important."

"Cleanliness isn't important?" Isabella grabbed a box of cereal and leaned against the counter.

"I make choices daily." Ming's voice held an edge. "I choose to go to work, do the accounts, pay bills, see my friends, go to church and... devote two hours on my day off to housework." She placed her dirty dishes in the sink, filled them with soapy water and smiled at Isabella. "You, however, have spent hours rearranging my cabinets, furniture and closets. Which adds extra time wasted to find stuff. I swear, you are becoming Mom." Turning off the faucet Ming poked Isabella's shoulder.

"Hey, that hurts." Isabella pushed her sister's hand away.

"Plus, you have no friends, no social life and when I invite you along, you refuse."

"I'm sorry I'm so awful." Unushered tears blur her vision. "I need...order."

"It's okay, sis." Ming wraps her arms around Isabella. "I promise to keep my stilettos in the closet." Isabella pulled away wiping her eyes with her robe sleeve.

"You better." Isabella gave an embarrassed laugh. Arguing with Ming was nothing like arguing with Ron. The thought startled her. When was the last time she'd expressed her displeasure and not been demeaned? "I've missed these fights."

"Me too." Ming grabbed a towel and flicked it in Isabella's direction. Giggles ensued.

8

BEYOND COMFORT ZONE

Dan sat on the edge of his bed slipping the liner on the stump of his right leg. He pulled the custom sock over his stump. Then attached the prosthetic leg in place and secured it with a locking pin. It had taken three weeks to get it back from repairs. He'd worn it a few hours the day before but today it needed to be worn longer.

"Man, I'm going to be sore today." Dan sat straighter, "Buck up, sergeant. What's a little discomfort?"

Brutus lays at his feet.

"Today's a new adventure."

Brutus' one floppy ear straightened to match the other ear. He focused on his master.

"Who am I kidding." Sweat formed on his brow. "Today I'll be the freak show."

He grabbed his pants with his left hand and together with his three-fingered right hand worked the left pant leg over the prosthetic. Then slipped the right leg into his pants and pulled them on. He'd debated wearing shorts. But he hated the stares. And his upbringing deemed shorts inappropriate for church.

"You think I look normal enough to avoid questions, fella." Dan stroked the dog's muzzle.

He steadied his footing before he took a few tentative steps to his closet. His right leg moved much smoother after the repair and his stub was for the moment pain-free. He repositioned his legs for maximum stability and pulled the blue dress shirt from its hanger. The remaining fingers his right hand ached from fastening the twelve buttons.

"Brutus, should I practice the sermon again?"

The dog moved closer nudging his hand. Dan stroked the canine pushing anxiety away with each touch. "You're right no need."

Dan flexed the right fingers, stretching his hand out with his left hand. The thumb and two adjoining fingers still struggled to grip and open completely. He hadn't adapted well to using his left hand. Once his fingers relaxed he added a clip-on tie. Dan preferred polos and T-shirts, less small motor skill involved. But filling the pulpit for his uncle required this little sacrifice.

"What were you thinking, Sweeney?" Dan combed his hair and ran the comb along his beard.

His curly blond hair touched his collar. "Should I get a haircut?"

Brutus huffed and Dan sighed. "Yeah, maybe not."

The long hair and short cropped beard covered the scar trailing his cheek. At least that wound was combat-related. He shoved keys and wallet in his pocket and continued moving to the door. Brutus bolted toward him waging his long whip-like tail.

"Woo!" Dan signal for the dog to sit. "Calm down." Dan stroked Brutus under the chin. The canine leaned in closer his tail pounding the floor.

"We have ten minutes for you to do your business before I have to leave." Dan opened the back door for his furry friend.

The fenced-in yard had been an unexpected blessing after acquiring Brutus. However, the dog had found the loose boards and other escape routes. A big dog running full out greeting strangers with whimpers, slobbery kisses and slaps from his wagging tail created drama.

"A new fence is moving up my to-do list." Dan groaned when his friend headed to the fence line. His shrill whistle got the dog's attention. Brutus moved away from the fence and back to business.

Dan didn't want any trouble from the neighbors. He needed Brutus. The dog's presence kept his PTSD in check better than meds. He set the stove timer and poured himself a second cup of coffee. Dan spoke to the house. "You may be ugly, but you're mine."

Childhood memories of eviction notices ran through his head. Dad couldn't keep a job, keep off drugs or keep a family. Dan glanced at the pant leg covering his prosthetic. How can a one-legged man keep a family? The timer dinged. His whistle brought Brutus running back inside.

"Behave yourself while I'm gone."

He patted Brutus and signaled for him to go to his dog bed near the couch. "You get the day off today, buddy. Relax."

The dog stood in his bed following Dan with his eyes.

"Don't need you joining in on the worship." He stepped over to give Brutus a final pat. Brutus settled in, his massive head resting on his folded paws.

He hadn't had a panic attack in months. Even without the service dog, Dan knew the warning signs and how to handle them. Today there was no danger, no trucks, IEDs or battle stations. He could do this. He had to. Being normal depended on it.

By the time, he reached his pickup truck, his gait had a slight limp. He'd splurged on the duo- cab silver truck. The purchase didn't erase his disability. But driving the truck gave him the illusion of wholeness. Trucks equaled masculinity. At least that's the line Steve had given him when he helped him pick it out.

Dan took the scenic route to Stone Church. His nerves need more time.

"What was I sniffing when I agreed to preach today? God give me courage."

Uncle Paul's bout with the flu had taken a toll. Dan was no preacher but his uncle wouldn't take no for an answer.

"I remember, Danny boy, the nice talk you gave for the youth group. You told me you spoke at a Veteran's group. You can do this."

"Why do I let my uncle talk me into these things?" His damp handkerchief did little for the perspiration on his neck. A phantom pain ached in his missing calf. His stomach churned.

He'd labored over the sermon not sure how this small congregation would respond to his style.

"Style, Dan you have zero style." He saw the reflection of his frown in the rear-view mirror.

A mini cooper swerving through traffic caught his attention. It followed on Dan's tail.

"Lord, keep that guy away from me." Sweat dotted his brow, his knuckles whitened on the steering wheel.

Watching his mirrors often until the tiny car turned down a side street. He exhaled the breath he was holding. Even in the large truck the fear of another crash loomed in his mind.

Slow your breathing. In, out, in out. Focus on breathing.

Tightness in his chest eased, his heart rate slowed.

Dan pulled into the parking lot of Stone Church an hour ahead of the congregation. This gave him time to walk with in the new leg before anyone arrived. While he loosened his muscles, he tried releasing the unpleasant thought stuck in the forefront of his mind.

Two tours in Afghanistan and Dan came home with two less fingers and a scar on his face. But the motorcycle tour with guys from his unit put him in Walter Reed VA Hospital. That was another reason to cover his prosthetic. He hated the "Thank you for your service" remarks because it always followed by, "How'd you lose your leg?" Explaining was just as uncomfortable as letting them think he lost it in the Middle East. Those thoughts accompanied him into the foyer of the church.

Dan quivered, shaking away the sad memories.

"Hey, there."

He turned from his view of the sanctuary, put on a practiced smile. "Well, Dickson Jones. How you doing, man? Thought you'd gone to meet your maker eons ago."

The impeccably dressed gray-haired gentlemen pounded Dan's back in greeting. "Don't think I haven't seen you sneaking in late and leaving early, young man." Mr. Jones said. "Mouthy as ever. Always told your uncle he needed to take you to the woodshed more often." He reached out to shake Dan's hand. Mr. Jones folded Dan's disfigured hand between both of his own. "Paul told me about the motorcycle accident. Glad to see God answered prayer." Before he released his hand, Dickson added. "Thank you for your service."

Dan nodded. The remark didn't sting coming from his uncle's old friend. Mr. Jones observation shamed him. Arriving late and leaving early before anyone noticed him kept the hated remark at bay. And drew less attention to his crutches and empty pant leg.

"I understand you're taking the pulpit today. Your uncle never mentioned you were a chaplain."

"Because I never was. It crossed my mind for a minute. But military intelligence and logistics were a better fit."

"Paul is trying to get you into the ministry."

"In his dreams."

"What are your dreams?"

His dreams were crushed with the IED and shattered with the motorcycle accident. His high school dream of playing in a band, unrealistic even if he were whole. And a career in the army didn't happen for a sergeant minus a leg. "I'm attending college right now. Business major."

"Very Good. What business do you have in mind?"

The same question he'd asked himself a hundred times "No idea really. My plans for a military career have changed."

"I'm sure by the time you've finished your degree, the right opportunity will come along." Dickson patted Dan's shoulder. "Come see me when you're farther along in your degree. I might have some ideas for you. Now, I need to get the programs folded before others arrive."

Mr. Jones toddled into the church office leaving Dan alone again. He walked the center aisle, trying to minimize his limp. Sweat trickled down his collar. At the third pew from the front Dan paused. He fished in his pocket for his fresh handkerchief and dabbed at his neck. A second handkerchief might not be enough today. If he sat in the front row, the trek to the pulpit was minimal. If the song leader had everyone stand to sing, perhaps no one would notice him move into position. "Father, I don't like this one bit. Way out of my comfort zone. Please have everyone focusing on my words and not my handicap. And please help my words be clear and minister to someone, anyone at all."

~

Isabella grimaced as Ming's car sputtered and groaned to a stop.

"So, discreet."

"Sorry." Ming extracted the key. "Well." Silence prevailed as they stared at the lime stone church with its ancient spire. "Are you sure?"

"I gotta do it sometime Mingy."

"But this church is so...so...old school."

"Maybe that's what I need." Isabella turned in her seat to face her sister. "Like Gramma's church. Remember Awana and Vacation Bible School?"

"Kinda. I was in 3rd grade. I recall Henri and you fighting over the lone bathroom."

"Yeah." Issy smiled at the memory. "That one year in Iowa—if you were in 3rd then I was in 6th grade—it changed my life.

"Well, I cried a lot because Carla and Ken were off at college."

"I hoped Daddy wouldn't find another job. I wanted to stay with Gramma forever."

"I wanted to go back to Missouri, I missed my school friends."

Ming straightened in her seat.

'Why can't you just come with me to Living River Community?"

"You know I can't."

"Issy, it's not Resurrection, It's not even Indiana."

"I know. I just..." Her shoulders slumped with the heaviness of the task.

"It's okay." Ming wrapped her arms around her sister giving a gentle shake. "It'll be all right." She smiled and winked. "Once you find a home church, I'm outta here. My friends think I'm deserting them."

"I appreciate all your support. You know you don't have to come with me." Isabella unlatched her seatbelt and continued staring at the edifice.

"I'd never leave you in a lurch in your time of need." Ming waited in solidarity. "Besides you wouldn't go by yourself."

Isabella looked at her baby sister and squeezed her hand, gathering strength from her presence.

"Well, we better get out of your car now before anyone notices this rattletrap and calls for a tow." Isabella watched the mock shock appear on her sister's face.

"Hey, be careful not to hurt Bernie's feelings or he may refuse to start later." Ming patted her hair and examined her face in the rear-view mirror before exiting the car. Isabella didn't bother.

"So, remind me again why we didn't take my nice new, quiet car?"

"Because I always drive. That way your forced to sneak out with me."

"Ha ha." Isabella laughed and slammed her door, trying the handle to insure it had locked.

The sisters approached the church hand in hand. "Six." Ming announced with a laugh. Counting steps. One of the mysteries that defined her unique personality.

"You are too funny."

"Look oak doors to the sanctuary, stain glass windows." She pulled the heavy handle and the two entered. "Red carpet. Even the coat racks are old." Ming whispered.

"Enough." She shushed her sister trying not to smile. Two older men stood at the door, programs in hand.

"Welcome, ladies." The rotund man bedecked in a black suit and floral tie greeted them. His ushers name tag said Richard "Glad you are here to visit us today. You can sit anywhere you like. Here's your bulletin and some visitor's cards to fill out." In true greeter style, he reached out to shake their hands with his right hand, as he held out the proffered paperwork with his left, a pasted smile on his face.

"The usher dance." Ming smothered a giggle while they found seats near the back.

"You're incorrigible." Isabella sighed as she slid in beside her sister.

Ming had a way of making light of every situation, which at times embarrassed her sister. But Isabella's reentry into church attendance was made far easier by her sister's silly barbs.

They settled into the pew while soft organ music played in the background. Isabella scanned the sanctuary. The dark wood reminded her of her childhood visits to Gramma's church. *This could be good. I found Jesus in Gramma's church.* A smile formed on her lips. Memories of ice cream socials, revivals and her sweet grandmother warmed her healing heart.

The service was so predictable that a stern look from Isabella kept Ming from giving a running commentary. Organ music gave the service a high church feel. Far different from the worship services she had attended since college. When the choir began, she knew she had stepped back in time. The gray-haired choir had trouble staying on tempo. She pushed the critical spirit that she'd acquired from her years on the worship team aside. Instead she set her focus on the hymn's lyrics. *Yes, Lord, you are a mighty fortress.*

Worship clicked by following the program. The use of hymn books rather than an overhead projection of the words took some getting used to. The song leader was less gray and what he lacked in musical skill he made up with enthusiasm. The organist was now playing the piano that Isabella noted was out of tune. *Stop it!* She struggled to turn off the musician's portion of her brain when the vocals were off key.

After the offering, the pastor limped to the front. Once he rested his Bible on the podium, he stood tall. The sun reflecting off his blond hair forming an angelic halo. Isabella wondered if the sermon was timed to begin when the sun's rays reach this point. Light from the stained-glass window of the good shepherd carrying a lost sheep created colorful highlights in his hair. He shuffled the papers, gave a nervous smile, scanned the congregation and cleared his throat.

"Before we get started I want to introduce myself to any of you who may not already know me. I'm Pastor Whitehall's nephew Dan Sweeney. Uncle Paul is still wrestling that nasty flu virus. Please continue to pray for him. If he isn't better by next Sunday, you'll be stuck with me again." A gentle chuckle filtered through the congregation. A thin elderly gentleman sitting near the front shouted out. "Danny Boy, you'll do just fine." Amens of encouragement rose in the sanctuary.

She heard the man clear his throat from her place in the back of the room. Isabella turned to her sister and pinned her with a scowl. A muted giggle threatened to escape through the fingers covering Ming's lips.

Bowing his head, he asked God to bless the word before he began. Isabella waited in anticipation to see if God would.

Dan skimmed his left hand through his hair before beginning. "Open your Bibles to..." His voice was deep and resonate like a well-tuned bass. His eyes flashed when he shared stories to illustrate scripture. Psalm 32:7. You are my hiding place; you preserve me from trouble. You surround me with songs of deliverance.

Isabella sat transfixed watching the light play through Dan's hair, her mind mulling over the verse. Aurora was her hiding place. She'd escaped to the refuge of her sister's comfort and encouragement. Safety and rest surrounded her there. When the sermon ended, she hoped no one asked her what was said. His voice seemed so familiar, comforting like another time when she'd needed the Lord's comfort. The Holy Spirit called to her spirit and she was enveloped in God's peace and care. *Thank you Lord for bringing me home.*

The benediction was given and the congregation rose. The pastor limped down the aisle to greet everyone at the door. When they stood to leave, no one greeted them. Ming shook her head in disgust. Isabella knew her sister was making red marks on her mental list of how newcomers should be received.

"What a bunch of stuffed shirts." She whispered as they leaned over to collect their purses and Bibles. "Where do you want to have lunch?"

"I don't care—you pick."

"How about Cracker Barrel?"

"That's fine."

"Really! I thought you hated the long lines."

"What? Where do you want to go?"

"Thought so, your mind was somewhere else. Don't tell me. You like this place?"

"Like isn't the right word. I sensed the Holy Spirit speak to my heart during the sermon." Isabella smiled deflecting her sister's eyebrow raise and added. "I'm coming back next Sunday."

Instead of slipping out the side door, they waited in line to shake the pastor's hand.

"Nice to have you two young ladies visit us today. I'm Dan Sweeney."

Isabella noted his left-handed handshake was firm. His right arm hid behind his back.

"I'm Ming Wilson and this is my sister Isabella."

"Sisters!" His surprised smile lead Ming to her traditional response.

"Yes! We were separated at birth. But our Heavenly Father brought us back together."

His laughter brought a sparkle to his sapphire blue eyes and caused the scar peeking out from the trimmed beard to take on a dimple-like quality.

"Ming has been helping me church hunt."

"I hope you ladies will visit again. My uncle loves fresh faces in his congregation."

"I'm a member of Living River Community but Issy was looking for something a little different."

"I believe I've found it. I'll see you again next Sunday." Isabella smiled

"I..." He paused staring at her for a few moments. Isabella, is it?"

"Yes, my family calls me Issy."

"Ma'am. Have we met before?" His face pinked. "Sorry, sounds lame but you look so familiar." Dan's face pinked deeper. Isabella raised her eyebrow and backed up a step.

Ming intercepted the awkward moment. "She may have a doppelganger out there somewhere."

Dan let out a gentle laugh. "Yes, of course. I apologize, ma'am, I didn't mean to make you uncomfortable. And if I haven't scared you off, I'll direct your attention to the bulletin. Stone Church has other meetings you might be interested to attend throughout the week. "

"I'll check those out." Isabella smiled waving the bulletin as they moved along to the exit.

Once inside the car Ming unloaded on her sister. "Seriously! You want to attend this old dead church?"

"It's not so dead. It suits me. My faith, like this church, still has a spark for Jesus. I'm coming back next week. Maybe there is more here for me."

"Are you referring to God or that cute pastor?"

Isabella swatted her arm as Ming made her old familiar tongue-in cheek face as she turned the key. Bernie sprang to life like her heart had inside the old church.

9

DREAMS AND NEW REALITIES

Sweat soaked Isabella's pajamas. Light from the street lamp on the corner peeked through the slit in the curtains. Taking several breaths, she threw back her covers and pulled open the curtains. The vacant street and silent neighborhood contrasted her nightmare.

Chords of the new worship music Ron had labored over still resonated in her head.

The last song he ever sang.

A shiver trailed through her body as she tried to shake the final image of the dream from her mind. Their baby's death and Ron's melted into one event the moment the song ended. Baby RJ and Ron dissolved before her eyes leaving her amid a staring, angry, faceless congregation. She swallowed hard, gulping air. The peace she'd taken to bed from her worship experience at Stone Manor lay puddled in the corner of her heart. Her faith had clay feet even far from its place of destruction.

The mega-church in Indiana had drowned her in their expectations for a pastor's wife. Maybe she'd let them. Pleasing people had always been her downfall.

"Sister Marklin, I've been praying. The Holy Spirit compels me to speak to you." Mrs. Graystone was part of Maureen's ladies group. Her orthopedic shoes were always chasing other people's business. "That outfit is a bit... over the top don't you think. If you were younger or at least not in a leadership role, it might be fine. But I sense God saying, 'Temper your clothing choices. Let

Modesty be your guide." She'd patted Isabella's shoulder and left her head held high.

The dress had a scarf hemline. The blue butterfly pattern flattering. She loved the dress. "I had no back-bone and let that old prune dictate my dress code."

She leaned against the coolness of the window. Her mind still trapped in memories.

Ron's position as worship leader and youth pastor kept him too busy to be with her. She volunteered to be his assistant. Hoping for time together. Instead, he'd pressured her into being the church secretary.

Ron's words grabbed her from the past. "Melinda, you belong to this congregation. They require special care. We've been tasked with this responsibility." She recalled her calendar back then bled with colors indicating the various commitments

A tear trailed her cheek. "Oh Ron, whatever happened to the wonderfully, encouraging man I married?" The whispered words echoed in her ears. Before his headaches, her husband treasured their time together. He'd walked through art museums without a word of complaint. Was it all a charade? Like a bad movie script. The husband becomes a cad once his won the bride. Did he ever care about her feelings? But there was the brain tumor.

"God forgive me for not seeing the signs."

She paced the floor willing her thoughts to turn off.

Her husband morphed from loving to manipulating and caring to demanding. The headaches increased, but he refused to see a doctor. Then RJ died and....

"Melinda, my love, service brings healing."

Maybe for him. Hindsight told her differently. Ron spent hours at the piano or guitar.

At first it was worship music and classical pieces. Then the music evolved, the guitar riffs shook the apartment.

A vivid picture of his cutting words filled her. The snow that day fell in rhythm with the chaotic chords.

"Ronny, turn the music down it makes my head throb."

Ron's disapproving glare stabbed her heart. "King David grieved for his son. This music helps me grieve for mine." Ron reached for the volume control than paused. "Maybe your headache is unconfessed sin, Bathsheba." The volume soared with his rendition of Black Sabbath.

Isabella paused before the window again. The distorted reflection in the darken glass reminders of the ghost from her past.

A month after their son's death he'd insisted she return to music practice.

"Ronny, why 'Standing on the Promises'? Her voice had cracked and tears came to her eyes with Ron's arrangement of the old hymn. The lyrics had taunted her grieving soul. The doctor's prognosis of infertility swept away with their son's birth. RJ had loved her unconditionally. Her little boy, God's promise, lay dead one morning in his crib.

"I can't sing, honey, not yet."

Ron turned and placed his hand on her cheek. "It's okay." The sweetness in his voice so soothing. He looked around at the other musicians. "We can manage without her, right guys."

Later, when he'd found her resting in their bedroom, the monster reappeared. "Just who do you think you are?" Ron pulled her up from the bed.

"You're hurting me."

"Not as much as you hurt the Lord. How could you embarrass me in front of the whole team?"

"Embarrass you." Isabella jerked her arm away, a red hand print remained. "I told you I was sad today. I begged you to let me stay home."

"If you'd tried a little harder, you could have overcome. I'm so tired of the crying and moaning. Our son is dead. Nothing's going to bring him back."

"How can you be so callous?"

"Callous… callous… King David rose up from weeping after his son died and went on."

His holier-than-thou responses were the undoing of their relationship. She'd given up so much for Ron. At first, the sacrifice of art, stepping out of her comfort zone at his side on the worship team had brought her joy. Over the years his goals smothered that joy and damaged their love. He'd push through his headaches to present a good front as a worship leader. Yet, he never even tried when she needed him.

Then there was the deception. He knew. He and Maureen knew. The bitter ache of betrayal formed in her heart. She wiped the wetness from her cheeks.

"Why hadn't he been honest?"

The streetlight flicked and died casting the room in total darkness.

Guilt ascends from the inkiness. She'd planned to tell him after church. Her mind rehearsed the words. A goodbye her heart to terrify to speak. Abuse had beaten away love. Isabella crossed her arms and leaned against the wall.

Verbal abuse that's what the grief counselor had called it. Yet it took her another year to recognize her mother-in-law held a master's degree in the subject. Hers was subtler, sophisticated and far beyond what Ron became before his death.

"*Dearest Melinda, whatever were you thinking?*" Maureen's eyebrows raised, she tssked her disapproval.

"*Please, I was thinking I'm in no mood for visitors.*" Isabella hated to be called Melinda. When Ron discovered her middle name, it became his pet name for her. Romantic.

"*Melinda, we Marklins, always practice hospitality. I've called Harriet back and told them you've changed your mind.*" Maureen patted her shoulder.

"*Maureen, I don't appreciate....*"

"*Ron said you'd gotten sullen after Jeffrey's death.*"

"*Please we called our baby RJ, never Jeffrey.*"

"*My Jeffrey never liked those silly initials.*"

"*It was his idea.*"

"*I suppose calling himself Ron after marrying you was his idea too.*"

"*I always knew him as Ron. You know His pet name for me was never intended to be for public use.*"

"*On the contrary.*" Maureen smirk filled her face. "*He told me Melinda sounded friendlier and less formal. He felt Issy was childish and Isabella too foreign.*"

She'd held her tongue while her neck warmed. Maureen robbed her earliest sweet memory of her husband, replacing it with Maureen's bigotry.

"*Now, my dear girl. Go change your clothes and fix your face. Company is the best remedy for grief.*"

Isabella crossed to the bed.

"Why did I stay for a year?" She crawled back in bed and the truth joined her. Guilt—plain and simple, kept her at Maureen's side.

"I told everyone we needed to go through the grieving process together. Find solace and hope while we rebuilt our lives." *Great plan. I blamed myself for our bad marriage. I believed all his lies and let his mother pour guilt on me for leaving her childless.*

Curling up under her comforter she pressed the pillow into obedience. Closed eyelids did nothing to shut the door to the memory trail her mind explored.

A memory movie played snippets of scenario of her mother-in-law, Ron or other members of Resurrection Church.

Turning to her side Isabella searched for a position to bring back sleep and turn off the past.

She'd finished her training for her new job. Tomorrow she'd join the morning team at Hobby Life. *Focus! My lock combination is 2714. Punch in with my social. Find the inventory list....* Anxiety ached in her shoulders and weariness brought a throb behind her eyes. "Oh, God, help me." She hadn't prayed herself to sleep in a long time. "Father, could you please pour out some of the peace I had Sunday?"

The alarm blared from the clock radio, sunbeams caused eye squinting and a moan escaped her lips. Her cottony brain disoriented for a few moments. "Well, I guess praying worked."

Ming's morning persona filtered through the closed bedroom door, her off-key voice sang with gusto—*This is the Day the Lord has made.*

"Well, that remains to be seen." Isabella shuffled off to the bathroom as the smell of fresh brewed coffee attempted to change her mood.

~

DAN PAUSED in the center of Hobby Life overwhelmed by its content. Model airplanes hung from the ceiling. Some with ten-foot wingspans. Toy trains traveled around tracks on a large table top town. It reminded him of Mr. Rogers Neighborhood.

Rows and rows of craft supplies. Scrape booking to jewelry making lined the left half of the behemoth store. While the signage for the right side boasted sewing and art supplies. Uncle Paul had asked him to buy a gift for his granddaughter. The request simple enough. His leg ached in anticipation of the search and retrieval mission before him.

"Hello, you look lost."

Dan flinched at the unexpected invasion of his thoughts. Noticing the familiar face, he smiled. "You're one of those twins who suffered through my preaching last week."

"Yes, I am. That's about the twin part, not the preaching part." She returned a dimpled smile.

He remained silent enjoying the radiant smile and divine chocolate eyes focused on him while he tried to remember her name. "Isabella—your name. But, I guess everyone here is your friend because your name tag says, Issy." Dan pointed at her lanyard dangling from her neck. Her tie-dye T-shirt with Hobby Life emblazon across the front contrasted her dress slacks and two-inch heels. He refocused on her face before she caught him scanning her attractive form.

"Isabella was too long for the font size they use on these name tags." She shrugged and smiled once more. "What can I help you with, Pastor?" She emphasized the word pastor.

Busted. "It's not pastor, just Dan." He found her smile disarming. Her closeness stirred feelings he didn't care to deal with.

He moved a step back which required a little more concentration with his prosthetic. Her hand reached for his arm then went back to her side.

Thanks, but I can do this. Warmth formed under his collar.

"I need to find a gift for a 10-year-old girl. Uncle Paul gave me no real direction except that she loves to make things."

"Aisles seven through ten are girls' crafts."

"Thanks," Dan made his way to the girl's section. The huge store stretched on for eternity as far as his prosthetic was concerned. By the time, he reached aisle seven perspiration dotted his brow. He paused to get a breath, then wiped the sweat with his forearm. *Man, am I out of shape.* The doctor had warned him to take it easy. He'd already spent several hours encased in the artificial limb while in class. *I should have waited until tomorrow. Oh, well. Accomplish your objective, Sweeney, and get this sore leg home and into the whirlpool.*

"Excuse me, Dan." Issy appeared beside him again.

"Ma'am, are you the ninja sales clerk? That's the second time you've snuck up on me."

"Sorry. You were deep in thought." Her chocolate brown eyes were laughing at him.

Deep in getting a second wind. Dan's breath caught when her smile spread to those gorgeous brown eyes.

"I've an idea for that gift." Issy pointed toward aisle eight. Dan refocused his attention and followed her.

"Wow! I've never seen so many beads in one place."

"Neither had I."

"I hope your idea is more than pointing."

"Of course." Isabella squatted to reach a lower shelf. The poise she maintained in those heels was impressive. Dan watched her retrieve a box and stand erect, no wobble. Funny the things he noticed now that his own balance was... less than normal.

"Jewelry-making starter kit. It has everything she'll need. There're instructions to make a necklace, bracelet, and key chain. I suggest this cording." She grabbed a package just above her head. Still managing to stay balanced. "The cord in this kit is cheap and can be pretty discouraging to use for the beginner."

"Thanks, ma'am. Much appreciated. Mission accomplished."

"If there's nothing else follow me to the cashier. We're giving every customer a 20% off coupon that's good for the rest of the month. Maybe your niece could use it for more beads."

"Cloe is my second cousin. My uncle's granddaughter."

"Right."

"Hey, will I see you Sunday?"

"I'll be there."

"I look forward to it."

Dan shook his head as she disappeared around a corner. "Smooth move, Sweeney." Dan wondered if he'd ever feel comfortable around women again. Not that he was popular. The few dates could be counted on his damaged right hand. And his one serious relationship took a 747 to California at the first sight of his scarred face. His further disability nixed the idea of dating, ever. This woman though...if he could remember who she looked like... their next conversation might be less awkward.

ISABELLA GLANCED toward the door from her place at the fabric counter just as Dan pushed out the exit door. She assumed by his polite use of ma'am he was ex-military. He walked with a more distinct limp today. She was glad she hadn't embarrassed them both by trying to help him when he appeared to lose his balance.

He seemed like a sweet man. *Where did that thought come from?* She still had wounds to mend.

But Dan's sapphire eyes so familiar. Sapphire, such a feminine word for a guy's eyes. Isabella's hands returned material bolts to their rightful place. While her mind search for a better word. *Soulful.* Dan's eyes were soulful. A great quality for a minister.

There was another reason to not even put him on blank list of possible relationship candidates. He was in the ministry. Claiming not to be a pastor. Ron refused the title. He may be subbing at Stone Church but I'd wager He'd jumped at the chance to fill an empty pulpit.

Isabella whatever you do, don't mention this part of your day to Ming.

She straightened the bolts of fabric, humming *This is the Day that the Lord has made.*

"Ming, you are so good for me."

10

STRUGGLING WITH CHANGE

The motorcycle roared with life underneath Dan. Military buddies' chatter echoed through the helmet's Blue-tooth. Another day of travel and this cross-country trek could be checked off his bucket list. Darkness shrouded the single taillights ahead.

Beyond the next intersection was the Holiday Inn. Revved engines sped through the green light. His mid-pack position was soon overshadowed by bikers passing on both sides. Dread filled the air as large headlights blinded Dan. Evasive action— left swerve on oily asphalt. Bike and body skid toward the oncoming truck. A silent scream. A heavy weight pressed against Dan's chest. Brutus whimpers break through the dream. Slobbery licks erase the panic.

"Get off." Dan pushed the dog away with the nightmare. He rose from the couch. And face planted on the living room floor.

"Stupid."

"Stupid."

"Stupid."

Dan's fist pounded out his frustration.

The crutches tumbled to the floor from the vibration.

"So much for watching a little TV before bed."

Brutus moved in, licking his face and snuggling close.

"Hey, boy, it's okay." Dan rolled over and sat up. He rubbed Brutus behind the ears. "Stupid dream. I forgot I was minus a leg." Dan hugged Brutus. Anger raced through his bloodstream. Scooting over to the couch, Dan heaved his body back onto the cushions. A hand-signaled sent Brutus to retrieved a crutch. Dan grabbed the crutch's hand grip and pushed off the couch with his left hand. He positioned the crutch under his right arm. Brutus waited with the other one. "Good job, good boy."

The crutches secured under his arms, he took a cleansing breath. "I'll let you out and then it's off to bed."

Brutus flew out the door searching the ground for the right spots. Dan watched the mutt for a moment. A few stars twinkled beyond the city lights. A full moon illuminated Brutus. Dan envied the dog. Free to run and play, no physical restrictions.

The sounds of TVs and children's laughter float from open windows. The spring night air held scents of new grass and smoke from backyard fire pits. Night shadows cast an eerie vision over his neglected yard. Tall grass, weedy flowerbeds and shaggy bushes. One more thing to remind him of his limitations. *My luck the city will fine me for my tall grass this summer.* Dan whistled for Brutus. The dog leaned close. The thoughts of fines and tight finances calmed with each stroke on the canine's head.

His disability and monthly settlement checks covered the bills. Working part-time as one of the geek squad at Techno World covered other necessary expenses like food and gas. The additional funds available with his VA loan were designated for home repairs.

Brutus sat at his master's feet staring at Dan. "Hey, boy, can you learn how to do lawn care?"

"What's that line from Mom's favorite book, *Gone with The Wind*?"

Brutus cocked his head and woofed.

"I'll think about it tomorrow for tomorrow is another day."

The phrase was his late mother's mantra when Dad was out of work or they were forced to move again.

Dan crawled into bed, pulled up the covers and switched off the lamp on the nightstand. He stared into the dark. The rustle of Brutus circling in his bed echoed in the stillness.

Dan poured out his heart in the darkness to the One who loved him unconditionally. "My life belongs to you, but this is so hard. Every morning I gotta remind myself that I'm missing a leg. Otherwise, I greet the floor with my face." Dan pulled his comforter close around his neck.

"Every day is a struggle. I come home exhausted from using the prosthetic. Phantom pain shoots up my invisible leg. I paste on a smile to show the world

I'm cool with all this." Dan sighed and turned to his side. "Lord, I hate it. Help me be normal." He fought a sob as Brutus crawled in bed beside him.

"Thanks, boy." The dog snuggled close. Tears damped Brutus' head. Dan wiped his face. His voice chocked.

"Forgive me, Father for being petty. There's guys in far worse shape." Dan spent several minutes praying for those men and thanking God for the provision of Brutus. After a time, calm came. One more pat on the furry head. Then a push sent the canine back to his bed. Dan watched the moonlight create odd shadows on his walls. Memories of childhood intensified his loneliness.

"Lord, if there was a wife in my future...someone...."

Dan shoved his right hand under his pillow and shifted position. His resolve to have no social life was melting under Steve's influence. Not to mention the sweet Hispanic woman he'd met at church and again at Hobby Life. Her features filled his thoughts as sleep took him.

~

DAN CLIMBED into his truck after class. His back ached in sympathy with his stump. After another long walk to the far end of the parking lot, George, a fellow vet's words hit home. "There's independence and then there's just plain stubbornness."

When it came to handicapped parking tags his pride needed to surrender. Tomorrow he would locate the right office on campus to request a tag. Then check online for the form to get a handicap license plate from the state. "I should have thrown the crutched in the truck this morning." A phantom foot pain added more discomfort.

Dan pulled into a parking space and changed into the purple Techno World polo before heading in. "Can't wait to get that degree." Although computer troubleshooting came easy, it wasn't the career of choice. Numbers were his first love. Accountants made good money. CPAs didn't need both legs. How pathetic. The minus column for his future always longer than the plus.

"I'll think about it tomorrow, after all, tomorrow is another day." Dan pushed open the truck door and eased to the pavement. The employee's parking lot was another long walk. "Definitely getting that sticker."

11

NEW FRIENDS

"Ok, it's time." Ming announced after dinner on Friday.

"Time for what?" Issy stacked dishes.

Ming stood by the sink watching the suds form.

"You know I hate your pregnant pauses." Isabella sat the dishes near the sink. "Please." She flicked a handful of suds at her sister. Ming returned the gesture, a suds battle ensued followed by giggles.

"I'll spill, I'll spill; I don't want to change my clothes for a second time." Ming used the dish towel to wipe her face and stepped away from the sink before continuing. "It's time you got a social life. I'm taking you to my single's gathering tonight."

Isabella took her sister's place at the sink. She didn't want to argue. Keeping her hands occupied might keep her mouth silent.

Ming dried a plate. "Before you say no, hear me out. The meeting is at Mary Hart's place, not at the church," She placed the plate in the cupboard and held up a finger. "So, you won't have mega-church meltdown." A second finger went up. "The group is older singles, less drama than when you were first single."

"How do you define less drama? Besides, I'm a widow. Isn't your group real singles?"

"How are you defining *real singles*? People who've never been married? We have a few divorcees and widows.

"I'm not looking for a relationship."

"You want to start over. Find yourself. It's easier to do with people around to help you along the way. We hang out together for the fellowship. We share the same values. Sometimes friendships become something more." Ming dried a cup. And Issy focused on the knife in her hand before handing it to her sister.

"Don't give me that look girl." Ming gave Issy's shoulder a playful slap. "Hey, it's a singles group. Not a dating service and not a friends-with- benefits group." Ming laughed at Isabella's feigned shocked expression. "You know you were thinking it."

"You've thought this out. Even thrown my own words back in my face." Issy pasted on a scowl. "One question."

Now it was Issy's time for a pregnant pause. She took the washcloth and wiped the table with a slow circular motion. Ming stood with one hand on her hip and the other extended rotating in a go-ahead fashion.

"You're killing me Talls."

Ming's reference to a school friend's teasing them for being short with the remake of *Sandlot's* classic line caused Isabella to laugh.

"What is on the agenda tonight?"

"It's game night." Ming said.

"Board games?"

"You know it." Ming's triumphant grin contagious.

Game night should give her more chances to laugh.

"Is there time to change?"

"Sure, Robin is always late. We usual give her an extra thirty minutes before we start the games. You go change. I'll make quick work of these dishes." Ming hummed Onward Christian Soldier. Issy bumped her with her hip before dashing to her room to change.

$\sim$

THEY ARRIVED A FEW MINUTES LATE. Ming took their jackets and purses to the bedroom. Isabella scanned the room. Noting the small clutches of people chatting. Dan and another man came in the door.

"So, you're a part of this group?" She noted the royal blue polo shirt paired with tan Dockers. The combination deepened the blue in his eyes.

"This is my first time. Steve invited me." Dan introduced his red-headed much taller companion. "This is Isabella." She liked the way he said her name. Like a caress. *Wow, cool it, girl.*

"You're Ming's sister right." Steve's green eyes appraised her. "You're not at all how I pictured you."

"Oh." What had Ming told this group? Did they envision a grief-stricken widow in black or... she didn't know what?

"I thought you'd look more alike being twins."

Isabella laughed. Steve appeared oblivious to his mistake.

"You do know Ming was joking." Dan patted his friend on the back trying not to laugh himself.

"No, Ming sounded serious."

Isabella felt sorry for the guy. "She's a pro at saying we're twins without cracking a smile."

Ming joined them. Giving Steve a wink. "Mrs. Crawford, who's in her eighties, said the same thing you did."

"Makes me feel so much better." Steve laughed and grabbed Ming in a bear hug. He looked over at Isabella. "You know she dared me."

"I believe it." Issy shook her head.

"I did not." Ming gave Steve a playful slap. "I told everyone we were like twins."

"See." Steve wagged his finger at Ming. "Nice to meet you." Steve shook Isabella's hand. "Do you prefer Isabella or Issy?"

"Issy to my friends. What do you do for living Steve?"

"I'm a lawyer slash wanna-be mechanic."

"Interesting."

STEVE KEPT the conversation moving while Dan observed from the sidelines. Issy bright pink blouse showed off her figure without showing her figure. Her black slacks fit well, not clinging like a few of the other women he'd seen tonight. Silver earrings danced when she nodded. Delicate fingers entwined the matching necklace when she listened.

"What do you do for a living?" Steve asked.

"Nothing."

Dan stopped observing and joined the conversation. "You're unemployed?"

"No...I work part-time at Hobby Life."

"But it's just temporary." Ming defended her. "She's a widow getting back on her feet."

"A few months ago, I decide Indiana had no more hold on me so here I am."

He liked the way her skin darkened when she blushed. Why did this woman turn his brain to mush?

Before the awkward silence grew Steve extended his hand to Isabella.

"Well, we're glad you're here. If you're looking for a church home Living River might be a good fit."

"I'm attending Stone Church. Have you heard Dan preach?" Issy smiled at Dan causing his neck to warm.

"He told me he was filling in for his uncle. So, he's got it going on as a preacher." Steve gave Dan a wink.

"No big deal. Uncle Paul is still recovering from the flu. He'll be back in the pulpit next week and I'll be sitting in the pews."

"Your uncle's been the pastor of Stone Church since we were teens. Any plans for retirement?"

"Uncle Paul lost his zeal for preaching when Aunt Sally died. I think it won't be long and he'll be retiring."

"Are you planning on taking his place?"

"Me, a pastor—not on your life." Dan caught himself before his voice went any higher. "Takes more courage than night maneuvers in Afghanistan."

"You're so good," Issy said.

"Thanks," He looked at his shoes. "If you got anything from the sermon... it was God speaking. Not me. I doubt my next sermon will be much better."

"Let me be the judge of that." Issy touched his shoulder sending a wave of pleasure down his arm. "Don't belittle yourself. I'd rather hear a man speak from his heart than a professional orator."

"Well, I'll take the compliment." Dan's mind blanked on any further conversation with this beautiful woman.

Nadia rescued the uncomfortable moment. "Robin is in the building. Let the games begin." Everyone chuckled, leaving Robin red-faced.

Mary's home had an extra-long living room. Couches rested against the walls. Card tables and folding chairs filled the space in the middle. The evening started with a round of Pictionary pitting the guys against the gals. The women were triumphant. Dan couldn't remember the last time he laughed so much. Isabella company added to his pleasure. She threw herself into the game. But appeared to have a hard time keeping the pictures simple. Dan had no artistic ability but Steve figured out biscuits and gravy from the blotches he drew on the paper. A timer buzzed.

"Time to switch things up," Nadia announced. "We have six tables and six different games. Each game requires at least four players. We gave each of you a number when you arrived. Everyone move away from the tables." Chairs shuffled, people moved.

"Heyward and I will place the games on the table with four numbers. Uno has five because we have an odd number here tonight."

Heyward added. "When Nadia says ready, find your number."

Dan and Issy found themselves at the Yahtzee table with John and Charles. John's collar length hair and studious appearance contrasted his competitive spirit. Charles, shy laughter when his dice found their pairing inspired playful trash talk. Issy's melodious giggles fueled the guys' verbal jabs.

"Come on, Chuck, you trying the rub the dots off the dice?" John slapped him on the back causing the dice to tumble out of the cup.

"Hey, I want a do-over." Charles scowled at John then noticed his dice. "All right." He high-fived Dan. "Never mind, I rolled a full house."

"Won't be long and you'll be wiping the floor with John." Dan winked at Issy. His dice spilled from the cup. "Yahtzee!" another high-five between Dan and Charley. "Puts you in last place, bro."

"Issy, see if you can't crush these pompous poodles." John gave a playful glare at his opponents.

"Poodle. That's the best you can do?" Dan laughed. The banter and fun reinforced Steve's words. Dan needed a life. This. Right here. Playing games, meeting new friends was what he needed.

Issy threw her dice. "I need sixes or fives. Oh, come on." She laughed at her own misfortune. Two more tries gave her four of a kind with threes. "Obviously, I'm the amateur here."

"Nah, just a kindergartener playing with the college guys." John bumped her shoulder.

"Whoa, Tonto, time to rein in the name calling horse." Dan's tone held no humor.

"Hey, it's fine. He's an equal opportunity trash talker." Issy smiled. John nodded and Charles laughed.

"Chill out, bro." Charles grabbed the cup shaking it hard, "Two more spaces to fill and I'll be the one claiming bragging rights."

Their last two turns played out with no fanfare or bantering. Same covered Dan after he over-reaction. *Smooth move, Danny Boy. So, high school.*

Issy took her last turn which concluded the game as the timer went off again. "That was fun. John and Chuck tied for first, Dan second."

"All right, step away from the tables," Nadia instructed. "We have snacks. Heyward, John, and Nathan will set up the video game stations. Everyone else help move the card tables and take a few of the chairs out into the dining room."

Mary pointed to the sign on the wall. "So, there is no confusion. Go through this door. Fill your plates. Exit through the other door back to the dining room.

"Thanks for the help, Miss Obvious." Steve laughed and feigned difficulty reading the sign.

"Well, the last time the gathering was at my house two of you guys whose initials are Steve and Nathan bumped into each other at the same door and christened my carpet with strawberry soda. Cost me a bunch to have it cleaned." Mary's declaration brought heckles and teasing from the rest of the men present.

～

MING AND ISSY found chairs along the wall of the dining room. "Thanks for making me come, sis. I think I'd forgotten how to have fun."

"I agree." Ming scooped bean dip with her tortilla chip. Her head bobbed in contentment as she chewed. Wiping her lips with her napkin she added. "If you want to experience some more fun, Steve is trying to get a group together to sky dive."

Dan and Steve appeared with full plates and sat on either side of the girls.

"Parachuting out of a plane is not my idea of fun." Issy shook her head then popped a grape in her mouth.

"Falling through the air from 20,000 feet is more fun than..." Steve's statement finished by Dan.

"Breaking your leg in three places while having a heart attack."

"Count me out." Issy popped another grape in her mouth.

"It's tandem skydiving. You're strapped to a professional. Relax and enjoy the ride." Steve balanced his plate on his left hand while his right hand imitated floating downward.

"And watch the ground rise up to meet you seconds before the chute gives you whiplash." Dan jerked his head to the side for emphasis before biting into a brownie.

"That confirms my no."

"Such a party pooper." Ming bumped her sister.

Issy bumped her back. "Not the first time you've accused me. I'm sensing a theme."

"Well, you are." Ming wink at her sister and Isabella raised her eyebrow and faked a frown.

"I sky dived once." Dan offered. "Never again."

"You chose Ruby as your tandem buddy." Steve said.

"Ruby was insane. She loved to push the envelope. Faked a faulty chute. At the last moment, she pulled the ripcord, and we missed a tree by inches."

"I remember how you looked when we landed. A ghost in sunglasses." Steve laughed. "I offered to trade partners."

"Yeah, well. I thought a grandmother would be safer than the marine you had."

"Army strong couldn't handle a little old lady."

Dan neck redden. He shoved a whole chocolate cookie in his mouth and chewed. Ming and Issy's hands went to their mouths in syncopated rhythm.

"Go ahead. Laugh." Dan pointed at the girls. "Don't injure yourself on my account."

In unison, the girl's laughter exploded. The men followed. They laughed until tears formed.

"All right, everyone the video games are ready." Nadia got the group moving toward the living room again. "We have Wii bowling and Family Feud for those who don't want to play whatever macho war game Hayward and Nathan have set up on the Play Station and X-box systems." Nadia crinkled her nose for emphasis before adding. "You can play, cheer the players on or sit around and talk. And if anyone needs to leave feel free."

Dan, Ming, and Steve joined Mary and Nadia and Charles to challenge another team in Family Feud while Issy enjoyed cheerleading. She couldn't resist whispering answers to the girls causing the men to declare her a cheater.

Except for the diehard video gamers, the party dwindled within an hour. Dan climbed into his truck as the sisters headed for their car. He caught Issy staring as he transitioned from the ground to the driver's seat. Humiliation fought with the smile he was trying to maintain.

"See you Sunday." Issy slid into the driver's seat of her Prius.

"Hey." Dan signaled for her to roll down her window. Her brow formed a tiny frown before the window opened. He cleared his throat.

"Want to go to the dog park with me tomorrow?"

"No."

Dan shrugged not knowing what to do with such a direct rejection.

"Wait." Her door flew open and she walked over to his truck. "That came out wrong. I work tomorrow." Issy gave an embarrassed smile. "Thanks for asking."

Dan forced himself to look her full in the face.

"Right... I'll see you Sunday."

He watched her slide back behind the wheel and returned the girls' waves as they headed out.

Dan pulled out of the driveway frustration wrestled with hope. He'd put himself out there coming to this party. *The dog park? Man, you are so lame. But hey, she didn't say no to his company or was work an excuse? Don't over think it.* His mind focused on all the smiles she'd given him that evening. *Maybe there was something there. But she smiled at everyone. Ugh! Rein it in Sweeney.*

12

CONFLICT AND FRUSTRATION

"Isabella, I need a word with you." Mr. Clayton's go-to statement when he wasn't pleased.

"Let me ring up this customer." Issy had been helping an older woman find more skeins of burnt orange yarn.

The woman hovered over her while she knelt beside the lowest shelf shifting through the bins. Mr. Clayton's rotund physique towered over her floor-level posture. Issy's mind flashed to a time when she'd broken an heirloom china cup. Maureen loomed over her. "How could you? A tear trickled down her cheek. "Immigrants. Disrespectful and careless. Shame on you." She'd left the room clutching the remaining saucer.

Issy pushed the vision away. Mr. Clayton's scowl followed her to a standing position.

Stepping back and giving the customer a practiced smile, he added, "Ingrid is at the register, finish up here and meet me in my office." Mr. Clayton directed a second smile and nod to the woman before leaving.

It took the customer several minutes to inspect the yarn. She held her sample up to each skein before declaring. "These are perfect." A contented sigh escaped her lips. "Thank you so much, hon." The woman placed the skeins in her cart and headed toward the checkout. Issy knelt to replace and reorganize the shelf before heading to the manager's office. She used the time to review her work performance for any reason for the summons to the manager's office. Before she could reach the back of the store, three different customers had approached her for help with finding things. Fifteen minutes passed before she knocked on the closed door.

"I called you to my office thirty minutes ago," Mr. Clayton indicated the chair in front of his desk. A frown etched his brow.

Even though the exaggeration goaded her, she passed over the urge to correct him. "A few customers needed my help."

"Fair enough." His expression relaxed, he folded his arms in front of him on the desk. "Miss Wilson, I understand you did the easel display yesterday. And restocked the clay?"

"Yes, sir."

"You must redo them."

"Why?"

"I gave you specific instructions, you apparently can't follow them." He leaned back in his chair. "You have developed a pattern of doing whatever you want whenever you want."

"That's not true... I"

The flat palm forward signal from Mr. Clayton stopped further explanation. His lips tightened.

"I'm not finished." Mr. Clayton lowered his hand straightened his back and his tie before continuing. "Hobby Life is a franchise. The displays are designed by professionals in the head office. You must follow the illustrations step by step. The success of Hobby Life lies in the pattern for store layout and displays. You can not deviate one iota. Secondly, each new display has a fixed completion time corporate mandated. In the short time, you have worked here, you have not completed one task within the time frame allowed."

"Excuse me." Isabella straightened in her chair matching Mr. Clayton's stiff tone.

"Those time frames are unrealistic. They don't allow for interruptions. Helping customers is our primary goal. At least that is what the training manual emphasized. I can't ask customers to wait until the display is complete to help them." She watched red rise like a thermometer from the manager's collar to his cheeks.

"But you can call someone not on display and stocking duty to help them." He grabbed the manual on his desk and flipped a few pages. Running his finger down the page, he turned the book around and thrust it toward her. "Right here in paragraph three, it explains how to use your walkie-talkie to get assistance for our customers."

"I feel it's rude to hand someone off when I am standing right there. There are times... last Saturday for example. We had a lot of coupons. There weren't enough customer service affiliates to help everyone."

"The guidelines state how many employees are to be on duty in each position based on sales." Mr. Clayton turned to another page. "Per these guidelines, we can't schedule more personnel until we reach those sales plateaus."

"But we won't reach them without enough staff for the number of customers we have." Isabella felt her pulse race. She pressed her point. "Last Saturday three customers complained about our poor service. One gentleman left his cart and huffed out the door. Another woman said it took less time to drive to Matthew's Crafts in Saint Charles to get her items than to get waited on here."

"Miss Wilson, you have made your point. Although I sympathize, there's nothing I can do. The franchise owner is the one authorized to deviate from the manual. When Mr. Crawford passed away, his wife wanted everything left unchanged. this discussion is waste of time. Now redo the display and re-shelf the clay." He opened the door ending the meeting. "And Miss Wilson if it is necessary to redo a display you have assembled one more time, you will receive written warning. This conversation was your second verbal warning." The door shut before she had a chance to ask when she'd gotten the first warning.

Isabella's work-day couldn't end fast enough. After the warning, her day had decelerated into a slow plod of disasters.

She'd tripped over a box.

Directed a customer to the wrong aisle.

Her face darkened as she watched a line form while she struggled to recall how to replace an empty receipt cartridge. Another associate completed the task.

She punched out and headed to the car, exhaustion heavy on her shoulders. Pressing the key fob, the door opened. Issy slid behind the wheel. Turning the key produced nothing.

"Come on. You're a new car."

She tried the key again—nothing.

"Don't be like Bernie." She put her tongue in her cheek imitating Ming's ritual for starting her Junker.

She glanced at the dashboard and the interior for any sign of the problem. The rearview mirror was cocked her way and its light switch on. "No." She rested her head on the steering wheel.

Her bad day started earlier than she thought. She'd misread her alarm. Fearing she was moments from being late, she'd thrown on her clothes and ran a comb through her hair before bolting out the door. In the parking lot, she'd noticed the correct time on the dashboard clock.

"Note to self, don't put make-up on in the car unless you remember to turn off the light."

A frustrated sigh helped release some pent-up tension from the day. "Ok, now what?" Talking out loud helped her gain composure.

"Ming should be home by now." Retrieving her cell from her purse, she scrolled to Ming's number. It rang several times and went to voicemail.

"Rats, she always leaves her phone on vibrate in her purse." Isabella texted her dilemma and received an immediate response.

I added a late appointment.

She should be here in a few.

I'll find a knight to rescue you. Hang tight.

Isabella grabbed iced chai tea from the cafe across the parking lot. By the time, she'd walked back to her car, a familiar truck pulled into the lot beside her car.

"Hey, my lady, I hear you are in distress."

How many guys did Ming call first? Shame sweep away the rude thought.

Dan opened the door and slid from the truck. After ensuring his feet were balanced, he reached behind the seat for jumper cables. "Get in and pop the hood."

She slid into the front seat and pulled the hood lever. Dan connected the cables. "Turn the key and give her some gas." Dan's dimpled smile when the car came to life sent a tiny shiver up her spine. What was wrong with her?

"Fair knight you have rescued me." *Lame. Don't think what you're thinking. No good can come of it.* "How can I ever repay you?"

Dan leaned in the passenger window that opened at her touch. "Go to lunch with me after church."

"If it's my treat."

"Deal." Dan grinned. "I have to ask. How did you kill the battery on a new car?"

"In short—make-up... light switch."

"You don't apply makeup while you drive?"

"No. I'm not stupid. A vision of Ron's scowl flashed across her mind. "I was parked right here and forgot to turn off my mirror light, okay?" How dare he suggest such a thing.

"Hey, I'm sorry I upset you. My mom had a bad habit of multi-tasking when she drove."

"You assumed all women do the same?"

"Well, no." Dan ran his left hand through his hair a look of desperate repentance washed over his face. "I'm sorry."

She pressed a smile on her lips, nodded and put the car in gear.

"See you tomorrow." Issy managed before rolling up her window.

She watched him through the rear-view mirror. Dan waved.

~

ISSY SLAMMED THE DOOR, making Ming jump. "Hey, I almost sliced my finger." Turning from the cutting board of veggies, she pointed her knife. "The landlord fixed that door once. Let's not irritate him with a second repair."

"Sorry." Issy grabbed a bottled water from the fridge and took a few sips before flopping on the couch. "I hate my job."

"What happened?" Ming continued the rhythm of chopping broccoli without looking her way.

"Yeah, well, the SOP is—to quote a teen co-worker—really wacked."

"Are you swearing sister of mine?"

"What? No? SOP means Standard Operating Procedure. It's the manual every business adheres to."

"I was teasing. I know what an SOP is." Ming grabbed a carrot and deftly chopped it.

"Well, it's Mr. Clayton's Bible. He can quote it chapter and verse." Issy sipped more of her water.

"Several people I know said similar things when they worked there. Since Mr. Crawford died things went downhill."

"No wonder Mr. Clayton is so irritating."

"Do you know Teresa? Skinny. Gray hair. Blue rimmed glasses." Ming continued stirring while Issy placed the name and description with a face.

"The manager of the sewing department."

"And a member of my church and part of my small group. Teresa mentioned in one of her gossipy prayers that Mrs. Crawford refused Mr. Clayton's offer to buy the place. She asked God to give him patience. Then mentioned, to God, how she thought everything would be better for the employees if Mr. Clayton could make the changes he wanted."

"So, Hobby Life is often a part of Teresa's gossipy prayers." Issy moved from the couch and threw the empty bottle in the recycling on the way to collect plates from the cupboard.

"When she isn't complaining to anyone who will listen."

"Nice to know I'm not alone." Issy pulled out napkins from the pantry to fill the napkin holder. "It's more than the SOP. I hate stocking shelves and trying to explain to customers why the paint they chose—because it was on sale—is not what they need for their project."

"You'd rather put your education to use." Ming set a hot pad on the table, the delicious smells of stir fry reminded Issy she had skipped lunch. Ming placed the wok on the hot pad. "You've got an art degree from one of the best art schools in the country. Working in a craft store is like doing a paint by number."

"Good word picture."

After blessing the food, Issy served herself. "I've lost my painting muse. Ron and the ministry chased it away. Music and evangelism were the two big ministry thrusts. No one cared I had an art degree." She stabbed a carrot. "Wait, I forgot, I was allowed to decorate a few tables for ladies' luncheons." Bitter bile mixed with her dinner at the memory. "My job was to minister alongside Ron whether I felt gifted or called."

"I thought you loved to sing. You have a beautiful voice."

"I used to love it when we sang in Gramma's small church. I enjoyed the informal worship. And being part of the youth choir. Ron focused on an excellent production. He wanted to put on a good show."

"You're serious, a good show?"

"Then he got obsessed with sounding professional and making CDs."

"You made CDs?"

"Five of them."

"Can I hear them?"

"No." Acid rose in her throat again. "Those were among the things I left behind. I never want to hear them again."

"Why? Doesn't the music remind you of your husband."

"Exactly. Those CDs represent the part of our marriage that was ugly." Issy's fork pushed rice around on her plate. "The day before he died I had packed my bag and hid it in the trunk of my car. I was planning on moving out after church the next day."

"Wow!" Ming's fork clattered onto her plate. "Not in a million year. You two were so in love."

"Those first few years. Two things changed that love... his mother and a brain tumor no one mentioned."

"I thought he died of an aneurysm—just a freak thing."

"Me too. This past year I found out Ron and his mother had kept the truth from me. Ron might have thought I wouldn't marry him if I knew." Issy took a swallow of water to still the burning in her throat. "

"Once we were married he maintained the charade. After RJ died his personality changed. The tumor grew. He'd get nasty headaches that made him mean. His ministry focus changed to making it big as a Christian artist. Ron didn't know the tumor had grown because he'd stopped going to the neurologist and was self-medicating."

"Why would he do that?"

"Worship leader was who he was. If the church knew about the tumor..." She set her fork aside.

"He kept praying for healing, believing God for a miracle. I'd assumed he was referring to the headaches. I had no idea how big a miracle." Tears blurred her vision.

"Had I known he had a tumor, I'd have dragged him back to his doctor." Issy pushed her plate aside and looked around the tiny dining area not focusing on her surroundings. Memories exploded in her mind of clues she never connected.

"The sad part." Issy pushed her hair behind her ears and refocused on her sister's attentive face. "When I saw Ron's doctor for my migraines, he dumped a soap opera revelation on me. My husband's tumor could have been removed when first discovered with no ill effects,"

"So, why'd he decide against the surgery."

"Ron believed his illness was his thorn in the flesh."

"That's crazy."

"The doctor showed me the pictures of Ron's brain and explained it all to me. Simply put, the tumor pressed against the reasoning parts of the brain." Confessing the fact brought more clarity to Issy. *He was ill, not evil.*

"That must have been tough. What was Maureen's reaction when you confronted her?" Ming held her cup in her hands, elbows resting on the table.

"Maureen said nothing at first. She never addressed an issue right away. She had to plot an answer in her mind. Three days later she presented me with a letter she claimed Ron wrote her. It said his wife was too young and frail to handle his cross to bear. He was glad his mother was strong enough to help him through the ordeal."

"He wrote that?"

"Of course, not. He always printed in block letters because his cursive was illegible. Maureen couldn't face the truth of her deception. She always presented her best to her friends at church and her women's club. My being frail served her purposes better than admitting she helped withhold surgery from her son."

"How insane." Ming cleared the table.

"When the doctor told me, my grief turned to anger. And here's the kicker. I had to prove we were married before the doctor could discuss anything with me. HIPPA laws and the fact he had change his marital status on his records."

"The doctor must have known Ron a long time."

"The doctor first saw him at sixteen. Once he moved to Missouri and worked at the folk's church, he quit seeing the neurologist. The tumor had stayed the same size for ten years. We visited his mother our first Christmas. Apparently, he saw the doctor then. That's when he took the job as Minister of Music at his mother's church. We went home and relocated." Once the cluttered closet was open, the uglies came tumbling out. "I know now we moved so he could be near his doctor. The one Ron claimed was treating his mother for migraines. The one he took her to every month. She'd move her appointment if he couldn't take her. I thought she was being difficult when she refused my offers to take her."

"Being a smother?" Ming cleared the table.

"Oh, she smothered him all right. I never knew how dependent he could be until I saw how close he was to his mom. At first, I thought it sweet. Then they stopped talking when I entered the room or Ron stepped outside to talk to his mom on his cell, I got jealous. Their relationship seemed weird and I blew up at him one day."

"I bet that went well." Ming formed bubbles in her palm from the dish water and blew them toward her sister. Issy batted the bubbles away. She appreciated her attempt at lightening the mood albeit lame.

"He laughed. Told me I was overreacting. He said his mother was delicate and needed to be handled."

"And..." Ming held the limp dish towel in her hand the last plate forgotten in the draining rack.

"He made love to me."

"TMI, Issy." Ming covered her head with the dish towel.

"Well, you asked." Issy's mood softened watching her sister try to keep from laughing.

"That was his solution to everything. Anytime we disagreed he persuaded me to make love by nightfall. After a while, it became one-sided sex."

"Hey, why are you telling your single sister this?" Ming finished drying the plate and retrieved the wash rag from the sink.

"Stop!" Issy grabbed the wet rag from her sister. "Use a fresh cloth to wash the table."

"Seriously, the rag is fine. How can you switch from discussing your sex life to a dirty dish rag all in one breathe?"

Issy shrugged and grabbed a broom. Silently, they finished putting the kitchen in order. Issy's milled over her sister's last words. How could she put those two things in the same sentence? Maybe the dirty rag was a symbol of her life? She pictured an acrylic painting with the sudsy dirty rag perched on the edge of a table with a weeping woman in a ragged dress crouched in a corner. If her art muse was resurfacing it was horrid and dark.

13

GETTING ACQUAINTED

Dan shook congregants' hands and half-listened to their comments while his mind reviewed last night's scenario. He'd angered her with his driving-while-putting-on-makeup comment. But she'd still said I'll see you tomorrow. Was the date still on? Did it mean I'll see you in church? It wasn't a date, just a thank you for helping her. *Oh God, help me. I need to complete my mission without acting weird.*

His objective: lunch with Isabella.

Before leaving the parking lot yesterday, he'd hit on an idea for a small homemade gift for her. Now secured in a gift bag in his truck, he second guessed the wisdom in presenting it to her. *Get your head in the game, Sweeney.* He smiled at Miss Lindy while she continued chattering. Her voice sounding like the cartoon adults in the Charlie Brown movies. All noise and no substance.

"I'll see you next week, Pastor." The woman squeezed his left hand as she toddled away.

"That's Dan." His words lost as her back moved toward the door. "Not pastor, just Dan." The pastor term stuck with this older generation. They were paying him a compliment for stepping into his uncle's shoes. It still felt uncomfortable.

Dan spotted Isabella still seated in the last row. He waved, and she smiled gathering her purse, and Bible. She wore a jean skirt with a royal blue top. Her ankle length black boots had three-inch heels. Why did short women feel they needed to add extra height with feet-killing heels? On second thought his cousin stood six feet, and she always wore killer heels. Women, who can figure.

"What?" Isabella stood, slinging her purse over her shoulder.

"What?"

"You were shaking your head."

Dan's face warmed when he realized how observant she was. "I was wondering how women can walk in those spiky things."

She laughed. "That's a relief, I thought you might cancel our date. Some hot old lady was making you a home-cooked meal."

Her joke broke the ice from the awkward moment from last night. Dan felt relief roll over him. She considered it a date. Score. Dan winked. "There were a few. But I turned them down. Didn't want the old widowers jealous."

Isabella's easy laugh warmed him. He opened the passenger door of his truck.

"Would you mind if we took separate vehicles?"

Not really a date. "Ok." Dan closed the door and walked her to her car. "Where do you want to eat?"

"I'm in the mood for seafood. Red Lobster? You're not allergic, are you?" She waited for his response.

Dan refocused on her question. Her floral scent beckoned him to lean in closer. He held her door open breathing in the fragrance. "Not allergic. Sounds good."

He closed her door and knocked on her window. Her window slid open. "The one on Route 59, right?"

"I don't know where that is. Ming and I went to the one in Saint Charles awhile back. I'll follow you."

Dan watched out his rearview mirror to be sure Isabella was behind him. He pushed the speed limit, and it appeared she drove like an old lady. There were no parking spaces available. They pulled into an adjacent lot. Dan fought embarrassment as she waited beside his truck. He concentrated on landing without jerky movements. The gift bag a bit crinkled by the effort.

"What's that?"

Her interest in the bag made Dan glad he'd not forgotten it.

"You'll see after we get seated."

Dan took her hand before he lost his nerve and they walked together. The hostess directed them to a booth near the back. "Can we have this table instead, please?"

A table for two.

"You sure can, hon." The hostess left two menus on the table.

Did Isabella know booths were a challenge?

The hostess couldn't see his prosthetic under his long pants. He held out Isabella's chair, then slid into his own.

The perky waitress greeted them. "Can I start you out with something to drink?"

Before she gave wine suggestions, Isabella asked for raspberry tea.

"I'll have iced tea with no lemon."

"I'll be back to take your orders."

"Order anything you like. It's my treat and I want the sampler platter. Don't you dare order the cheapest thing on the menu, either." Isabella shook her finger at Dan.

"Hey, I'll charge your battery anytime." Dan hid his blush behind the menu hoping she didn't catch the unintended double meaning. "I'll have the lobster and steak combo." Folding the menu, he found his composure. The waitress reappeared with their drinks and took their orders.

"So, tell me. Who is Isabella Wilson."

Her face blanched white before answering. "There's not much to tell. I grew up in a variety of states. My dad was a geologist, and he moved from place to place while he did geological surveys for oil. I graduated from high school in Iowa. I attended the American Academy of Art in Chicago. Met my husband Ron at a church there, married right out of college. We moved to Indiana where he was Minister of Music at a mega-church. He died from an aneurysm, and after living with my mother-in-law for a year, I moved here.

Her recitation of the facts interrupted by the waitress. Relief registered on her face. The waitress arranged their food and an extra basket of biscuits. "Enjoy."

"Your turn." Isabella fidgeted with the table service. "Who is Dan Sweeney?"

"I grew up here. My parents died in a plane crash just before 9/11."

"How awful for you."

"Yeah, well... I lived with my older sister until I graduated from high school. One semester was enough college for me. I planned a career in the army. But I lost my leg, and they booted me out."

"Why? Wasn't there another job you could do? After all, you lost a limb for your country."

And there it was—the snake that always bit him. Best to set her straight now.

"I didn't lose my leg for my country. Even if I had, I didn't have enough rank and the right pull to keep my career."

Dan sipped his tea before continuing. He didn't look up from his glass afraid of the pity he'd see.

"I lost these two shorter fingers for my country." He held up his deformed right hand. She nodded and remained silent. "There's a scar on my cheek from an IED explosion in Afghanistan." He pointed to his bearded right cheek. Dan refrained from listing the myriad of unseen wounds like his PTSD.

"What's an IED?"

"Improvised explosive device. That's a fancy term for a homemade bomb."

"Oh."

"I didn't qualify for an MOS in combat anymore but they found me other work."

"MOS?"

"Military Occupational Specialty." Defining terms for her lessened the awkward feeling of sharing his pitiful life. "I was the logistic liaison for two years. My last leave I was home riding my chopper. That's a motorcycle."

She flashed him a grin and rolled her eyes. Dan relaxed a little more.

"An inexperienced semi driver fell asleep at the wheel. He swerved away from my biker buddies and me. But overturned his cab trapping my leg between the cab and my bike. I spent a year and some months in rehab at Walter Reed VA Hospital. Received an honorable discharge and free college. So, I'm working on a business degree."

"Would you two be interested in dessert?" The waitress' timing was perfect. He didn't want to talk about himself anymore. Even the abbreviated version bothered him.

"Let's go somewhere else for dessert," Isabella asked.

"Sounds fine with me."

The waitress left their check. Isabella slipped cash into the bill folder.

"Where did you have in mind?"

"My place, I made a to-die-for German Chocolate cake. We could enjoy coffee and let the lobster settle."

She was inviting him home. It was a date. Dan reached for the gift bag he'd laid at his feet. "Before I forget, I wanted to give you this. You'll need it if you are ever late for work again."

Isabella eyed the bag before opening it. "I love it." Dan had fashioned a sign that clipped to the vent tines in her car, written in calligraphy across a small pre-made plaque.

"Be sure to turn off all lights before exiting the vehicle." Isabella read aloud.

It sounded lame to Dan's ears.

"You are so thoughtful." She showed it off to the waitress when she picked up the leather holder. The waitress nodded and gave her for-my-customer's-only smile.

Dan laughed.

"You had to be there."

The waitress took the payment and departed. Thy headed to the exit. Isabella matching her steps to Dan's. His leg felt heavy after sitting. He found his stride by the time they'd reached the vehicles.

DAN FOLLOWED ISABELLA HOME, parking in the driveway behind her car. Ming's over-the- garage apartment sat at the back of a lot. The home in front appeared to be subdivided into apartments. He recognized Steve's car parked next to Isabella's. There was a black Toyota truck parked behind a two-tone Junker.

The long flight of stairs was a chore for Dan but he kept a consistent stride and made it to the door a few steps behind Isabella.

"I'm sorry, I forgot about the steps." Embarrassment colored her face.

"No worries." Dan breathed in fresh air attempting a smile. She entered first giving him a moment to gain his footing and composure. Disappointment settled on his shoulders when he saw Steve along with John from the singles group sitting around the dining table.

"Hey, Sis, did you leave any cake for the baker?" Isabella lifted the cake cover lid.

"What kind of sister do you think I am?" Ming grabbed two more dessert plates. "Besides having you all kinds of mad at me after I begged you to make the cake well.... it wouldn't have been pretty." A giggle followed the opening of the silverware drawer. "You'll have to use spoons."

Dan shook hands with the guys and sat in a kitchen chair, glad for the respite. "So, what are you guys doing here?"

"We're are claiming our pay." Steve scraped cake crumbs onto his fork. "Mindy's car wouldn't start after church. John helped me install a new starter."

"I made spaghetti in exchange for their hard work." Ming handed the slice Isabella had placed on the plate to Dan. "The cake was their tip."

"I guess food is the acceptable pay for car repairs." Isabella gave Dan a cup of coffee and placed hers on the table. Retrieving her dessert, she slides into the chair next to Dan. "Dan drives a harder bargain. We ate at Red Lobster."

"What did you have to fix to score that?" John went to refresh his coffee.

"I gave her car a jump. Her battery died." Dan thought better of teasing her about her make-up blunder.

"Wow! Mindy, you are so cheap. And to think I passed on that when you told me your sister was stranded." John sat again and grabbed the sugar bowl adding three teaspoons to his coffee.

"Passed up? You are so full of bologna." Steve took his plate to the sink. "Let's get the facts straight. When I called, you told me your shift didn't end for another two hours. Even though cops have been helping damsels in distress with car problems since the first automobile."

"You're a cop?" Dan pegged John for a computer geek after the singles game night.

"I work for the Fox Valley Park District."

"He's a wanna-be real cop. He chases love sick teenagers out of the park after curfew." Steve moved his chair out of John's reach.

"Ha ha." John pushed his plate to the center of the table. "You have no idea what I do. We assist the local police or the Sheriff's department. We deal with drug dealers and other scumbags in the park. Fox Valley Park District has 164 parks, not to mention nature trails we have to patrol."

"I had no idea" Isabella turned giving her full attention to John while he shared stories of his daily activities.

Jealousy crept through Dan. A whole cop is far more appealing than a broken soldier. He ate his cake in silence opting not to get another cup of coffee. The leg ached from the trek up the stairs and his limp would be more prominent.

John's cell phone dinged before he could begin another story. Pausing to check it, he pushed his chair back. "I got to fly."

Steve rose too. "I'll follow you out. I still have your tools I borrowed last week, in my car."

The two men hugged Ming and Isabella. Hugging was a more accepted departure than a handshake these days. Dan hated the ideas of those two getting to hug Isabella first. *"Pull it together Sweeney. Act cool."* He wrestled the envy monster back in its cage.

Ming waited until the sound of their footsteps were muted before she whispered. "John's got a date."

"So?" Isabella took John's dishes to the sink and brought the coffee pot to the table and refilled Dan's cup and her own before adding soapy water to the sink.

"I forget you guys aren't one of us." Ming sat on the kitchen chair with her leg tucked under her. "John has been on that Christian dating site. What's it called? Pairing.com or perfect fit..." She flicked her hand to dismiss her confusion and barreled on. "John keeps meeting these loser girls for coffee. They start with coffee in case it doesn't work out." Ming looked over her cup at them.

"Really, sis, you gotta milk this one. I could care lesser than less about John's love life."

Dan repressed a smile. She wasn't interested in John, even if he leads an exciting life. Or was it she was interested and didn't want to hear his dating exploits?

Ming's frustrated sigh echoed through his foolish thoughts.

"Ok, ok. Well, the last one—this girl, Becky--made it to a second date... They're meeting at the Gilman nature trail. She loves the outdoors too."

"That's nice." Isabel plastered on an animated smile.

"Okay, I get it. You really don't care. A little faked interest would have been nice."

Isabella started to wash the dishes.

"Stop right there." Ming pushed her sister away from the sink with her hip. "I got this. I made the mess, I'll clean it up. You have company."

"If you're sure." Isabella grabbed both their cups.

Dan push his irritation aside. Why did she take his cup? Was it pity or just what it looked like, moving their cups. Did she think he couldn't balance a cup of coffee while he walked? His leg was rested enough to make the transition from table to living room with ease.

Dan took the straight back chair. Isabella had placed his coffee on the end table between his chair and an overstuffed chair.

"Are you sure you don't want the other chair? It's more comfortable."

"No thanks, I'm good." Dan noticed the chair was well-loved making it easy to slip into its recesses and hard to extract yourself.

"Inquiring minds want to know." Isabella' words reminded him of an interview he'd done once. He hoped the subject wasn't his disability anymore.

"You're not a member of Ming's church, and you don't often attend their singles group. How do you and Steve know each other?"

Relief brought a smile. This was a safe subject.

"We grew up together. His folks moved to Prestbury and he attended Kaneland High his senior year. We still hung out together on occasion. When I joined the army, he was the one guy from our old gang who kept in touch. After I bought my house here, we hooked back up. He's a real estate lawyer."

"How long have you been back?"

"Depends on which time. I bought my home while I was still in the service. I hadn't decided to reenlist. I figured I could always rent it." Dan reached for his coffee cup. Here he was talking about himself again. But Isabella's questions didn't pinch his heart as they had when others had asked. No way could he talk his home in Aurora without talking about his loss.

"For the past few years I took my one month leave and did remodeling. Six months after the last leave I was fighting for my life in Walter Reed ICU. After rehab I got a medical discharge. Steve and some of his friends had finished the projects I started—like the bathroom so I could move in."

"I've been here two months. It must be wonderful to get reacquainted with childhood friends."

"Some have moved away from the old neighborhood. I took a drive through the area, saw one of my old neighbors sitting on his porch. Mr. Gomez remembered me, we talked. Said all the other neighbors had moved away."

"Did you look up your friends?" Isabella gave Dan the same attention he had given John earlier. Leaning forward in her chair, eyes fixed on him.

Pastor's wife training or real interest? Stop it. Sadness wrestled happy memories before he continued.

"If I wanted to visit the cemetery."

"Oh, I'm sorry." Silence wrapped the conversation for a few moments. Isabella shifted in her chair. "I asked because my family moved so much due to Dad's work I didn't develop those life-long friends. I'm a bit jealous of those who do."

"I had two close friends. Steve was one and Ray the other."

"Have you seen Ray since you've been back?"

"No." Ray's crooked smile and laughter passed through his mind. "He's in prison in Marion, Illinois." Dan saw another apology coming. "Don't be embarrassed for asking. It's just life. Steve's folks moved him out of the neighborhood to avoid gang influence. My folks got me involved with youth activities and sent me to my Uncle Jim's farm in Waterman during the summers in high school."

Dan finished his cake frustrated that another conversation had a depressing theme. "I should take off. Thanks for dinner and the cake was awesome."

"I'll walk you to the door." Isabella rose from the couch retrieving the slippers she removed when she sat down.

"Promise you won't watch me leave." Dan hoped his voice had a teasing tone. He wished he'd have left with the guys. Steve knew how to help him down the stairs.

"Ok, I guess." Isabella's confusion led to the question he wanted to avoid. "Why?"

"Your steps are real steep. I'll need to go down my backside. Don't want to feel any more humiliated than I do telling you."

Instead of apologizing again she smiled. "I understand. I'll see you next week if not sooner."

Dan sat on the stair landing. No one from the neighborhood was watching. At the bottom, he used the railing to pull himself upright. He found his balance and walked to his truck with even strides.

"Ah man, I missed a hug." He shook his head then headed out of the driveway.

"What did she mean? See you next week if not sooner? They hadn't made plans. Was she hinting for another date. Sweeney, *you are such a grade-A loser.* His pride kept him from catching the hint if it had been thrown.

14

A NEW OPPORTUNITY

The sun dipped below the horizon. Dan pulled his truck in front of Steve's law office. Brutus jumped out of the cab as Dan positioned his crutches. A frantic call from his friend and an offer of more money than he'd make on his geek squad shift had compelled him to call in sick. Guilt nettled with the lying. Well, it was a half lie. The stump did hurt. That's why he'd opted for crutches. He felt exposed hobbling along toward the entrance. It took skill to balance the backpack of tools while he navigated. Brutus walked just outside the motion of his crutches.

"Thank God you're here." Steve held the door open. Red hair rumpled and tie askew. "We've been wrestling with the technology fiend and it's whipping our rears."

Steve showed him to a desk. "Let me take that." Steve place the backpack on the desk and gave Brutus a pat.

Dan lowered into a chair and placed the crutches along the floor next to the desk. Brutus laid his head on the crutches, eyes fixed on his master. "Good boy."

"Let's see our patient."

"Well, she's jammed up and sneezed on all the computers in the office," Steve said.

"Sounds like a virus, pun intended. There's three nasty buggers. One comes through your email with the subject line: 'you have to see this.' Another attacks your PC if you play games on unsecured sites and the third grabs you if you're into porn."

"Well, I can't speak for anyone here but my Dad and me. Don't play games at work and never check out porn." Steve scratched his chin. Then moved toward an adjoining office. "Hey, Crystal. Did you open any emails with the subject line...?" Muffled conversation filtered through the closed door. The look on his friend's face in the doorway told Dan everything.

Steve sighed, loosened his tie and plopped in a chair. "Now what?"

"Judging from the script running across the screen you might want to interview all your suspects."

"What do you mean?"

"There's more than one virus."

"Oh great. Dad and the other senior partners will flip. They never...well, at least my Dad never backs up anything. They rely on their assistants to do it."

"Crystal is one of them." Dan grinned at the grimace on his friend's face. "Sad to be you."

"No joke. If you can't get these puppies up and purring by tomorrow a big real estate deal will crash into a pile of—"

"Puppies don't purr." Dan laughed as he clicked the unresponsive mouse.

Steve crossed his arms as Dan reverted to keystrokes.

Confident the mess could be fixed. He enjoyed letting Steve sweat. There was a satisfaction in being needed.

"Can it be fixed?" Steve paced and jiggled the keys in his pocket.

"Sure, it'll take time. I'll need something from you."

"Anything, bro."

"Your feet."

"Sure. What do you want me to do?"

"Be ready to run out to the truck for my case if needed. Might have to trash the system and buy new."

"Please don't say that." Steve smacked his head.

"No worries." Dan laughed.

Steve sat at the desk, head in hands.

"Get me some coffee."

Steve leaped from the chair heading for the break room. "Coming right up."

"Also, you'll be on Brutus duty. I don't want to stop working."

Steve sat the coffee cup next to Dan. "I'll get a bowl of water. What about food?"

"He's working. Brutus won't eat until I'm safe at home again."

Twelve hours later and two pots of coffee, the systems were running slow but working. All important documents backed up and the Internet access was secure.

"I'll give Dad your recommendations for computer upgrades and here is the check."

"Good thing my class isn't 'til two. I'm going home and try to sleep."

"You insisted on all the coffee. Besides didn't the Army train for sleep deprivation?"

"Ha ha."

"Thanks for coming on short notice." Steve held the crutches.

Dan puts on his backpack. Swiveled the office chair way from the desk. Then positioned the crutches under his arms. Brutus rose from sentry duty. Once Dan's stance was secure, Steve gave him a brotherly hug. "You saved our bacon."

Dan made it home before his eyeballs blurred. Brutus waited until he filled his food bowl, gulped the kibble then raced for the back door. Dan opened it and threw a few of Brutus' toys into the yard. He filled a cement water bowl near the back door, He'd leave the dog in the yard while he napped. Things would be quiet until the kindergarten kids with their parents walked home. Brutus couldn't see the kids with the six-foot privacy fence, but he'd bark and whine at the sound. That should wake him for sure. If he left his friend in the house, he'd snuggle on the bed and wait for his master to wake up.

Dan pulled the check from his pants pocket and laid it on his dresser. It was larger than a week at his job. "Don't need both legs to earn a decent wage." Maybe working on computers held more promise than he'd first imagined. Wages from Tech World didn't reflect it. Dickson Jones' question about business and the idea of exploring more computer science classes floated around in his foggy brain. The macho image he'd wore as a soldier needed discarding. A vison of a macho computer tech fought for a place in his future. Fatigue pushed to the forefront.

Frantic barks interrupted his musings. "So much for my brilliant idea."

Brutus stood barking at a cat perched on the fence. Dan's shrill whistle called him.

"Really, dude."

His companion crept into the house, tail between his legs.

"It's ok, Boy." Dan rubbed Brutus' head then signaled for him to stay down. "Go to your bed." The canine's soulful eyes had no effect on his master. "Not today." Dan reinforced his words by shutting the bedroom door leaving the dog alone in the living room.

Setting his alarm and turning the volume to its loudest setting, Dan curled up on his bed not bothering to change out of his clothes. He fought the urge to fetch Brutus when the business idea kept spinning around in his mind. Restlessness could lead his brain to the "what if "stage. Which often included scenarios of failure and fear, sometimes panic attacks. Instead, he opened Pandora on his phone and selected a file marked sleep music.

~

THE ALARM BLARED, startling Dan. Deep brown doggie eyes stood over him. "I'm up, I'm up."

"How'd you get in here?" He pushed the furry beast off the bed. "Tomorrow I'm going to the hardware store to get a new door knob." Part of the service dog training was opening doors. He'd changed the handle on the utility room so his friend couldn't escape when Dan wanted him out of harm's way. Brutus lay on the floor, paws over his eyes at his master's declaration. "It's ok, boy." His tail beat the floor.

Dan still felt awkward working with a service dog. Many of the skills Brutus learned benefited his previous owner. The child needed aid in so many ways. Dan didn't need as much help. A service dog drew attention to his disability.

Dan sat up remembering to grab crutches before heading to the bathroom.

He maneuvered his wrinkled clothes off and stepped into the handicapped-accessible shower—a walk-in tiled area. The bench was removable for wheelchair use. The shower controls were near the bench and three shower heads sprayed water. This bathroom was one project Steve and his friends had completed while Dan was at the VA hospital. It had been hard on his ego, but he needed it completed so he could come home. He'd argued with Steve over the shower design. Dan felt a few modifications on the existing shower would be sufficient. But Steve's logic had won him over.

"A shower should relax and relieve stress not just get you clean."

A wet soapy surface and a one-legged man a dangerous combination. Sitting on the bench he let the water jets knead the ache out of his shoulder and invigorate his sleepy mind. Maybe when the last class ended at nine he'd be awake enough to drive home. A dream still lingered on the edge of his mind. For once it wasn't a nightmare of IED and truck crashes.

The background music still played in his head. Jeff's funeral unfolded before him. His sister had signed him out of rehab, and driven to the big Megachurch in Indiana. She was nowhere in the dream. But he relived every moment. Dan's body ached from waiting in the long line in his wheelchair.

After saying goodbye to his old friend, he'd slipped over to the widow, a slight Hispanic girl with the saddest chocolate eyes he'd ever seen. He'd joined in her tears. The widow's weeping flowed to the deep hurts in his own heart, bringing peace for the first time. Something resonated in their shared loss. More than the loss of Jeff. All the pain they'd both suffered entwining their hearts and the God of all comfort received their tears.

"What was her name?"

The question amplified by the shower walls. The weird part of the dream was the sad widow morphed into Isabella Wilson. He recalled her name started with an M.

Toweling off on the chair in front of the sink he pondered the dream. So, weird. Isabella did have gorgeous chocolate eyes. They held sadness. But Jeff's widow had stirred him out of his funk. He'd determination to overcome. It's' why he came back to his hometown to attend college, and wanted to help other disabled vets start over.

The dream cycled his thoughts while he dressed and attached his leg. Somewhere in a drawer or box there was a thank you note with her address. "I could look her up and see how she's doing. God, is that what the dream means?" Before he could wait for an answer, he saw the flashing red numbers on his alarm clock. "Man, I must be moving slow."

Dan did a wobble dash to his truck and hit the college parking lot with minutes to spare. A car had just vacated a primo parking space in front of the building. He plopped in the last empty seat in Business law class before the bell rang. Focused on the professor, the dream evaporated into the recesses of his sub-conscience.

15

DOUBLE DATE

Dan pressed the Bluetooth as he drove home on Friday. After the third ring, Steve answered. "What's up, bro?"

"Not much. Want to do something tonight?"

"Like skydiving." Both men laughed at the dig. Dan could hear Steve's assistant talking in the background. "Hang on." Steve's voice faded then returned. "Sorry."

"Interested in doing something tonight?" A smile formed as he recalled high school where the whole gang sat around asking that same question.

"Any other night. I got a date with this girl I've had a thing for forever. Man, I'm stoked."

"Sounds great." Jealousy drenched Dan's mood.

"So, call Isabella and make it a double date."

"I doubt she'd be interested."

"What makes you think that?"

"Seriously...we're not going there." Dan gripped the stirring wheel.

"Do I have to slap you through this phone?"

Steve's response might have been funny when Dan was whole.

"You don't get it." Dan scowled at the red light. It couldn't change fast enough. He wanted to slam on the gas for emphasis.

"Yes, I do. You're being a coward. My hero has a yellow streak."

"You've got mega low standard for heroes." At last the light changed. A patrol car appeared in his rearview mirror. *Really, Lord!*

Dan could hear Steve slam his office door. "Are you serious? You came back from death. Restarted a new life. Not to mention saving my tamales at work the other day. Call her and she will go."

"I still think…"

"Stop thinking and be my wing man. My dates with Mindy. You know, Issy's little sister. Took a lot of begging to get this date. If you come along, she won't feel obligated to rush right home so her sister won't be alone."

"Not happening."

"Then I'll call Ming and ask her to ask her sister."

"You do and I'll send my hero superpowers raining on your rear." Dan sighed. *Trapped.* He had too much pride to have his best friend ask for him. "Ok, but when I suffer rejection humiliation, it's on you."

Dan hung up with Steve as he turned into the driveway. Before he lost his nerve, he called Isabella.

THE GUYS JOINED the girls at their apartment. Isabella and Ming were standing outside. *Great, pity for the gimp. Sweeney, act like a gentleman.* Dan handed a single coral rose to Isabella. The florist had explained coral roses spoke of getting to know the recipient better. Her nose pressed against the petals. "Let me run upstairs to put this in water."

"Wait." Ming pulled a vase from behind a bush. "Use this."

"How girl scouty of you and weird." Isabella placed the flower vase on the lowest step.

"Scotty, the landlord's five-year-old son likes to pick his mom's flowers and leave them on the step for me. I left the vase out here for him, so the flowers aren't wilted by the time I get home." Ming took Steve's arm. "Don't look so embarrassed. I didn't expect any from you."

"You don't think I can be romantic?" Steve pouted.

"I have no idea. I do know you and pollen are enemies. Flowers are last on your romantic list."

"Wow! Impressive memory" Steve smiled. "My romantic gift is on the seat."

"Oh." Ming headed for Steve's BMW.

"I assume we're taking separate cars?" Isabella asked.

Dan bristled at her thoughtfulness.

"What do you think?" Steve watched Mindy reach in through the window. The daisy patterned dress clung to her.

"This is too much, Steve." Mindy's voice a whisper. She flashed a Pandora bracelet. "Look, the four charms I picked out." The girls admired it then Mindy turned to Steve and leapt into his arms. "You remembered I was saving money for one of these." Mindy pulled away, a cute blush forming on her cheek. "I think we should go in Steve's BMW."

"I think we should go in separate cars." Isabella countered.

Dan caught the what-were-you-thinking look she flashed her sister.

"Hey, no worries. We can go in Steve's car." Dan placed his hand on the small of Isabella's back and guided her to the BMW. "The back seat is spacious, limo-style." Dan opened the door while admiring her silky floral dress—a deeper blue than her sister's. She wore silver jewelry. The floral scent added to the vision of perfection. She slid into the back seat. He got in behind Steve. Steve's height set the front seat further back erasing the roominess for Dan. Getting out would not be smooth.

"Steve, what is it we are seeing again?" Dan attempted to straighten his leg, the prosthetic pressing too hard against his stub. He avoided eye-contact with Isabella. Afraid he'd see pity as he struggled to get seated.

"South Pacific. Remember back in the day."

"Yeah. This should be fun."

Ming turned to smile at Dan and touched Steve's shoulder. "Why didn't you mention we were walking memory lane? I thought we were just going to East Aurora High's musical because we both love old musicals."

"I promise not to sing along." Steve grinned into the mirror at Dan.

Dan laughed. "Mindy, pull his handkerchief out of his pocket and gag him. No way he can resist singing his rendition of *There is Nothing Like a Dame.*"

"Bet." Steve's wink in the rear view a dare.

"Ha. You're on."

"Hey, Sis, we are out with a couple of high rollers." Isabella glanced at Dan. "It must be great to have those kinds of memories to revisit."

"We are so jealous." Mindy agreed. "Dad moved with his job every few years. We begged to stay at our grandparents during high school just to stay at the same school long enough to graduate."

"It took four years to get into a clique. After graduation, we moved away." Isabella said.

"Man, the parking lot near the building is packed. I'll drop you guys at the door."

Before Dan could object, Mindy added. "We'll save you a seat. We'll try to get close to the front."

Dan crawled out of the backseat steadying himself as Steve pulled away. Entering the auditorium, the ladies found seats fifth-row center. He'd forgotten the limited leg room between rows. A phantom twinge in his missing foot reinforced the doubts about his seat.

Isabella and Ming chatted together. "Why so many empty seats when there is no parking?" Ming twisted left then right, taking in the moderate crowd.

"This is the final show. There's a basketball game in the gym." Dan looked around the auditorium remembering all the fun.

"A basketball game and a musical on the same night?"

"Student body is three thousand students. Lots of activities going on. Even night classes." Steve said.

"Big contrast to our alma mater. We had three hundred kids in the whole student body." Isabella smiled and Ming nodded agreement.

"Here's an interesting factoid." Dan pointed to the stage. "Largest high school stage in the state of Illinois. There's a huge backstage area. We got a convertible on the stage for *Grease*."

"Impressive." Mindy turned and waved. Steve jogged to their aisle and squeezed by a middle-aged couple on the end of the row and sat next to Mindy.

The lights dimmed, and the curtain rose to the opening notes from the orchestra pit. Nostalgia cloaked Dan while he watched the high school students recreate the various scenes. The teen playing Luther Billis ham it up in coconuts and a grass skirt. When his character, Lt. Buzz Adams appeared, he almost recited his favorite line but refrained waiting for Steve to sing out any minute. Unlike Dan, Steve still pursued his love of music. His guitar collection was growing. Dan hadn't bothered with his deformed hand. The depressing thought interrupted by humming. Stretching his arm behind Isabella he whacked Steve with his program.

"Caught you."

"Humming is not singing."

"A technicality."

"Shh." The man seated next to them scowled as he adjusted his hearing aid. The girls suppressed giggles while the guys feigned coughs.

By intermission, Dan was ready to stretch his legs. Struggling to his feet he smiled at the ladies. "The Athletic Club sells snacks during intermission. Can I get you anything?"

"I'd like to visit the ladies room. Grab a soda. Please." Isabella waited for Ming to exit the row.

"Sure thing. Bathrooms are up the hall on the right."

"Bottled water, please." Mindy gave Steve a sweet smile before following her sister.

"What is it with women and public restrooms?" Steve took small steps up the aisle matching Dan's gait.

"Beats me." Dan shrugged and picked up the pace.

Steve handed money to the pimple-faced kid manning the cash box. He pocketed two candy bars and picked up one bottled water and a soda. "Issy's into you."

Dad ignored the declaration as he grabbed two sodas. Isabella had been a pastor's wife. Politeness and attentiveness were part of the job description. He pushed his doubts deep and smiled when the girls appeared.

The guys handed off their drinks.

"I think I'll get a Butterfinger." Mindy eyed the candy.

"Tad-ah." Steve pulled the treat from his pocket.

"My hero." Mindy laughed. She smiled before tearing off the wrapper and taking a bite. Her expression shear ecstasy. Steve's crooked high school boy smile made Dan smile.

He watched the interaction between the two and still couldn't believe this was their first date. "How long have you known each other?"

"In years or in person?" Mindy asked.

"Well, now I'm confused?"

"This is Sir Red?" Isabella asked.

"In the flesh." Steve pointed his finger like a gun for emphasis.

"This is the mystery girl from the internet you mooned over in high school?" He shook his head in amazement.

Steve grinned. "The one you were convinced was some middle-aged male perv."

"Well, I'm insulted." Mindy laughed.

"That was your mom not me." Dan laughed and glanced at his watch. "Intermission is over."

Once settled back in their seats, Mindy finished their story. "Steve and I met on the now defunct Neighborhood website during junior high. We've been messaging each other and sending emails forever. When I wanted a change after cosmetology school and a crummy breakup, Steve suggested I come here."

"And it took two years to get this date." Steve added as the lights dimmed and the curtain rose.

Dan envied Steve's good fortune. He'd found the girl of his dreams. Had a job he loved and seemed comfortable in his own skin. Life had been easy for his friend. Envy compared their lives.

His parents died leaving piles of debt and no insurance. The money put aside for college settle the estate. His sister was a newlywed. Living there felt awkward. The Army offered him free college. Then when he wanted a military career he lost his leg. Now ten years later he attended classes with a bunch of 18-year-olds. Laughter brought him back to the present. *Get your head in the game, Sweeney. Forget about what you don't have. Right now, you're on a date with a beautiful, smart woman.*

≈

THE FOURSOME HEADED to Panera's for coffee and conversation after the final curtain. Isabella had taken the seat behind Steve giving Dan the roomier place behind Mindy's seat. Dan smiled, trying not to overthink her actions.

≈

"PANERA'S IS MY FAVORITE SPOT," Mindy announced as Steve opened the door for the ladies. "You can sit here for hours and no one bothers you."

"Let's take the couch and chairs near the fireplace." Isabella headed in that direction. "I'll save us seats."

"Get us Chai tea, guys." Mindy plopped on the couch next to her sister.

"You've been quiet tonight."

"Have I?"

Mindy sat facing the counter. "The guys have a line ahead of them so you have five minutes to tell me what's up?"

"It feels weird."

"What feels weird, Panera's?"

"Not funny. Isabella resisted rolling her eyes. It feels weird to be on a date."

"You'll get used to it. Dan's a great guy."

"Maybe."

"What does that mean?" Mindy spotted the guys and pasted on a smile.

Isabella more than happy to set their awkward conversation aside. A great guy can wear a mask. At first, Ron was a wonderful man. He'd sweep her off her feet, showered her with affection, then turned into a control freak. Granted, there was the tumor. But maybe he was always a control freak—his mother was.

"Earth to Issy." Mindy's shoulder bumped her, the simple action helped dislodge Maureen's scowling face from her mind.

"Sorry." Isabella smiled at her sister to help close the door on the visit to another sad place.

"Dan was asking if we'd want to go see Steven Curtis Chapman next weekend."

Uneasiness crept up Isabella spine. She noticed the decadent brownie next to her cup of tea. Taking a bite of the brownie and chewing slow kept the answered delayed.

"I don't know. I need to check my schedule." *Coward.*

Large music concerts were on her permanent to-be-avoided list. Too much of Ron's life focused on pleasing crowds of adoring fans. Hard to believe churches had worship leader groupies. Ron did. Exploring concert memory lane would end in disaster.

Isabella saw disappointment in Dan's eyes. She thought fast not wanting to hurt this man who stirred her in ways she didn't want to admit. "We could all checkout Brookfield Zoo tomorrow. I'm off." *Some one stop me.*

"It's too cold for the zoo." Mindy wasn't helping. "Besides, I always work on Saturday."

"How about the Shedd Aquarium then?" Isabella couldn't believe the words coming out of her mouth, Ming had already declined.

"I've got paperwork I need to finish tomorrow for a closing." Steve smiled at Dan before adding. "Doesn't mean you two can't go without us."

"Sounds like a plan." Dan smiled and winked.

A blush warmed her cheeks. A foursome was safe. What had she done? Backing out now would hurt Dan's feeling. Especially, when her big mouth ran away with her good intensions. "The aquarium it is." She produced what she hoped was a sincere smile.

16

AQUARIUM AND DISASTER

I sabella finished crafting her hair. That's what it felt like after adding hair product and using a flat iron to recreate what Ming had done. She missed no fuss long hair. "Oh, well. Hair can grow back." The mirror showed a younger reflection. A smile formed at the happy thought. Lots of new choices had crafted more happiness into her life.

The phone chirped. Dan's texted he was downstairs. Scooping up her phone she responded. Was this date a good choice? Her trust-o-meter binged in her heart.

Isabella applied a soft lip gloss. She wore bootleg jeans bejeweled on the back pockets and her low-cut black boots. A pink scarf over a gray top completed the outfit. She grabbed her purse and hurried out the door. Half-way down the stairs, she remembered she forgotten to lock the door.

~

DAN WAITED beside the truck to open the passenger door for Isabella. Watching her sudden rush back up the stairs made him wonder about his outfit. Jeans and army emblem t-shirt wasn't too under-dressed? She fished in her purse, produced a key. Dan exhaled. He appreciated the suggestion to wait downstairs. Watching her descend in spiky heels both amused and amazed. She looked like a fashion model. While he felt like a model for Hillbilly Gazette.

"You look beautiful." Her skin darkened with the compliment.

The blush faded but Isabella's eyes retained their gleam. Dan set the GPS for Chicago. Anticipating heavy traffic, he'd prayed for God's grace that no semi-trucks or crazy drivers would freak him out.

Dan hurried to the driver's side. Grabbing the hand hold on the door he pulled himself into his seat. "Have you been to the Shedd Aquarium?"

"No. But I love aquariums. Are you the man on a mission type?"

"Do a quick step so we can say we were there?" He threw coins in the toll booth basket.

"Yeah, like a school field trip."

"Never fear, I plan on making this day last." Dan kept face-forward afraid of the reaction to his playful words.

"We could check out the dolphin show."

"That's a plan." Dan smiled and glanced her way. A smile meant his gaze. Nervous tendrils invaded his happy thoughts. *Don't mess this up, soldier.*

ISABELLA FOUGHT the awkward feelings whirling inside. She closed her eyes for a moment. Since childhood, closing her eyes to experience the smells, sounds, and textures around her gave her a better perspective. In this case, the smell of Dan's musky cologne, the motion of the truck and music playing in the background. She had vague memories of closing her eyes to the ugliness of the poverty before the Wilson's adopted her. Somewhere she recalled a sweet voice encouraging her to enjoy the better parts of the world she could not see.

"Are you tired?" Dan's baritone interrupted her thoughts.

"No." Her neck warmed with embarrassment. Straightening, she cleared her throat. "My parents shared their love of museums and zoos with us. We had a yearlong membership to the zoo for when we lived in Cincinnati. "We'd ride our bikes there every Saturday."

"Neither of you became a zoologist."

"Ming is allergic to fur. I found drawing animals more interesting."

"I'd like to see your drawings."

"There stored at the folks." The memory of the box tucked in the corner of the attic reminded her of the sacrifice she made for love. *Why did love have to be so one-sided?* The Chicago skyline came into view and with it a resolve to guard her heart while she enjoyed this excursion.

DAN FOUND a parking space close to the entrance. Isabella jumped out first. Her purse formed a barrier between them as they walked into the aquarium.

Isabella was earnest about her slow tour. It wasn't just for his benefit. She read plaques, sometimes pausing at a tank for ten minutes. At the coral reef tank, Isabella pressed her face against the glass.

"See the clown fish?" An orange, black and white fish flitting by.

"You mean Nemo."

She laughed at his reference. "The Percula Clownfish."

"You know its proper name?"

"That would be Amphiprion Oceallaris."

"Hmm, tell me more." Dan stepped behind her placing his arms around her waist. His breath tickled her neck causing her to shutter and move away. An anxious look reflected in her eyes. *Shift to neutral. Don't scare her off.* Her composure resumed in seconds along with the narrative.

"The clownfish is found in the waters of the Indo-Pacific. It eats plankton and crustaceans. And it loves to swim among the tentacles of anemones." Isabella fell silent, staring at the clown fish.

Dan noticed her face reflected in the tank. A smile of joy lit her lips. "I love watching them. The variety of colors in this tank is breathtaking." After several minutes, they resumed walking.

At the dolphin area, Dan found himself mesmerized by the white whale. His slow maneuverings in a confined space spoke to Dan. The whale appeared calm. It radiated to him as he watched this giant. "I'm enjoying this more than I thought I would."

"I'm glad." She smiled and took his hand. Dan loved the feel of her soft small hand in his. "If we leave now we can watch the diver feed the fish in the coral reef environment."

Dan was surprised how well he was doing. The long rest on the bench near the dolphin tanks helped him get a second wind. After the presentation at the coral reef, Dan looked at the time on his cell phone. "Hey, no wonder my stomach's been calling. Want to grab a bite?"

"There's the sign to point the way." She tugged him forward. Dan resisted at first, planted his feet and tugged her back. A playful giggle bubbled from her lips. His laughter broadening her smile. They followed the sign to the cafe. After a lunch of burgers and fries, they headed for the dolphin show.

"How come no salad?"

"What? All women eat salad?"

"No, I didn't mean." Dan blushed at his blunder. She looked too awesome for someone who ate fast food.

"I don't care for pre-made salads in plastic containers. At least the burgers are fresh. I love a good salad if it's fresh and only in warm weather."

"Let me guess, you eat soup when it's cold."

"That's when it's the best."

On the drive, home the two sat in comfortable silence.

"A penny for your thoughts?" Isabella's voice startled him.

"Sounds about right."

"Let me guess. Nothing."

"Not a thing." He couldn't tell her she consumed his thoughts even when they were together.

"There's a hundred on mine." Isabella leaned her head on the backrest.

"My mother once said humans had shoe boxes in their heads to store their thoughts. If you opened any one of the boxes in a man's brain, it's empty." Dan wiggled his eyebrows at Isabella.

They laughed together.

"So, tell me lady fair what you were thinking."

～

ISABELLA SQUIRMED AT THE QUESTION. Her thoughts a betrayal of her earlier resolve. This had been the best date. Not once did she compare him to Ron. Guilt and doubt wrestled with those positive feelings. Dan was a special guy. He may be wounded on the outside but his heart, pure gold. The thought made her sad. She didn't deserve even the friendship of a guy like Dan. "Thinking about all the interesting aquatic life we saw today. I am still amazed."

When Dan reached for her hand, she moved it to her lap. "Keep both hands on the wheel please."

Dan jerked back his deformed right hand.

"I'm sorry. It's... Multitasking of any kind while driving scares me."

Dan's sweet understanding smile melting her resolve more. Leaning back on the headrest she closed her eyes again. His scent filled the truck cab. A memory to take home. One to add to the positive side of the tally sheet her trust issues kept. Opening her eyes again she watched Dan drive.

"What?" Dan's neck colored.

"Thank you for a lovely day."

"It's not over yet." Dan glanced her way not daring to take his eyes off the road. "I know this great place for coffee that has a fish tank."

"Not sick of looking at fish?"

Dan said nothing. Hoping his spontaneous choice was a good one Pulling into his driveway.

"Is this your home?"

"Yes, still needs work. It was in foreclosure so I got a good price."

"Does it have a basement?'

"No ..." Dan almost said do I look like a guy who wants a basement. Why do I always assume it's about my handicap? "It's got a crawl space."

"Show me what you've done." Isabella waited at the door while Dan pulled the key from his pocket. Holding the screen door open with his back, he unlocked the door and let her pass through first. The peaceful scene exploded into a scream.

Brutus had greeted Isabella by planting front paws on her chest, Hysterics followed. The canine retreated to his bed in the corner, covered his eyes and whimpered. His date dashed out the door. Dan followed her. "Hey, I'm sorry. You should see how repentant he is."

Isabella stood there with her eyes closed. Tears stained her cheeks. Dan reached for her. At his touch, her eyes flew open and she ran for the truck. "Keep that monster away."

"He's really a teddy bear, Issy."

"Take me home." She crossed her arms, fire and fear fought in her eyes.

Clicking the key fob, the doors unlocked. Isabella leaped into the passenger's seat and waited for Dan.

Once on the road, she broke their silence. "I'm sorry. If it isn't obvious, I'm terrified of dogs."

"I'm sorry, I thought I mentioned Brutus."

She stared out the window. Dan felt the cab fill with tension. "If I had known. I would have put Brutus in the utility room."

"Why do you have such a big dog? Even if he were tiny I'd be afraid. But, little dogs can't eat me."

Dan would have laughed if it weren't for the edge to her voice. *Now what do I do. Thanks a bunch, buddy.* "First, statistically, small dogs are more aggressive. Secondly, I got Brutus to assist me. When I first came home with my prosthetic, I didn't want an aid. But if I fell, I had a problem."

"Brutus is a service dog?" Isabella's voice softened.

"Not as well-trained as I'd like. My friend Kyle got him from a family who had an autistic child. The boy died of cancer and Brutus didn't handle the loss well. Kyle thought we might hit it off better. He senses when I'm depressed or on the verge of a panic attack, and knows how to help me up when I fall. He's also a big baby and gets his feelings hurt easily." Dan reached for her hand but she moved closer to the passenger door. Still looking out the window her voice filled the cab.

"My parents could never figure out why I was so afraid of dogs. They adopted me when I was six. Before that, I lived on the streets of Managua, Nicaragua. They got rid of their dog because no amount of persuasion would keep me from screaming in terror every time they let him inside. Years later we were watching a documentary of my birth country and they showed packs of dogs fighting in the streets. That's when I remember dogs biting me to take my food." She turned toward Dan. "I haven't screamed like that since I was a child. I think having my expectations on something good and then being greeted by a monster dog pushed me over the edge."

Arriving at Isabella's apartment Dan turned to her. "I hope Brutus isn't a deal breaker if I ask you out again." He took her hand in his and kissed her palm. "Again, I am sorry about ruining a perfect day. Let me make it up to you."

"Every thing's fine. I'll see you in church tomorrow." Isabella jerked away and got out of the truck.

"Bye."

She ran up the stairs and was out of sight in a flash. Dan slammed his good hand on the steering wheel hard enough to regret it before pulling his truck out of the driveway.

Isabella stepped inside and closed the door pressing her back hard against it. Kissing her palm reminded her of Ron. The first time he'd done it she melted. After a while, she learned it was a prelude to criticism. She closed her eyes and rewound to a moment on their date where Dan stood behind her, eyes on the coral reef. Recalling his arms around her waist, feeling protected and cared for made her smile. Sadness seeped in and washed it away. "How do I explain my reaction?"

"You don't," she answered herself.

Isabella sat on Ming's couch, a cup of sleepy time tea in her hand. Ming was still out. She'd texted earlier that Steve had called and they were going bowling. Isabella had missed her by minutes. Glad for the quiet, she changed into lounge pants and a Cubs T-shirt she'd found in her sister's drawer. Sipping her tea, the knot caused by too much reflecting on the past squeezed tighter. "Father, help me."

She reached for the stereo remote. The last few bars of an instrumental filled the room. Her feet in fuzzy slippers shuffled to the kitchen for a snack.

Bringing a bag of cookies back to the couch the music changed. She ate one of the generic chocolate chips and sipped some more tea. The unfamiliar worship song ended and the chords of a new song began. The hair on Isabella's neck stood on end, her teacup shattered on the floor. She clicked the stereo off. Those first notes told her she couldn't listen. Not that song, not now. "Father, I am so weak. If I don't listen to his favorite songs, bitterness won't grab at me." A memory skirted around her prayer and covered her mind like a mist.

"Melinda, you were off a beat on the harmony line." Ron's lips formed a firm line.

They were still in the church parking lot when he began his critique of worship. Usually, he mentioned each team member and his analysis of their performance. Today it was all her fault. Feeling small, she pressed against the passenger door and watched the storefronts pass. She caught Ron's glare reflected in the passenger window.

"Are you listening?"

She nodded, tears forming in her eyes.

"Melinda, look at me." Ron's sharp tone made the tears flow harder.

Dashing them away with the back of her hand before looking at her husband, she turned her chin still quivering.

"Please, don't cry, all you ever do anymore is cry." His prickly words gathered momentum. "If you'd control your weeping and focus on the music, you wouldn't take everyone out of the moment with your flat notes."

"When I focus on the words I am singing, God touches my heart and I cry. I'm sorry. What am I supposed to do... shut myself off from the whole worship experience so the music is flawless?"

"No. That's not what I mean. Just try holding it together. If you can't, stop singing until you can. The rest of us will cover for you."

"Then you'll be doing that a lot."

Isabella remembered the rest of the trip home in a blur. Ron's lecture on her inadequacy and lack of respect for his position in the church increased as he accelerated. Soon blue and red lights appeared in the rear-view mirror. Ron morphed into a repented gentleman for the officer.

"I hadn't realized I was speeding. My wife was crying. We lost our child recently, and I was trying to sooth her. I guess the emotions of the moment gave me a lead foot."

She never forgot the sympathetic look the policeman gave her and his warning to drive more carefully. Ron had used her to get out of a ticket and rubbed more salt into her wounded spirit by reminding her of RJ's death. By the time, they got home she was too angry to speak. She'd locked herself in the bedroom and Ron had gone to spend the day with his mother.

"Father, what can I do. Everything around me brings back his hurtful words. The man I thought I loved took everything from me. Can't you erase these last few years from my mind? I know, that's a stupid request." The broken cup sat in a pool of creamed tea. "Mom always said hard work was good for the soul."

Isabella reached for paper towel and the broom determined to sweep away the memory along with the broken cup. After cleaning up the mess she searched through Ming's large collection of CDs. Isabella found a remix of classic hymns. Pouring a fresh cup of tea, she put it in the microwave to reheat.

As the carousel turned warming her brew, she let the music soak into her soul. Ron didn't care for old hymns and sometimes added them to the worship mix to appease those who did.

Isabella loved the classic hymns she'd learned in her Gramma's church. Knowing Stone Church used hymnals allowed her to let her guard down. Someday she would have to allow those worship songs that once had a profound impact in her heart back into her life.

"Knowing what I should do and doing them are two different things."

The CD ended, she turned off the stereo and set her teacup in the sink when the happy voices of Ming and Steve came through the door.

"Hey, sis, didn't know you were a Cubs fan?"

"Ha, ha. You two have a nice time?"

"I dusted the floor with her." Steve's eyes sparkled as he teased Ming.

"Yeah, right, you keep believing that." Ming kissed him on the cheek before removing her sweater. Issy's heart ached. *Does the promise of forever love exist?* She pasted on a smile.

"You guys want some cookies?"

Steve helped himself.

"How was your date?" Ming sat on the couch next to Steve.

Issy sat in the overstuffed chair and wrapped the throw from the back around her. It covered the embarrassment of being dressed for bed.

"Fine. He seemed to enjoy himself."

"You going out again?" Steve's question put her on the spot.

"I don't know." Her face warmed and she stared at her house slippers noting the flower on the left slipper was missing a petal.

"What's not to know?" Steve's tone defensive. Issy shifted in her seat before answering. She was in no mood for a pro/con discussion about his friend.

"He has a monster dog."

"Oh." Ming's eyebrow flexed in understanding.

"Brutus is a teddy bear." Steve laughed.

"That's what Dan said."

"You don't believe him."

"Let's just say that was not my experience."

"Oh man." Steve's expression convinced her it was time to end this conversation.

"I'm heading to bed." Issy escaped, the throw trailing the floor behind her, before Steve had a chance to build his defense for the behemoth dog.

17

STEPPING BACK AND MOVING FORWARD

M ing's clippers glided over Isabella's hair.

"Are you going out with Dan again?"

"Ah ha! An ulterior motive for squeezing me into your schedule."

"Maybe, but you were getting shaggy. Why not take advantage of my cosmetology expertise often?"

"Remember those words when the advantage taking has reached a climax." Isabella watched her sister recreate the same cut she'd done weeks earlier.

"Your highlights still look good. We should schedule for a redo in a couple weeks." Ming fluffed her sister's hair and checked for stray stands before running mousse through it. "You haven't answered my question."

"I don't know. I'm not sure what possessed me to accept the first invitation."

"Didn't you invite him?"

"Well... But... I can't break myself of demonstrating gratefulness in a tangible way. A simple thank you would have been less complicated. Then you insisted on the double date.

"Wait. You refused to go with Steve and I when I asked. Something about being a third wheel."

"Then it felt wrong to turn Dan down." Isabella hated how much she was still Ron's Melinda. "Then you and Steve put me in an awkward position."

"Hey, you could have said Sunday afternoon and it would have been a foursome."

"Funny, how you think of it now."

Ming grinned and shrugged her shoulders. "Was it so painful."

"Well no."

"Told ya." Ming's smirk goaded.

"Anyway." Isabella scowled. "I'm still trying to figure out who I am."

"Maybe Dan is part of that."

"Maybe a distraction. Ron robbed so much of my identity. And I let him. There were times I sensed God giving me direction. Instead of standing up for my convictions..."

"You'd wimp out."

"Exactly. You sure you weren't watching my life through the window?"

"If I had, Ron would have gotten more than a piece of my mind." Ming placed her right hand with the comb on her hip and swept the curling iron across in front of her.

"For sure." Issy laughed.

Ming nodded. "You know it." Then resumed styling Issy hair. "Has Dan called?"

"Twice. My cell is off at work. I haven't returned his call because I don't know what to say."

"How about the truth?" Ming used a generous amount of hair spray and removed the cape from Isabella's neck. "Tell him you've got a lot of baggage from your marriage. You need time to discover your solo, before you explore a duet."

"Clever music analogy." Isabella hugged her sister. "Thanks." She grabbed her purse from the ledge near the styling chair while Ming grabbed a broom. "How much do I owe you?" Ming kept sweeping. "You're not doing this for free." Issy placed money on the tray as Mrs. Crawford toddled in.

"Hello, Mindy's twin."

Isabella smiled at the elderly lady. The woman wore a burgundy pantsuit and carried a huge lime green purse.

"Ah, what's your name again?"

"Isabella."

"Tell me, Isabella, you work at Hobby Life, right?"

"Yes."

"Do you know anyone who comes in there who paints murals?"

"Why?"

"My senior Sunday School class repainted the nursery room at church. We thought a mural would be nice but none of us have that gifting."

"Isabella does." Ming chimed in before she could object.

Mrs. Crawford clapped her hands. "Is what Mindy saying true?"

"Well...." Isabella turned her head so her sister could see her irritation. "Yes." Mindy gave a satisfied grin behind Mrs. Crawford's back. As much as she tried, she couldn't feel angry for the interference. Maybe, this was her chance to get her muse back.

"When can I see the wall?"

"We can't pay much." Mrs. Crawford hopeful expression on the verge of comical.

"Let me do it as an offering to the Lord." *If my muse doesn't come back, it will less humiliating.*

"You are an answer to prayer." Mrs. Crawford hugged her then sat in Ming's chair.

"Work your magic. Got a hot date tonight."

All three laughed. "Gertie, Agnes and I are going to play Bingo at the VFW in Batavia. Would you young ladies care to join us."

"My shift starts in an hour." Isabella said.

"Wait." Mrs. Crawford fished a business card out of her purse. "At my age, it's easier than remembering my number."

The card was pink with a picture of the cartoon character, Maxine, in the corner.

"Call and we can arrange a time." Mrs. Crawford grabbed her arm. "Tell Mr. Clayton to be good to you or he'll answer to me."

Laughter followed Isabella out the door. It wasn't until she was changing in her bedroom she realized the woman was *the* Mrs. Crawford who owed Hobby Life. Nothing like the image in her mind formed by her boss' complaints.

❧

FAITH COMMUNITY CHURCH was six blocks from Ming's apartment so Isabella had opted to walk. The square one story building look circa 1980's, blonde bricks and geodesic stained-glass windows. Mrs. Crawford met her in the parking lot.

"Good to see you, Twinny. Follow me." They entered by a side door.

The sanctuary pews were blonde wood. The blue carpet had seen better days. Mrs. Crawford opened the door to the former nursery. Bright yellow paint accosted Isabella's artistic sensibilities. "My, this color is..."

"Horrible. Bill and Warren thought it was the perfect color for a kid's room." Mrs. Crawford's swung her cane miming whacking the two offenders.

"Well, no need to turn on the light."

Mrs. Crawford cackled and patted her arm. "I like you, Twinny."

Isabella surveyed the area. The yellow overpowered the room. She wished she'd been asked before the base was applied. "Well, right off I have no ideas. Is there a theme?"

"Emily suggested Jesus at Gethsemane. Warren thought of David and Goliath and Mildred mentioned a montage of Jesus life."

"For a nursery?"

"Who said anything about a nursery class?"

"You said you were painting the nursery."

"Right. The confusion is my fault. This room was the nursery, now it's for the middle school class. The new nursery was the pastor's study, it's closer to the sanctuary. The pastor does his preparation at home. With cell phones now we can bother him anytime day or night." Mrs. Crawford laughed at her own words. "The young couple's class soundproofed the room and added a TV so the moms don't miss the service."

"Before I do any sketches, what is the goal for this group of preteens?" The art muse smiled.

"Dearie, I haven't the faintest idea. But I'll have their teacher give you a call."

ISABELLA LEFT Mrs. Crawford with a lighter step. The mid-day sunshine matched the joy in her heart. She could do this. Her feet followed the patterned of a chalked hopscotch. A giggle escaped her lips. Painting a mural for a church she'd never attended—what a happy thought.

A horn blasted her happy moment out of her head, she jerked and located the sound. A large black truck pulled alongside her. The passenger window opened.

"Want a lift?" Dan leaned toward the open window, his smile wide. She smiled even as her heart beat a fleeing rhythm.

"I only have a few blocks."

His lips shaped into a playful pout. "I'm headed in your direction. Come on."

She climbed in the passenger side. Her better judgment lecturing her. "Thanks. It isn't necessary. I like walking."

"Haven't seen you in over a week."

Isabella's guilt rose to the surface. Three sleep deprived nights in a row kept her in bed on Sunday. Not to avoid Dan. Or was it?

"I know...about that..." Ming's reminder to speak the truth whispered in her ear. "Let's stop at the park up the road. The one near the bridge. We can talk."

Dan nodded. His furrowed brow a signal to tread lightly.

The truck pulled into the parking lot and they walked toward a bench near the Fox River. The quiet grove of trees behind them gave the privacy Isabella desired. The sound of birds and a motorboat would record in her mind as the backdrop to a conversation she dreaded.

"I've been thinking about you." She began.

"Nice to know." Dan surveyed the ground as they walked placing his prosthetic with care.

"Maybe not." Isabella sighed as she perched on the edge of the bench. Dan lowered himself next to her.

"Go on." His lips formed a thin line.

"I haven't returned your calls because I wasn't sure how to respond."

Dan remained silent.

"I like you, Dan, you're a great guy but..."

"I know... it's not you, it's me." Dan finished her sentence. Turned away, and crossed his arms.

Isabella hated this scene. A reminder of the past. Ron argued, nagged and bullied until he got his way. Tears fringed the memory. A need to discover if Dan was different gave her voice.

"Let me explain."

Dan shifted his position. Stretching his legs out in front of him.

"Go on." Dan stared at the ground.

"I spent seven years in a marriage. The first year was wonderful. Then things change. I lost every bit of myself trying to please Ron and everyone at church. After his death, I moved in with Ron's mom. Maureen is ...troubled. She stole the remnant of my self-esteem. Young, confident me is buried in here. She touched her heart. Reconnecting with that person is something I need to do on my own."

Squirrels chasing through the trees drew their focus. Isabella waited in the awkward silence. Dan turned toward her. His expression unreadable. "Won't you let me be a part of that discovery?" Dan pushed her stray hair back in place. The tender touch both warmed and worried her. Ron often used gentle caresses to get his way.

Isabella sighed and turned away. A gentle breeze brought God's unseen presence. "I let a man join me on my journey. He was so confident. In my insecurity, I depended on him too much. I trusted his guidance more than the nudging of the Holy Spirit."

"I understand, Isabella." Dan slid over a few inches giving her space.

"Good." She turned toward the river the stressful moment flowing with the current downstream.

They sat in silence watching the river. A leaf drifted wherever the waves took it. Isabella wished she could trust God to take her wherever he wanted. She wasn't sure Dan was that direction. But what if... Apart from Ming who else did she hang out with? The leaf followed a bend in the river disappearing. She touched Dan's hand, he turned toward her.

"I know it sounds lame but can we stay friends. I need friends."

Dan remained silent long enough to send a tinge of fear up her spine. She braced herself for sarcasm and anger.

"I need friends too." Dan smiled, his eyes sad.

"I'm glad." Relief spilled over her. More silence. She waited for the other shoe to drop. Fear tried to capture her heart, she wrestled to win calm.

"How do you want us to be friends?"

Dan's practical question was not what she expected to hear.

"I don't know. Any ideas?" She waited.

"Well, if you need a battery jumped, I'm your man." Dan's smile tense.

"Sounds good. Friends also grab a bite after church." She added.

"So, you still want to see me."

Isabella wrapped her arms around her chest. "Friends only. And I don't have to be friends with your dog."

"That could be a deal breaker." Dan's voice had no mirth.

"I'm sorry if that offends you." Isabella turned so Dan couldn't see her tears. Why did she care so much?

"Hey." Dan touched her shoulder. "Hey, I was teasing." Dan wiped the errant tear from her cheek.

"Brutus will be sad. But he'll be fine." Dan's voice gentle.

"You realize I don't care if your dog is sad." She took a cleansing breath.

"You're not the only one who doesn't like Brutus. But, no one else has run away screaming."

A knowing smile passed between them. He squeezed her hand then released it. Her empty hand mourned the change in their relationship. She rubbed it across her jean clad leg trying to erase the shadow of his touch.

Together they walked side by side, a few feet between them, back to the truck. Quiet filled the truck cab during the short trip. Isabella jumped out once he parked in front of Ming's apartment. Her keys hid in the bottom of her purse. She knew without looking Dan watched to be sure she got in safe before he pulled away. The door closed behind her. The sound of tires on gravel emphasized her loneliness.

"I'm so sorry, Dan."

Tears followed her to the bedroom and leached over her comforter, along with wails long buried. Her small fist gripped the comforter. "Why God? Why did you let Ron ruin my life? Soil my heart toward anything good."

Isabella knew she'd made the choice to marry Ron. Her family had reservations. Her Dad even offered her a trip to Paris if she postponed marrying Ron for a year or longer until they were better acquainted. "Father, forgive me for not heeding my Daddy's counsel." Paris was an artist's dream vacation. She knew herself well back then. Her passion for art would have kept her from Ron. Her starry-eyed choice had been influenced by a charismatic man. In the end, self-loathing replaced her art gifting. Regret washed her face for several more minutes.

"Enough of this." Isabella rose and shook her head. In the bathroom, she wiped her face and ran a comb through her hair. Then she sat at her desk and opened her laptop. Clicking on Skype she dialed her dad.

"Daddy, I love you."

He blinked and the words—I love you too, baby—appeared on the screen.

Isabella ached for her father's hug. Something ALS had robbed from him. She didn't understand how the computer device that Ming said Dad worked by blinking his eyes worked. But she was thankful they could still communicate.

"Daddy, I have a painting gig."

"Wonderful!!!" filled the comment bar.

After filling him in on the mural project she took a cleansing breath. "Please forgive me. I should have listened to you when I graduated." *Dad had been right about everything.*

She watched him blink and waited for his response. Isabella's heart hurt watching this once strong man struggle to communicate.

"Child, remember God works all things for His good. Even bad marriages and ALS."

"I'm not sure I believe that anymore."

What kind of daughter says things like that to a dad with ALS? I'm horrible.

"Daddy, I didn't mean..."

"Trust Him." Her father's face filled with fatigue.

"Daddy, I should go."

His blinking intensified.

"Call Mom. She can explain." Dad's smile weak but full of love.

"Ok. Love you."

"Love U 2."

His pre-programmed answer came in seconds. His eyes spoke of deep concern for her.

The screen went blank. Glancing at the time in the corner of her screen. Had it been an hour? They'd said so little. Dad's painstaking blinks to type had worn him out. Yet he still trusted the Lord. "Dad your faith amazes me. God help me to trust like Daddy." When the prayer left her lips, a warm hug from her Heavenly Father surrounded her.

Pushing the negative aside, she grabbed her sketch pad as ideas flowed for the mural.

~

DAN CLICKED THE TV REMOTE, channel surfing, Isabella's words fresh in his mind. She wants to be friends. Her eyes had looked so determined. Dan knew she was sincere when she admitted her need to find herself again. But it still felt like rejection. He hadn't dated much before he lost his fingers. After the loss of his leg his sometime girlfriend left.

Wives and girlfriends of soldiers he met in rehab couldn't deal with the sudden disability. Maybe somewhere below the surface of her words Isabella couldn't either. Maybe after she found herself she'd push Dan further out of her life. What place could a one-legged man have in her life? He hated himself for thinking it.

She said she wanted friends—needed friends. "Father, you know it's always been all or nothing with me. I don't think I can do just friends."

Dan shut off the TV. Brutus nuzzled his hand then crawled up on the couch to lay his head in Dan's lap. Dan stroked his head. "Well, buddy. We gotta figure out a plan. I want Isabella in my life. If, and that'd be a huge miracle. If we became more than friends. Well, she needs to want you too." The dog's big brown eyes stared up at him. Then he licked Dan's face. "Down. I love you too. Let's go out." His friend ran to the back door.

~

TWO WEEKS later Dan sat watching Steve, Ming, John and his date Laura bowl. The sound of music drowned by the clash of pins falling matched his mood.

John groaned. "I missed the spare."

Dan related well with the lone bowling pin. Rather than play he volunteered to keep score. The automated scoreboard made his job nothing more than an observer. His heart hurt watching his friends interact. He missed Isabella. Stubbornness kept him from calling first. She wanted this friendship thing. Or did she?

"Dan, want to help me get snacks?" John headed to the concession.

"Sure thing." Dan reached the counter just as John placed the order.

They got their drinks while they waited for the food. Dan reached for his wallet but John waved him away. "This is my treat. Besides, I'm on a date." John handed the money to the clerk and nudged Dan.

"Hey, man, where's Issy?" John took a sip of his Dr. Pepper. Leave it to John to address the elephant in the room.

"I have no idea."

"I thought you were dating."

"Nah, we're just friends." Dan tried not to choke on the words.

"Oh, that stinks." John patted Dan's arm. "So, what you going to do about it?"

"Nothing."

"Well, that would be a big mistake."

"Look if she wants this friendship thing to work, she needs to make the first move." Boy, did that sound dumb when he said it out-loud.

"Hey, I know the feeling. You gotta be proactive." John placed a hand on his shoulder. "Talk to her, keep in touch, bring her thoughtful gifts."

"Sounds like dating to me."

"Maybe, but Laura is here today because I made that friendship angle work for me."

"She's not your cyber date?"

"What? No. That was not one of my brightest ideas. My lame attempt at stuffing my feelings. I'd almost given up on winning Laura. We met a few years ago. John pointed at Dan. "She only wanted to be friends. Reject city. It's been a tough road. Then she admitted we had a connection. A connection I'd sensed the first time I saw her."

"Did you date before you did the friends thing."

"Yeah, and it tore my heart out when she *just* wanted to be friends."

"So, how..."

"Prayer, bidding my time, helping her when she moved. Her then boyfriend was too busy to help. But he showed up for dinner later. A dinner I bought by the way. He messed with her head bad. It took a year of friending her before I asked her out again. That's when she realized we were good together. I'll tell you one thing. I sure took prayer more seriously."

The clerk handed them trays of snacks and the two carried them back to the others. "Stay the course, bro."

"Isabella's different. She had a bad marriage."

"The more she needs a real friend." John nodded toward the door. "Wonder if her ears were itching."

"What?"

"You know the old saying 'If your ears itch someone is talking about you."

Dan turned to the door, Isabella waved. Ming jumped up and gave her a hug as the men joined the group.

"I wish you'd have come sooner. You're a better bowler than me." Ming sat and patted the spot next to her.

"I'm too tired to bowl. I've been on my feet for hours." She kicked off her heels and pulled a pair of tennis shoes out of her tote bag.

"Can't we persuade you to play?" Laura pointed to the electronic score-board. "Our scores are abysmal."

"Abysmal —you must be a school teacher." Issy laughed.

"Senior English and American Lit at West Aurora High." Laura shook hands with Issy. "Please help us out here."

"Tonight, I'd make your scores worse. I worked on a display case for three hours. My arms are sore from painting before I went to work."

"What are you painting?" Dan didn't recall her mentioning any painting projects she had. But then again, he hadn't seen her since the let's be friends talk. And anything she may have mentioned before those fatal words had disappeared from his mind. She'd missed church last Sunday which made Dan more determined not to be the one to call first.

"One of Ming's clients asked me to paint a mural for her church's new junior high Sunday School class."

"You promised to let me see it when you're done." Ming took another sip of her soda before grabbing her ball and heading for the line. A squeal escaped her lips as her ball wiped out all the pens. "A strike, Sis you're my good luck charm."

Dan found his voice again. "I'd like to see it too."

"Absolutely, you can both come. I should be finished by week's end." Her face glowed with excitement over the project.

Dan half-listened. He watched her tiny manicured finger dance, empha-sizing her words. Even in her tie dye uniform shirt she looked gorgeous. Dan felt subconscious in his shorts. His prosthetic exposed. Up until she arrived he'd not thought about his leg. Get it together man.

"Did you enjoy your weekend away?" Steve's question caught Dan's attention.

"Yes and no." A sigh escaped Issy lips. "It was great to see family. Catch up with Carla and the rest. But seeing Dad... his ALS has taken so much from him. Yet, he has a wonderful attitude about life."

"When did you leave?" Dan felt stupid thinking she'd skipped church to avoid him.

"I caught a late flight on Friday and came back Monday morning. A spur of the moment thing."

"Another example of the new Issy," Mindy said. "No planning."

"Right, If I had I'd have remembered my toothbrush," Issy said. Dan looked at his drink when she turned toward him. He felt foolish realizing he'd been staring.

"Maybe you could help me out tomorrow."

"With what?"

"The mural."

Was this a lame attempt at doing the friendship thing.

"But I have no artist talent whatsoever."

She smiled at his confession.

"No worries. None required."

"You should do it, Dan," Ming interjected while she cuddled closer to Steve. The two laughed, the couple's playfulness brought jealous heat to his chest.

"She asked me this morning but I have clients on schedule all day."

So much for thinking I was her first choice. "What will I be doing?"

"You'll see it'll be fun." Issy smiled and turned to watch the bowlers.

John winked at Dan "Lots of friendly fun."

18

NEW FRIENDS AND HUMILITY

Isabella's fingers stretch to reach the last can of artichoke hearts on the top shelf of the canned foods aisle.

"Need help, Twinny?"

The familiar nickname brought a smile to her face.

"Mrs. Crawford, how are you? So, nice to see you."

The tiny gray-haired lady wore green slacks and a softer green pullover sweater. She rode the motorized shopping cart the store provided.

"Let me help you, dearie."

"If you can grow a foot." Isabella stretched once more no closer to completing her quest.

"Stand aside." Mrs. Crawford touched her arm. Isabella watched with amusement when she produced a metal rod. She extended it to its full length and pressed a button on the side. A clawed hand captured the can.

"Cool. I need one of those."

She took the can from Mrs. Crawford and placed it in her cart.

"I see you know how to cook. No microwave meals in your cart. I on the other hand..." Mrs. Crawford cackled at her own joke.

"My sister loves cooking with fresh ingredients."

"So, Mindy is the chef at your house."

"When she's home. I work part-time so I have the time to cook."

"Where do you work?"

"Don't you remember I told you, Hobby Life?"

"Yes. She touched her temple. My mind doesn't hold information like it used to." Another chuckle rose from her lips, she patted Isabella's hand. "Do you like it there?"

"It's a job." Her face warmed when she realized again who the wizen lady before her was.

"Hmm. You should be creating art instead of selling art supplies? I've been stopping by the church every morning to see what you've accomplished. It is amazing. So, life-like. As if I could walk right into the African village or the Chinese houseboat. So much detail."

"Thank you. Your words are high praise. I haven't picked up a paintbrush in a few years. I'd forgotten how much a part of me, creating art is. A light to the world. That's a powerful mission statement for young people."

"The kids thought of it themselves. They support a few missionaries through bake sales and such. This summer they hope to go on a mission trip to Arkansas to help with Vacation Bible School."

"Wow! My junior high Sunday school did well to stay quiet while the teacher gave the lesson."

"There's a lot of that too, according to Angela. Their teacher's my niece." Mrs. Crawford patted her hand. "You remind me of her, kind hearts."

"Thank you."

"Do you have business cards?"

Isabella shook her head.

"Well, get some so I can pass them out to my friends."

"Why would your friends want them?"

"Because we are on the Aurora Art Council board of directors." Mrs. Crawford smiled. "Please call me Clare."

"Ok."

"Now, get out of the way, Twinny. I need to finish shopping, it's almost time for Wheel of Fortune."

Isabella smiled. Hearing Clare refer to her as kind was a balm to her soul. Ron had often called her selfish or mean-spirited. Anytime she didn't want to do things his way the verbal arrows flew at her character. Even his mother referred to her as selfish when she'd mentioned moving out.

The thought of Maureen alone brought back guilt and her hand on a bag of chocolates. "I don't need you." She weighed the bag in her hand, then placed it back on the shelf. She turned the corner to find herself in line behind Clare.

"We meet again." The older lady dismounted the scooter cart and waited for the clerk to unload it. "Isabella, I thought of something I wanted to ask you." She shifted through her purse before she picked up her thought.

"I've got a brilliant idea for a new job for you. My nephew has been after me to eat better. He's threatening to hire a companion for me. Would you be interested in being my companion?" Clare unzipped one of the two zippers on top of her purse. Rezipped it. And did the same with the other zipper.

"A little cooking, cleaning, and listening to an old lady's chatter." She shifted through the second compartment and retrieved her checkbook. "It'd be a live-in position." Clare leaned toward her, a smile forming. "I'd let you set up an art studio in one of my guest rooms so you can work on art while I nap."

Issy's mused nodded approval. *Father, is this your will for me?*

"I'd pay you more than you make at Hobby Life and you'd have lots of free time to paint."

"Sounds interesting." She gripped the shopping cart handle to hold back her excitement

"Can I let you know in a few days?"

"Lovely." Mrs. Crawford handed her signed check to the clerk who filled in the amount. She put her checkbook back in her purse and fished around for something.

"Unlike you I carry business cards. It makes it easier. Sometimes my hands shake." Clare gave her the card and zipped her purse shut while she spoke. "Don't lose it, you'll need that number to call me."

Isabella tucked it in her own purse next to the one she'd already given her.

DAN AND STEVE wandered through Sports Mart. Steve held two different running shoes in his hands. "I don't know, this running shoe is $20 more than the one I just tried on. They look the same. You were a sprinter in high school, give me your expert opinion."

Dan examined each shoe, envy burning a hole through his calm demeanor. He'd love sprinting, jogging, racing to the finish line. The cost of a running attachment prohibitive on his budget.

"Either pair will give you good support. The wear of the shoe is more about the shape of your feet."

"My feet are little pigeon toed so the inner part wears faster. So, if I get the more expensive ones they'll wear out the same."

"True." Dan slapped his friend on the back. "For a basketball jock, you're pretty bright."

"I'll get these, then we can head to Home Depot." Steve tucked the shoe box under his arm and headed to the cashier.

"Are you still trying to find the ultimate grill?" Dan hoped it wouldn't take too long. He'd promised to help Isabella later. Dan fastened his seatbelt in Steve's BMW.

"Nah, I'm installing my dad's old one on my patio. He upgraded to an outdoor kitchen. That's way above my pay grade or cooking ability."

"Yeah, your dad's a grill chef. Hope he invites me over for his to-die-for steaks." Dan's mouth watered at the recollection of summer afternoons at Steve's house. His dad took every opportunity to grill out, and the food was phenomenal. "All you need is a small Weber to cook hot dogs and burgers."

"Well, yeah... but I'm used to my dad's old set up."

The two pulled into the Home Depot parking lot.

"So, what are we looking for?" Dan took care pulling himself out of Steve's car.

"Let's look at mowers."

"You sure your car's trunk is big enough for a mower?"

"Never thought of that." Steve shrugged heading toward the entrance. "I can come back with your truck."

"No, we can come back. You can't drive it."

"Who says it wouldn't be fun trying to drive your modified jalopy?"

"Could cause you to get pulled over by our men in black."

"You mean blue."

"No, Aurora cops have black uniforms." Dan gave his friend a gotcha gunpoint hand signal. "Hey, why do you need a mower? You live in a condo."

"Well, someone's birthday is coming up and his yard's a weed factory."

"Hey." Dan held his emotions in check. "You don't need to buy me a mower. I can hire a neighbor kid to do it."

"Have you noticed the neighbor kids in your hood are under the age of five? Besides you like doing stuff for yourself."

Dan remained silent. How could he explain he didn't feel sure-footed enough to push a mower even if it was self-propelled? There were lots of ruts in the backyard and the front yard was sparse on grass and heavy on rocky terrain. "I think the timing is wrong. My lawn needs lots of work yet."

"True." Steve scratched his head, a habit Dan knew he employed when he was holding something back.

"What?" Dan crossed his arm determined not to move until Steve confessed what was on his mind.

"The singles' class decided to take on a project. Nathan suggested we help a Vet. And..."

"I got nominated." Dan felt the heat on his neck "Other vets are more deserving, I'm not your guy." Dan turned to walk away.

"Stop right there." Steve's tone reminiscent of a drill sergeant. "Don't you dare throw that I-lost-my-leg-at-home-not-on-the-battlefield junk at me." Steve grabbed his arm. "Maybe you didn't take down some warlord, but you served well."

Dan began to object but Steve held his hand palm up. "Don't you dare make their desire to bless you turn into an awkward I'm-too-macho-to-need-help moment."

Steve's accusation rang true. Dan remained silent while his friend drove his point home.

"Hey, you said the landscaping was in the budget and if you did the work yourself you'd save a bundle. You pay for the materials and we help you get your yard in order in no time. Chad said he'd install a new fence. That was on your to-do list?"

"Yes." Dan felt like a whiny jerk after Steve's upbraiding.

"So today we order the riding mower you will need to keep your pristine yard in shape." Steve headed toward the display just inside the door.

Dan had to admit checking out mowers with Steve was fun. They both agreed the Mini rider with hand controls fit the bill. It had close maneuverability making trimming minimal. Steve gave the clerk his credit card and arranged for it to be delivered to Dan's home. Not dealing with loading and unloading the mower into his truck was worth the small delivery fee.

"When's this project supposed to start?"

"Two weeks from today."

"Good that gives me time to price what I want and have it delivered that Friday."

"Sounds good. Let me know if I can help you, Bro."

"Hey, is your dad changing out his patio pavers?"

"You want them?"

"If they are still in good shape."

"Dad's having the new stuff installed next week. If the old pavers look good, we can get them Tuesday."

"And you can help me clean them before the gathering of the gang."

"Oh man, I have a heavy case load."

"Hey, you told me I have to receive this blessing without complaining. Joy will overflow my heart next Saturday when you help me clean the pavers."

"I have a date."

"We can start early in the morning and finish in plenty of time for your date."

"Fine." Steve lengthened his stride and grinned as Dan matched him. "I'll be there."

"Let's go grab a burger, my treat." Dan offered.

"It better be." Steve laughed. "I think I'll have a shake and a sundae too."

Dan gave his friend a little push causing Steve to totter. "Want to borrow my crutches?"

19

WORKING ON FRIENDSHIP

"Knock, knock." Dan peered into the classroom the secretary at Faith Community had shown him. "Amazing! Everything looks so lifelike."

"Thanks." Isabella pushed her hair out of her eyes with the back of her hand. "Your timing is perfect."

"Are you sure you want my help? I'm no artist. I'll mess it up."

"See the paint over there." She pointed toward a roller pan on the floor in front of the last remaining yellow wall. "There's enough white paint to finish the undercoat."

Dan squatted to examine the can. He concentrated on balance while prying the lid open.

"The edges of the other walls are taped and tarped so you don't have to worry about splatters on the other walls."

"I'm no expert but shouldn't you have undercoated the walls first?"

"Yes. But they'd done the yellow before they decided on a mural. Once I finished the mural on the first wall the board decided to do the opposite wall."

"Now it's the whole room."

"Yeah. I couldn't say no. I had so many ideas and now I can use all of them." Isabella's smile of satisfaction lit up her face. "It's been a pain, though. The two painted walls were dry enough so the tape wouldn't disturb paint."

"Tarping should do the trick." Dan got to work painting the wall. "Never seen anything like this before. Awesome."

"You haven't studied the masters. This is amateur in comparison."

"Well, I know what I like." Dan stared at an African village scene. "The veins on the old guys ... so detailed." The Chinese houseboat seemed to move before his eyes. "The facial expression on the Asian dude is... I don't have words. Cool sounds lame."

Each wall illustrated three different scenes from around the world. Let your light shine, the theme, woven into every scene. The three-dimensional quality drew him into the settings. "How did you learn to draw life-like people?"

Isabella stroked paint on a blond boy in a wheelchair. That one dab of paint added depth to his face. "Studying the real thing."

"How so?"

"We studied anatomy and how the body moves. Then we painted nudes. Observing how the muscles flexed and the toes bent. Things like that." She kept her eyes on her work.

"Did I hear you right—nudes? You painted naked people." Dan's face warmed as the words passed his lips. A revelation of this woman he'd never imagine in a million years.

"Yes. I know it's a controversy among Christians. Good Christians don't look at pornography or paint naked people. The two are not synonymous. Most of the school's models are average people. They have scars, flabby skin, and irregular features. The reasoning is to help develop an eye to capture movement on the page in a realistic way. Immature people would think... well, you know." She turned to Dan. "It's like someone studying to be a doctor or nurse. They see naked people as part of their job."

Dan remained silent letting the idea sink in.

"There are those who abuse the art by painting vulgar realistic pictures. A photographer taking pornographic pictures after he has learned how to capture light on the human form is the same. So, I can either strive to become the best artist I can or settle for less. If I had wanted to limit myself to still life— you know flowers and landscapes maybe I could have skipped the human form portions. Although, the school I attended didn't permit it. The curriculum required students to experience every aspect of capturing life in artistic form."

Dan decided he'd asked one too many questions. Sounds of his roller spreading white paint over the yellow filled the silence. "It'll need more coats of paint."

"After the white dries, I'll add the background colors and the layers of paint will cover it."

Dan had two more rows. Then what? Did a friend hang around and talk? Would he be in the way?

"Good job, I'll tackle that wall after it dries. Could stay and start on the base colors. I'd appreciate it."

Score. Dan did a mental fist bump. "Sure. Hey, have you had lunch."

"No. Are you offering to make a food run?" From her place on the floor she smiled up at him. She was adding details to the wheelchair.

"Sure. By the time, I bring it back and we take a lunch break, this wall should be dry."

Dan went to a nearby sandwich shop and brought back two six-inch sandwiches. Hers was a vegetarian and a meatball sub. They sat on the front steps watching the traffic go by while they ate. Dan stretched his prosthetic leg out in front of him. He noticed a flick of paint on the artificial flesh. "It's nice out."

"I needed a fresh air break. It gets stuffy in that confined space with the paint fumes. I'd turn on a fan to clear the air, but then the paint would dry too quickly."

After a few bites of his sandwich, Dan noticed this beautiful woman had a smug of green paint on her cheek. Using the tail of his shirt he dabbed at the paint. Isabella startled expression changed to a smile. "Thank you."

Touching her cheek drew his eyes to her lips. Time to refocus on something else.

"At the bowling alley, you mentioned you spent a few days with your family. Something you said about your Dad intrigued me."

"What was that?"

"You said your father had a great attitude. What did you mean?" Talking about her dad might make her sad. He didn't want to ruin a perfect day. Tiny flicks of color sprinkled across her nose and her eyes held no sorrow.

"I mean he has ALS."

"Dad has a joyful light in his eyes, even though others have to help him. My niece and nephew attend to his personal needs. Mom feeds him and waits with patient calm as he shares his thoughts. Pops told me he is grateful to have such a loving family around him. He feels the touch of Jesus every time someone helps him. Makes me ashamed of my reactions to my own trivial trials."

"Wow."

"Yeah, that's about the size of it. If he can walk through this awful thing unafraid with his hand in the Masters, At least, I can try while building this new life."

Dan didn't know what to say. Shame washed over him as he stared at his prosthetic. Conviction filled him. He needed to relax when others offered help. So many of the guys in the VA rehab were worse off. Rehab gave him back so much. Her father didn't have that chance. *Lord, help me be... better.*

Dan and Isabella spent several minutes focused on eating. By the time, he'd pushed the last piece of sandwich into his mouth she was gathering up their garbage.

"Thank you so much." She smiled and pushed a stray hair behind her ear. "Most days I work through lunch then go home and eat a whole box of cookies."

"Glad to be of service." The lighter mood lifted his spirit. Dan followed her back to work. Now the part that proved he was no artist would begin. He ran his hand over his short beard while he listened to her instructions.

"This is paint by numbers. I'll draw out what I want and put a dab of paint in each area. All you have to do…"

"Is follow the pattern. Paint by number." Staying in the lines. That he could do. He watched her draw the boundaries of the various colors.

Once again, they were working in companionable silence. Isabella's sigh drew his attention. She was up on a ladder painting some leaves on an oak tree. "What was that for?"

"I love doing this. It's invigorating. I feel more alive than I have in years."

"I'm glad." Dan dipped his brush in a quart of light blue paint. He removed the drips from his brush on the lip of the can before spreading the color.

"That's the other thing. Having someone encourage my joy. I appreciate it so much."

Maybe John had something. Dan's competition was a dead man. If he could prove to Isabella, he was a different. He was feeling happier than he had since before the accident. Since before his parents died. Spending time with Isabella reminded him of a verse. "A merry heart does good like a medicine…" The peace her presence brought to his heart grew more each time they were together.

DAN SORTED THROUGH THE MAIL. Throwing ads in the office trash and placing bills in the inbox basket on his desk. A blue envelope remained. Carmen Morgan's new address appeared in the corner. Carmen had been his cheerleader during rehab. She was the only one he knew who wrote letters anymore.

Placing the envelope in his lap he rolled his wheelchair into the kitchen. Dan poured a cup of coffee and settled at the kitchen table to read her letter. Carmen's chatty letters always lift his spirits. Her sweet smile and gentle yet bossy care during rehab had helped him walk again. Mrs. Morgan's cinnamon skin always glowed with good cheer and her wide variety of dangling earrings started many conversations.

He turned to Brutus who lounged at his feet. "Hey Boy, Carmen will be in the area visiting her son and wants to stop by for a visit."

Brutus raised his head, cocked it to the side, then rested it on his front paws.

"You've never met her, but she loves dogs so you're in for a treat."

The dog's tail thumped on the floor. Dan patted his head. "You're a good boy, yes you are." He moved the massive, furry head side to side as he spoke making the canine tail pound harder as a whimper of joy split the air.

"You love it when company comes to see you, don't you, boy." Brutus turned on his back for a belly rub.

The letter mentioned the date of her arrival. She'd be here during the week of the thank-a-vet landscaping project. A tinge of guilt prickled his conscience. He'd skipped last night's singles' group activity on purpose. Carmen deplored cowardice. Dan pictured his friend and he recalled their first meeting.

"Well, soldier, I see ya been gazing out the winda again. Don't find no encouragement from staring at a brick wall." Carmen's voice pulled Dan from his melancholy. "Why you wastin' time when you could be gettin' back to livin'?"

Dan's recovery had reached a plateau. Body ached all over from therapy. He felt like an old man whose cane was too short. Dan stared at the zebra striped scrubs with matching zebra earrings.

"I'm your new coach."

"What?" Dan wondered if he'd heard right.

"Well, I prefer to call myself a coach rather than a physical therapist because at this point PT is a swear word on your lips." Carmen's full-belly laugh made Dan smile.

"You got that right." Dan scooted up in his bed, giving his visitor his full attention.

"I told them to fit me for a wheelchair. I'm done with therapy."

"That's why you got assigned to me. I have a flawless record. Every soldier I work with walks like nobody's business."

"Haven't heard nobody's business used since I was a kid."

"Well, you're going to hear it a lot from me. Cause it ain't nobody's business but your own how well you succeed. But it will become my personal business if you wreck my stellar record."

Dan had burst through the melancholy and kept Carmen's record intact. He admired the woman's tenacity. She'd started college when her youngest started high school and completed her degree the day her first grandchild was born. Then chosen to work at the VA when her oldest son lost his arm to an IED in Iraq. Dan remembered Carmen's constant admonition.

"Don't let shame keep you from having a full life."

The reminder jarred him back to the present. He reached for his cell phone.

"Hey, Steve, where's the Bible study this week?"

DAN WAITED for Steve to arrive before getting out of his truck. He hated asking for help. But he knew he'd block everybody's way as he worked his way up Mindy's stairs alone. Steve grabbed Nathan, who'd pulled up behind him. They were the same height and formed a chair with their arms to carry Dan upstairs. "Man, you're heavier than you look." Steve groaned as he and Nathan help Dan stand.

"All muscle." Dan hoped his words sounded cocky rather than agitated.

"What gym do you go too?" Nathan asked.

"I have a room set up at home."

"You've got more self-discipline than me. I have Matt over there as my workout buddy otherwise I'd never do it."

Dan appreciated the praise. It helped him relax among these new friends. This was his third time with the group. The other two times he'd sat by Isabella. Today he joined Nathan and Matt on the couch. Isabella sat on the floor in front of Ming's chair.

Steve opened the meeting. "Tonight, we will spend some time in the Word and the rest of the meeting will be a planning session for our Vet project." Steve nodded at Ming. She opened the time in prayer then everyone opened their Bibles. Steve led a short devotional.

"Unless anyone has anything else to add, we have snacks in the kitchen made by Issy and Laura." Steve nodded in their direction. "Thanks, Ladies. After we grab some food we want to spend the rest of the evening discussing next weekend's project."

Everyone helped themselves to the refreshments and found their seats again. Dan chose the veggie and dip. He'd skipped working out the last couple days and didn't want to risk weight gain which created stub chaffing. It was easier to maintain his weight than have the artificial leg refitted.

"All right." Steve got everyone's attention. "Pull out paper or your phone to take notes on what your responsibility will be next week. Laura is passing out a copy of Dan's punch list."

"What's a punch list?" Nadia looked around. "Okay, how many of you are willing to admit you don't know." A few men along with the women raised their hands.

"A punch list is all the things needed to get the job done." Steve turned to Dan. "Did you bring your landscape drawing?"

"I have it here." Dan pulled a folded paper from his Bible and spread it out on the coffee table. "This is what I envision the yard looking like when we are all finished."

"Wow! It's awesome." John came closer to take a better look.

Soon everyone had taken extra time to look at the drawing.

"Can we really get all this done?" Robin asked.

A few others expressed concern.

"Well, Dan, you're the expert."

"Yeah, right." Dan shook his head at Steve. After a little struggle, Matt and Nathan help pull him out of the large indent the guys had made in the sofa. He perched on the edge.

"We can focus on key things first. The front yard's sod and sprinkler system are being installed by professionals on Monday. So, that can be checked off the punch list. A new fence is second and then we roll the backyard, reseed and build the patio. If we have enough time and manpower." Looking at the ladies he added. "Or woman power. We could plant the flowers and trim the bushes."

Steve tapped his iPad. "We planned on starting on Friday with the fence. John, Matt, Nathan and Tony plan on knocking that out in a day. If any of the women want to start planting flowers on Friday, you can plant the front yard. And not be in the guys' way."

"What if I want to work on the fence?" Laura rose from her place next to John. After depositing her plate in the sink, she added. "I helped my Dad build our fence. I can hammer a pretty mean nail."

"Can you hammer a nice nail?" John's remark earned him a slap on the shoulder and laughter from the group.

"Ok, whoever, male or female who wants to help with the fence or flowers on Friday be there," Steve said. "The rest of us will gather early Saturday morning." Steve tapped a new note on his iPad. "And our Vet will feed us breakfast."

~

DAN WASHED THE LAST PLATE. Delaying his departure until everyone left. He preferred to leave on his own power without an audience watching him.

"Thanks, for helping." Isabella stuffed the last plastic cup in the trash.

"I can take that when I leave." Dan's mind working out the logistic of carrying a full bag of trash on his lap.

Isabella tied the trash bag. "No worries. I've got to roll up my car windows."

Dan didn't argue. He watched the soapy water drain, taking some of his pride with it. "Can I help you with anything else?"

"No. I appreciate you stepping up. Ming walked Steve out to his car which means she'll hang out there for another hour at least." She grabbed the kettle off the stove filling it with water. "Would you like some tea?"

"Sure." Dan was glad for a temporary reprieve from tackling the stairs. Private moments with Isabella had been scarce since he'd help her paint. "Are the murals done?""

"Yes. We could run by and see it tomorrow. Faith Community's junior high classroom grand reveal is next week. They've asked me to come as their guest of honor."

"I can say I knew you when." Dan watched her place a floral teapot on the kitchen table and two matching teacups with saucers. "Those are lovely. Which is a word I don't ever use."

"I got them at an estate sale Clare told me about. I can get you a mug if the handle is too small."

"It's fine. So, we'll plan on seeing your amazing room tomorrow. Can I take you to lunch before we go?" Dan didn't want her to think it was a date. "A girl got to eat."

"You'll get no argument from me. You pick the place this time."

"Cool. I'll bring my camera to commemorate the day." Dan mixed a little sugar in his tea. Stirring the spoon with gentle turns in the fragile china.

"Dan it's sturdier than it looks. Relax." Isabella giggled.

Dan used the thumb and forefinger of his right hand to pick up the cup by its handle. "Hey, cool. A new skill for my right hand. A mug is too heavy." Dan wanted to bite the words back. What a stupid thing to mention.

"Then we can share tea from my feminine china more often." Isabella toasted him with her cup before taking a sip. Dan toasted back amazed at how she adapted to his disability. Most people either overcompensated or attempted to ignore it. Isabella accepted his limitations. He wished he'd meet her earlier. Before the accident. She'd have been the girl to stand by her man. At least he hoped she would. If she'd ever see him as her man. The silence

resting between them reminded him of Uncle Paul and Aunt Sally. Quiet cama-
raderie.

"A quarter for your thoughts." Dan placed his hand on hers waiting for a
response. She looked at their hands and disengaged hers. Dan hoped the slow-
ness was a sign she liked it being there.

"Aren't thoughts worth a penny?" Isabella gazed into his eyes and for a
moment he got lost in hers.

"Twenty-first-century inflation." Dan gave an awkward laugh.

"Cute." She looked away for a moment. "Hey, I want to ask you something."

Dan sensed she needed a moment to put her thoughts together. Her brows
collide and her shoulder sag before she straightened her back. "I'm thinking
about moving."

Dan's heart crashed into his chest. "Back to Indiana?"

"Of course, not. Why would you even think that?" She gave a momentary
scowl before continuing. "I think Ming needs her space. Steve comes over every
single night." Isabella stretched out the last three words for emphasis. "He
stays for hours."

"So, you're tired of chaperoning."

"I never thought of that. I am tired of hearing muffled voices into the wee
hours of the night when I'm trying to sleep. Do you think it would hurt my
sister's feelings if I got my own place?"

"She'd be the better person to ask. But I imagine she's lived alone before
and will be fine when you leave." Dan finished his tea and carried his cup to
the sink. Together they washed and dried the tea set. "I'd be glad to help you
look. What did you have in mind?"

"A condo with great light. I've got my muse back so I want a room to paint
with lots of light."

"I think Laura's a real estate agent. She might be able to help."

"I thought she was a school teacher?"

"That too. She does the real estate thing on weekends and through the
summer. She's helping John find a new place."

"I forgot, she mentioned John was a tough client." Isabella smiled and
patted Dan's shoulder sending a warm shiver down his arm. "See you've helped
already. I'll bring my iPad and we can check out places over lunch."

"Sounds like a plan."

Dan mentally bound down the stairs with excitement while his back side
made slow progress. At the last few steps he slid to the bottom. And pumped
his fist in the air as he stood firm. More time with Isabella. This friend thing
wasn't so bad.

20

HOUSE HUNTING

I sabella tied her pink scarf again. Today she couldn't get the scarf to lay right. In frustration, she tugged off the scarf and exchanged it for the blue combo pre-fold, no fuss. She'd awakened from a restless sleep. The moving conflict wrested in her mind she needed to give Mrs. Crawford an answer. Isabella wanted her own place. But she fought the age-old battle of pleasing people.

She spoke to her reflection while she combed her hair. "I haven't ever lived on my own. I went from my folks to my aunt in Chicago when I attended college, back home, married, Maureen's home then Ming's. Never ever lived on my own. At twenty-nine it's way past time."

She added a light pink lipstick and stepped back to check the hem of her pleated black skirt in the mirror. She'd found this classic at a thrift store. Satisfied her white boat neck shell top had no wrinkles, she sat on her bed to pull on her black sling backs.

"Dan will roll his eyes at my heels, I don't care. I love these shoes."

Why did she care what Dan thought? They were friends. Some friend's opinion mattered. *I'm so needy and pathetic.*

Isabella had added quite a few pieces to her wardrobe and four additional pairs of shoes. Ron and Maureen had controlled her wardrobe. Her late husband wanted her to look more professional. In his confused mind, it bounced between pastor's wife persona and performer. Her mother-in-law encouraged drab. Now this wardrobe was of her own choosing.

"God, is it wrong to want to choose my own home too?"

~

ISABELLA ARRIVED moments before the service started and took a seat at the back of the sanctuary. She'd heard Dan preach three more times since her first visit to Stone Church. Today an unfamiliar gray-haired gentleman stood near Dan. This must be his uncle. She'd enjoyed Dan's easy-going way of sharing. Hearing his uncle preach might give her a better understanding of Stone Church.

A new pianist started the service. A young woman with obvious ability. The hymns flowed flawless from her fingers. The choir still managed to sharp or flat at least once every hymn. The soloist was a few beats behind the pianist.

Isabella stopped following along in the hymnal and let her heart hear the words. She closed her eyes sensing the zeal and the solemnity of the various choir members. During worship, her Lord whispered. *Trust me. I love you with an everlasting love.* Could she trust? What did that everlasting love feel like? Before her heart could explore it further the music concluded.

Reverend Whitehall's sermon was to the point, peppered with illustrations matching the age of most the congregation. The pastor's monotone presentation caused a foggy sleep to come over her. Isabella's eyes flew open, and she straightened her spine. Shame colored her cheeks and lodged in her stomach. Gentle snores resonated around the room, lessening her guilt.

She glanced at her watch. A mere fifteen minutes had passed. Above the pastor's head the stained-glass window glowed from the sunlight's reflection. The halo of light she'd noticed on Dan the first time he'd preached didn't look the same on this sage old man.

Her thoughts focused on the craftsmanship of the window glass. Her artist eye taking in every detail. The first notes of the benediction reconnected her with the service. *Father forgive my rudeness. And please don't let anyone ask my opinion on the sermon.* The word *trust* still echoes in her mind. Was that God's sermon for her?

One of the elders gave the closing prayer. Reverend Whitehall used that time to position himself at the sanctuary door.

Reaching for her purse she looked for Dan. He waved and paced himself behind a couple. The husband slowed his steps to match his wife's walker. After a few minutes, Dan appeared at the end of her pew. "My uncle wants to meet you." Dan took her hand and together they followed behind the same couple. "I already told him we had plans today so he wouldn't put you on the spot with a dinner invitation."

Once the couple moved away Reverend Whitehall took her hand. "You must be Isabel?"

Isabella smiled not correcting the mispronunciation of her name. "It's nice to meet you, Reverend. I am so glad you're well."

"As am I, child." Releasing her hand, he reached for Dan's right hand. Not bothered by the missing fingers. "Members of the congregation mentioned you did a fine job of filling the pulpit. I'm proud of you, son."

"Thank you, sir."

"Perhaps another time. Bless this old man. Come for a time of food and fellowship."

Isabella watched guilt pass across Dan's face. "I'll come by tomorrow for a visit."

"That's my day off. I'll run by the store." His uncle smiled and turned to Isabella.

"Will you be joining him? I'd love to get to know my nephew's special friend."

Isabella noticed Dan's blush.

"I have to work tomorrow night. Perhaps another time." She shook the pastor's hand once more, hoping this kind man couldn't tell she was fibbing. Her shift ended at five. The special friend remark was uncomfortable.

It bothered her more when she realized she'd allowed Dan to hold her hand in public implying something more. Yet, his presence comforted her. Their hands seemed to find each other. Being proactive, Isabella wrapped her arms around her purse on their way out of church.

Dan placed his hand on the center of her back and escorted her to his truck. His touch sent a tingle through her. "Where would you like to eat?"

"You pick, but I need to get my tablet from my car before we go." She walked to her car parked a few spaces away. This gave her time to compose herself. Heading back to the truck she was thankful to see Dan in the driver's seat. He'd left the passenger door open for her.

"It takes me awhile to get situated, I hope you don't mind."

"Fine by me." Isabella kept her tone nonchalant fumbling to fastened her seatbelt. "Where are we eating?"

"How about Golden Corral?"

"Ming said that place closed."

"I forgot. How about Ari's?"

"How about Panera's?"

"What happened to—I get to pick." Dan laughed.

"Sorry." *Ron's controlling spirit might be contagious.* She folded her arms across her chest and pasted on a smile. I was thinking Panera's is less of a hassle to get our food. There are outlets to plug in my tablet if the battery dies."

"Makes sense." Dan pulled on to Galena Blvd headed toward the Panera's on Orchard Rd. "Hope it's not too crowded."

The line near the door move at an even pace. By the time, they reached the counter Isabella had figured out what she wanted. "I'll have a broccoli cheddar soup and an asiago apple salad and chai tea."

Dan spoke before she had a chance to get the total. "And I'll have the Reuben with tomato basil soup and coffee." Dan pulled out his wallet and handed the girl his Panera's card.

"You are entitled to a bakery treat for 99 cents today with your purchase." The cashier smiled.

"We'll take two cookies." He paid cash for their purchases. The cashier gave him a beeper.

"I have enough points for a free sandwich next time." Dan grinned at her as they moved to collect their drinks and find a seat.

Isabella grabbed the beeper when it binged and collected their food. Dan took the chair leaving her the booth bench. "I could have got those." Dan scowled and took his plate from her.

"I could have paid for my own food." She scowled back.

"Touché." Dan laughed.

"I need to be independent too, Dan."

"I know. My parents raised me to be a gentleman."

"You are. But my daddy always made sure I had money before I left for a date." Isabella stabbed her salad with her fork. "Not that this is a date. I mean...."

"No worries." Dan waved off the comment and took his first bite.

After that awkward moment, she steered the conversation onto safer ground. The upcoming reveal of the youth group room and the debate he took part in during his philosophy class. Once the food was consumed, she opened her tablet and found Laura's website. Dan refilled his coffee and ordered her another tea.

After looking through several condo offerings, Isabella shook her head. "The virtual tours aren't helping." Dan gave her a sympatric look. How refreshing not to be scoffed at or chastised for indecisiveness. "The trouble is I don't know what I'm looking for."

"What kind of place did you have in Indiana?"

"An apartment. The church had subdivided a large Victorian to provide housing for various staff members. We were the lone married couple. Our apartment was the third floor and the attic. The attic bedroom had one small window, poor ventilation, and no light. The third floor was drafty in winter and stifling in summer and the lighting came from the north."

"The opposite would be lots of light, cool breezes in summer, no drafts in winter and windows."

"It's a start." Isabella closed her tablet. "I think I'll call Laura and ask her to show me a few places. I need to feel the space.

"Feel it?" Dan's dimples flashed and his eyes focused on her.

"You have to close your eyes to feel the space." She felt her smile widen as she returned his gaze. *Oh. Lord, I am not ready for this.*

"Let's give Laura a call and set something up." Dan reached for his phone. Isabella touched his hand.

"I'll do it tomorrow."

I'm sorry." Dan's blush was so endearing. "Army trained me to take charge. This is your gig not mine."

"It's ok. There is something else I need to do today and I want to ask your advice." She stared at the empty cup in her hand. "Mrs. Crawford offered me a job as her companion and a place to stay. But I need to be on my own."

"And want to let her down easy." Dan touched her fingers sending comforting reassurance to her heart. "Can you take the job and live on your own?"

"I can afford to live on my own if that's what you mean. Whether Mrs. Crawford wants a part-time companion off-site is another story."

I'm sure if you explain why you want your own place she'll understand. She must think a lot of you to ask. I'm sure having a companion has to be a hard step to take."

"Want to come with me?"

"Really?"

"I know it sounds weird but I'm a coward using the word no. You can keep me from changing my mind."

"I've got your six." Dan took her hand as they walked out of Panera's.

DAN SETTLED into the driver's seat while Isabella called Mrs. Crawford. He'd dodged a bullet when he tried to take control of her house hunting. Not the guy in charge, not the sergeant commanding a room full of logistics specialists.

Sitting beside him was a beautiful woman desperate to find her own path. Boy, how he could relate. After ten years in the army, he'd worked hard at the same thing. Dan still didn't know his college endgame. One thing he knew for sure he'd guard her six and be her wing man on this mission.

Isabella put her cell phone in her purse. "Clare said to stop by now."

He watched her take a deep breath and let it out slowly. Dan patted her shoulder with his right hand. She smiled. He removed his hand and shifted the truck into gear.

"Where to?"

She handed Dan a slip of paper.

"I know the street."

They drove in silence.

Mrs. Crawford live in an old Italianate on Downer Place. It sat on a large lot in an older neighborhood that had held its value over the decades. Dan pulled into the circle drive. Isabella exited the truck before he could open her door. Another reminder they were just friends.

If I were any good at reading women I'd know what having her back meant.

He reached the porch steps as she rang the doorbell, enjoying the view of her slender legs disappearing into her pleated skirt. She patted her hair in place as she waited for Mrs. Crawford. He stepped up beside her wanting so much to slip his arm around her waist. He'd hold her hand if it wasn't wrapped around her purse.

A short wizen gray-haired lady in a lavender sweat suit answered the door. "Twinny, you brought your boyfriend."

Dan noticed her blush and tried to keep his smile in check. She glanced his way. Did he detect a slight shake of her head?

"Clare, this is Dan Sweeney, a friend."

"Come in, come in. Let's sit in the parlor." Clare opened the solid oak door wider as she pointed toward the room.

Dan scanned the antiques cluttering this one room. His mom had loved antiques and at this moment the identity of every piece of décor came to mind. Three tiffany lamps of various sizes sat on an octagon table in one corner, an ornate bookcase full of knickknacks and a hutch displaying lots of filigreed framed photos filled the opposite wall.

Clare indicates the tiny floral love seat. The two sat side by side. Dan scooted toward his side of the chair so Isabella could rearrange herself in a more comfortable position. He watched her straighten her back, cross her ankles and place her hands in her lap before speaking. It projected elegance. "I wanted to discuss your job offer."

"Excellent." Clare clapped her hands and leaned forward in her matching floral chair.

"I am considering taking the job as your companion. I like you and it could be quite interesting."

Clare laughed at her remark. "I agree, Twinny."

"I don't wish to live here, though."

Dan noted the catch in her words before she explained why it was so important for her to have her own place. Clare listened and smiled with satisfaction.

"I understand completely. I shared a flat with three other girls before I meant Harold. We had a gay old time." Her hand went to her mouth. "That didn't mean back then what it does now." She chuckled, her wrinkles deepening as her eyes sparkled. "We spread our wings and learned a few things about life."

Isabella shook her head. "I've learned quite enough in recent years. But I'd like the chance to decorate my own place."

Clare roses from her chair. "I'd like to see that too. Come with me." She led them through her house. The dining room had a large table and china cabinet. The kitchen was large enough to prepare a huge banquet. She took a key off a hook near the back door. Then continued out the door. A walkway led to a small cottage behind the house. "This is the care taker's cottage. It's been empty for a few years. As far as I know the electric and plumbing are in good shape. It needs a good cleaning and a facelift." Clare opened the door and found a light switch. The inside surprised Dan with its roomy open space. The nine-foot ceilings had a few cracks, the windows needed caulking and the carpet replacing. It smelled musty with a faint cigar scent.

"This place is interesting." Isabella's eyes surveyed the room.

"Interesting enough to live here?" Clare's eyes sparkled anew.

Dan watched to see Isabella's reaction. She closed her eyes and stood still. No one spoke. Dan waited for her decision. He'd back her up if he saw that expression. There it was. A smile spread across her face as her eyes opened.

"This place has real possibilities. I wish it had nice southern light."

"Come, come." Clare guided her past the small kitchen to a door off to the left. "This room was added by my late husband for our daughter when she married. She and her husband lived here for a year before they bought their own home. Barbara used this room for her plants. She loved this southern exposure." The ceiling to floor windows allowed the sunlight to trail along the walls. The white walls a bare canvas. Isabella sighed and turned to Dan. He nodded, delighted she cared what he thought.

"Who will be responsible for the repairs?" Dan hoped his question wasn't stepping over the line.

"If Isabella wants it, I can have a carpenter in here tomorrow. She can move in as soon as it's finished." Clare smiled at Isabella. "Twinny, you can decorate any way you like. I'll give you an allowance for that. Promise you'll come work for me before you move in. That will give me time to get used to having someone tell me what to do. You can meet my nephew; he'll tell you what he expects." Clare winked and gave Isabella a nudge before adding. "Then we can make our own rules." The three laughed.

"I'll give my two weeks' notice and tell my sister my plans." Isabella hurried ahead wandering through the house examining every corner. Clare and Dan followed behind at a slower pace.

A screech echoed from the bathroom. Dan and Clare rushed to the door. Isabella stood on the toilet seat, hands pressing the wall behind her. "A mouse. I hate mice." Isabella pointed to a now empty corner.

"I'll get an exterminator," Clare assured her as Dan extended his hand to help Isabella down.

"I have one question." Dan steadied her before releasing his hold. "How in the world did you jump up on that toilet seat with those heels?"

Both women laughed. Isabella gave him a playful smack on the shoulder as her face blushed darker.

"Twinny, this one's a keeper." Clare declared. She placed her hand on Dan's arm for balance as they headed toward the front door.

21

MASSAGE, ADVICE, AND LANDSCAPING

Dan sprawled on his couch absently petting Brutus. The dog's body wrapped around his master's shoulders. Canine eyes closed, a contented moan rumbled in response to the strokes.

"Boy, in a couple days the house will be crowded. You need to be on your best behavior. No jumping on Isabella." Dan turned and lifted Brutus's head to look him in the eyes. "Keep your distance. She'll warm up to you. I hope."

Brutus's penetrating gaze told Dan he was trying to understand. "Up."

The dog gave a gruff sigh and slid off the couch.

Dan scooted into his wheelchair and rolled into the kitchen to finish the last of the coffee. Pain shot down a non-existent appendage. "Oh, Man." He rubbed his stub. Brutus came to offer comfort. Dan grabbed the dog by his jowls and moved the massive head side to side. "I had to be the macho guy."

The last three evenings he should have opted for his crutches or wheelchair. But instead, he'd worn his prosthetic too long and helped Isabella decide what colors she wanted in her new home.

"Greens are always nice." Ming had flipped through the color swatches.

"Not happening." Isabella had showed her the white chips.

"You're an artist and you're going for white?"

"White is always a great base coat. I have big plans, Sis." Isabella tilted her head letting her hair fall over one eye. Dan had resisted pushing the strands behind her ear.

"It's your house." Ming had pushed the green samples aside.

"And the artist side of your sister will make that house fantastic." Dan's encouragement was rewarded with a smile from Isabella and a sigh of resignation from Ming.

"Promise I get a private tour before anyone else," Ming asked.

"Sure thing."

Dan loved the way the sisters interacted and supported each other. He wondered if adopted siblings had an extra special bond. Ming's whole attitude had changed after the initial announcement of Isabella's move. Unlike his sister who still maintained his military choice was a mistake. Forget the fact he lost his leg on American soil.

He suspected Steve had something to do with Ming's quick recovery. Dan had been doing his weekly system check when Ming had stormed into Steve's office unannounced.

"It's not fair," She'd whined as Steve took her into his arms. "I just got my head above water and now I need a new roommate."

"Babe, it's not happening tomorrow. You have plenty of time to interview new roommates. We can put an ad on the church website's announcement page. God will provide."

Dan had noted Steve's protective nature. How he longed to have Isabella seek him out in times of trouble. Paint chips support didn't come close to what he had witnessed.

"You're right. Issy needs her own life and as much as I love her, I'd like a roommate who works nights so I can have the apartment to myself when I come home. Maybe I'll move to something smaller."

"Why not turn the attic of your shop into an apartment. It makes no financial sense to rent an apartment and pay a mortgage." Steve's idea had delighted Ming and the two discussed plans for the renovation. Ming had blown Steve a kiss as she exited.

"I'm so jealous." Dan focused on packing his tools.

"I'm a blessed man." Steve smacked his friend on the shoulder. "Once Issy has her own place, things could heat up between you two."

"We'll see."

Dan liked the idea of visiting Isabella without climbing fifty stairs. He'd counted them on his way up and as he sat gliding down. If he used his upper body to pull himself up he made better progress. But the extra exercise left perspiration stains on his shirts that were as embarrassing as having help from his buddies.

He planned on helping Issy paint tomorrow if his leg felt better. If it didn't, he'd have no choice but to cancel. Humiliation followed the thought.

"Well, Brutus." The dog perked up and focused on his master. "If I'd swallowed my pride and used my crutches or this wheelchair when my leg tired, I'd have avoided the pain now."

Brutus woofed.

"Yeah, rub it in." Dan signal with two fingers and Brutus brought over his empty water bowl. Dan filled it and placed it on the doggie place mat near the back door, careful not to spill.

He'd worn shorts around Isabella a few times. How would she respond to seeing him legless? "I think she'll be ok with it. But I'm not ready yet."

Brutus finish his water then sit staring at his food bowl.

"Fine. Typical dog. More interested in your own comforts than my love life." Dan grabbed the bowl and placed it on his lap and rolled over to the plastic container of dog food and flipped the lid open. He measured two scoops of kibble into the bowl and rolled back to the mat.

"If you're so smart, how come you haven't figured out how to serve yourself?" Dan laughed as Brutus moved his head from side to side waiting.

"Ok, boy." Dan pointed at the bowl. "Eat." Brutus inhaled his meal and then licked the dish for a few minutes.

"Hurry up. Michelle is coming soon to give me a massage."

Michelle always loosened the tight muscles he'd overexerted allowing him to sleep pain free. Having her come to the house helped, too. He'd slip right into the hot tub after. Pure bliss.

His phone buzzed. Michelle texted she was outside. Dan open the utility door, "In." Brutus trudged slower than a dog twice his age. Michelle had strict rules, no dogs, cats or kids greeting her at the door. "Unless they're my client, I don't have time to be sociable." She'd once said.

"It's open." Dan stayed back as she wheeled her portable massage table into his living room. Michele's T-shirt advertised *Mom's Massage, I make it all better*.

"How are you feeling today?"

"Sore."

"Of course, you are." Michelle laughed while pulling the portable massage table out of its carrier.

He removed his shirt leaving on his shorts. Once the table was ready he climbed on. She assisted him into position with his face in the donut pillow. "Have any special complaints?"

"I overdid and now my back and leg muscles are cramped.

He stared at the floor while she stretched and rubbed the muscles on his neck and back. "How's the grandkids?"

"Adorable." Michelle entertained him with a few stories of her three- and four-year-old grandsons. When she'd finished her update, silence filled the room for several minutes as Dan relaxed under her firm ministrations. "Got a girl in your life yet?" Michelle's question brought him out of his dreamlike state.

"Sorta. I guess. It's complicated."

"Let me guess. Her last relationship left her in a bad place. She likes you but isn't ready to admit she loves you. She just wants to be friends."

"How'd you know? Got your grandsons spying on me?" Dan tried to make light of her on-the-nose observation. His laugh came out contrived.

"I lived it." Michelle helped him turn over and adjusted the bed. Moving his right arm over the sheet she began a gentle stretch starting at the shoulder and working down his arm. "I treated my Jonny the same way. My first husband was heavy-handed both in word and deed. When he left me, I almost did a happy dance. Except I needed a job to care for my daughter. He left me nothing, and I didn't bother to take him to court for child support."

"Why not? It's your legal right." Dan groaned as Michelle pressed a pressure point releasing the tension in his upper arm.

"He'd left the state. I didn't need the aggravation trying to fight him and I couldn't risk more abuse. I went to school to be a massage therapist and a nail specialist. That way I could keep my schedule booked up at the salon. The first year we lived with my cousin. But by the second year, we had our own place. During that first year, I met Jon. He taught at Cleo's school. He was a widower and his daughter Mary is Cleo's age. They became besties, which threw the two of us together a lot. We went on one date and I got cold feet. I told him friendship was all I wanted. He's the total opposite of my ex in every way. When we first meet, he made me nervous. Hank was small but very strong. Jon is a big ole' teddy bear but back then I thought he was a giant. I didn't want him angry at me. But, he became the friend I needed. His gentle ways and quiet manner stellar opposite to Hank. After three years, I knew Jonny was the one. That Christmas I wrapped up some mistletoe and gave it to him. He kissed my breath away and has been doing it for over twenty years. Be patient, son, she'll come to see what a great guy you are."

Michelle had never shared her personal life beyond her grandbabies with Dan. Was Isabella like Michelle? Did she expect me to respond to her like her late husband? *Lord, this is the second witness you've sent my way.* Hope warmed his heart. "I'm trying to stay friends." He said. "It's hard. Isabella is so confusing. One minute she's holding my hand the next she takes the seat across the room."

Michelle arranged the sheet around his left leg.

"I know she doesn't hold my disability against me. But I can't help wondering when she acts all weird."

Michelle spread more lotion on her hands then pressed her thumb on a knot.

"Hey, not so hard." Dan's words came through gritted teeth. Her pressure lessened.

"If she's had a bad relationship, your handicap could be a plus."

"What do you mean? She feels sorry for me or I'm not a threat."

"She's can see your heart. That first physical attraction comes later. At first, I didn't want anything to do with Jon. His physical size was an initial turn off. Once I got to know his heart everything about him became a turn on."

"TMI." Dan's laugh turned into a grunt. "Lighten up your touch." Michelle finished the massage and stepped back. Dan rose and dangled his leg over the edge. The massage had left him a little too relaxed. Michelle moved the wheelchair next to the table and locked it in place. Dan transferred himself. "Do you really believe any woman can look past--?" Dan pointed at his stub.

"Not if you keep making it an issue." Michelle folded her sheets. "Quit trying so hard. Focus on your other qualities. Maybe then you won't overwork your leg and back trying to pretend your leg is flesh and bone." Dan watched her fold up her table, put it back in the carrier, and onto the wheeled cart. Michelle hadn't wasted words getting to the core issue. "Shall we make another appointment for next month?" Michelle looked at her tablet.

"Better make it two weeks. I got a landscape party planned." Dan pulled his shirt back on, noticing the pain gone in his shoulders.

"Wednesday at 5:30? Don't forget to ice any tender places." Pointing with her stylus she added. "Don't overdo it before then because I am booked solid." Michelle wrote the appointment on the back of her business card and handed it to Dan.

"Thanks." Dan followed her to the door. "See you a week from Wednesday."

Dan released Brutus from the utility room into the yard. Dusk was forming and Brutus' black coat hid him in the shadows of the fence. "Well, Lord, I guess I should take inventory of my good qualities and see if any of them could entice Isabella to consider me as more than a friend."

∾

FRIDAY MORNING the guys plus Laura arrived early and by lunch had the old fence down and post holes dug for the new one. Dan took Michelle's admonishment as he cleaned the dirt off the old pavers Steve had dropped off earlier in the week. Rather than pushing himself, Dan took a break to pull lunch together. "Need any help?" Laura strolled into the kitchen. "I've forgotten how labor-intensive a fence is." She washed her hands at the sink.

"There's paper plates in the cabinet next to the dishwasher and chips in the pantry. I got fruit and sandwiches on the table. There's bottled water too."

Nathan, Matt, and Tony joined them at the kitchen table. After Dan said a blessing over their lunch, everyone dug in. Laura left the table to take a call from John. She stepped outside and returned with a container of cookies. "I forgot I left them in the back seat. John made me promise to save him some." She managed to set three aside before surrendering the rest to the guys. Together they cleaned up and went back outside to finish the fence. By four the prefabricated fence sections were affixed to the fence posts and Matt was hanging the gate.

"Done and done." Matt announced when the gate latch clicked. "I got work tomorrow so I won't be around for the yard party."

Dan shook his hand. "I appreciate the awesome job you did."

"Anytime, Man." Matt grabbed his tools and headed to his car.

The others soon followed. Nathan and Laura planned to return the next day.

"Listen, you've done a lot already. Take tomorrow off." Dan said.

"I got nothing better to do." Nathan smiled as he headed out the door.

Laura put her purse on her shoulder. "No way. I love working outside." She gave him a sideways hug. "I have a condo. This is fun." She grabbed her container from the kitchen counter. "Will Issy be here tomorrow?"

"I don't know. She's afraid of dogs." Dan opened the utility door and Brutus gave a happy wag and leaped up to plant doggie kisses on Laura's face. "Down." Laura's commanding voice brought instant obedience from Brutus.

"You're good." Dan smiled.

"My Dad raised and trained German Shepherds for police work." Laura patted Brutus.

Dan let him out the back. "Maybe you could talk to Isabella."

"I'll give her a call and see if I can't persuade her to come. But if her fear is based on a dog attack, you might want to find a place for Brutus to stay until the crew leaves tomorrow."

Dan watched Laura's car pull away from the curb. She was right. All the company would get him excited. Good behavior would flee with his joy over company. There was nowhere to drop Brutus off. A sigh escaped his lips as he glanced at the rooster clock. Carmen was due in an hour. He grabbed his cell phone from the counter and placed a call to East China Inn as he headed to the shower.

~

DAN QUICKENED his step to the door as the bell rang for the second time. He pulled his polo shirt down. His hair was still wet from his shower. Dan opened the door to a warm bear hug from Carmen. "My, my, don't you look like a shaggy dog."

He pulled her inside. "As beautiful as I remember you."

"You do know lyin's a sin." Carmen laughed as she made herself comfortable on the couch her eyes scanning the room. Dan missed her trademark animal print scrubs. Her civvies were still colorful. She wore a floral print blouse, black slacks and open-toed shoes showing off her red toenails. A small white rose decorated the index fingers of her matching manicure. Unlike Issy Carmen preferred gold. Five bracelets, a multi-stranded necklace and a large gold hoop earrings gave a flamboyant flare which matched her personality. *Sweeney, you got it bad. Since when do you notice women's clothes.* Carmen's voice refocused his thoughts.

"You done good for yourself with this place." That familiar million-dollar smile lit up her face. "Where's your baby?" Dan stared for a moment. Had she read his mind?

"I think you said his name is Brutus."

Relief flooded Dan as he released his furry friend from the utility room. Carmen rose and signaled for Brutus to sit. For once he didn't hesitate. She knelt and hugged the big dog, cooing to him and patting his head. Then found a sit on the couch. The whole-time Brutus remained seated, at her signal, he curled up at her feet.

"Wow! I've never seen him so well-behaved." Dan laughed. The doorbell rang and he retrieved their dinner from the delivery guy. The dog remained at Carmen's side. After closing the door Dan took the food to the kitchen. "Where have you hidden the real Brutus?"

Carmen laughed. "I have a little secret. Brutus and I are old friends. You remember my tellin' you Darrell was a dog trainer?"

"Yeah."

"My son trained Brutus for work with people with disabilities. I dog sat this guy a few times. I was sad to hear little Connor died. But Brutus found a good home with you."

An idea flashed through his mind. "Would you mind babysitting Brutus tomorrow? I have a bunch of people coming to put in my landscaping." Dan back paddled realizing how rude he must sound by asking a favor when she came to visit him. "I'm sorry, I wasn't thinking." Dan ran his fingers through his hair. "I guess he'll survive a day in the utility room."

Carmen raised an eyebrow. "Brutus will be miserable." She grabbed her phone from her purse on the floor near her feet. "I'll give my youngest son, Jamal a call while you set out dinner. He has a labradoodle and a big back yard. I'm sure Roscoe will love a playmate for the day."

The arrangements were made. They caught up over egg rolls, sweet and sour chicken and fried rice. Dan hadn't laughed so hard in a long time. Carmen always told the best stories. The ones about her late husband were hilarious. "My, my look." Carmen glanced at the wall clock. If I don't get a move on, Darrel's going to lock me out like he does my grandson Tyrone when he misses curfew." He savored the hug from his old friend. "Glad you could come."

"Me too." She patted his arm gracing him with another of her sweet smiles.

"Jamal and I will be by at seven for Brutus' play date."

"I appreciate this."

"Roscoe will be thrilled."

Carmen kissed Dan on the cheek and gave him another bear hug before she left.

22

NEW YARD, NEW JOB, HAUNTING PAST

Brutus left moments before the work crew arrived. John held a Starbuck's coffee and his hair stuck out in awkward angles. "Not a morning person." Dan laughed as he held the door open for them.

"That bad, huh?"

John tried smoothing his hair.

"I told you so." Laura retrieved a comb from her purse and kissed him on the check. John followed Dan's pointing finger to the bathroom.

Laura placed two boxes of Dunkin Donuts on the kitchen counter.

"Thanks. I got coffee and store-bought Danish." Dan open one box as the doorbell played the Star-Spangled Banner announcing the rest of the crew's arrival.

"Issy will try and make it later," Ming offered as they gathered around the breakfast treats. "She works this morning."

"I see Brutus isn't here today." Steve poured a cup of coffee.

"Yeah, I arranged a play date for him with a labradoodle."

"I'm texting Issy. She'll be so relieved." Ming's fingers flew over her phone keyboard.

Dan felt weird at her response. Even if Issy became more than a friend, there was still her fear of Brutus. "If you've all gotten your sugar high, let's get started."

ISABELLA KNOCKED on Mr. Clayton's office door. A muffled voice answered her. She opened the door, hoping the noise she heard was an invitation to enter. Mr. Clayton's scowling face glared at his computer. "Isabella, what can I do for you?" His expression lost its scowl as he greeted her.

"I could come back at the end of my shift if you're busy."

"No, please come in. This stupid accounting program is going through updates so it keeps freezing. I'll give it time to reset itself before I call tech support." Mr. Clayton pushed his chair away from his PC and signaled for her to take the empty chair in front of his desk. "What can I do for you?"

"I'm giving my two weeks' notice. Mrs. Crawford has offered me a position as her companion on a part-time basis."

"So, you can't work here too."

"No sales clerking, sorry. I've found my art muse and this will give me time to paint. I've found a beautiful home offering perfect lighting."

"Painting is your hobby."

"I have a BA in Art."

"Of course, you listed that on your application. I've got an idea." Mr. Clayton leaned forward, his chair groaned against his weight. "Would you be interested in teaching a few art classes? Say one night a week and on Saturday morning?"

"I'll see if Mrs. Crawford is open to the idea. Let me think it over. If I say yes, I'll need another two weeks to get used to my new job before I take on those classes."

"Works for me. Gives me time to advertise the classes."

"I haven't said yes yet. How much will it pay?'

"Because of your degree, you'll receive more than others who teach art and craft classes. I'll put together a contract." He slid back to his computer and tapped a few keys. "Once I get the tech guys in here to fix this mess."

Isabella couldn't believe her good fortune as she stepped back to the cash register. "Thank you, Lord." At last, she'd found her calling. She hummed through her shift and raced home to change. Her first thought was sharing her good news with Dan. The idea startled her. Ming would be supportive. But. Dan. Dan would understand. He was trying to rebuild his life. He was the first person in a very long time to praise her art ability. The man supported her dreams without trying to pressure her into changing for him. Art was not his gifting yet he respected her. Warmth flowed over her at the thought of sharing her good news with him.

∽

Issy PULLED into Dan's driveway. She exited her car grabbing two buckets of chicken and closed the door with her backside. Ming leaped from her place near the flower beds. "Glad you could make it, Sis."

"I have soda in the trunk if anyone wants to grab it."

"Steve," Ming called her boyfriend away from helping John trim bushes. Ming took her sister's keys and popped the trunk. "Steve, get the soda out of the trunk and bring it in the house. Hey, everyone. Lunch!"

Issy smiled as everyone put their tools away and headed into the house. John and Nathan each took a bucket from her hand and Dan held the door open for her. She reached up and pushed his hair out of his eyes. "I quit my job today."

∾

DAN SAVORED her touch on his face. "You look happy." He closed the door behind them. Her face glowed.

"Mr. Clayton asked if I wanted to teach a few art classes."

"Wow! Are you going to?" Dan went to the sink to wash his hands. Issy matched his pace as she continued to share.

"I wanted to ask Clare first, but I'm sure she'll cheer me on."

Dan washed his hands and Issy handed him a paper towel. "Where are you hiding Brutus?"

"I thought Mindy text you."

"Oh, that's right. In my excitement, I forgot." Issy handed a paper plate to Dan.

"Aren't you eating?"

"Too excited. Maybe later."

Dan loved seeing her this happy. Issy shared her news with the rest of the group. Everyone congratulated her. She beamed under their praise. After lunch, work resumed. Issy helped Ming finish the flower bed while Dan started seeding the backyard.

∾

Issy HELPED Mindy finish a row of pansies. When Nathan approached. "Hey, Issy, I gotta show you something."

Issy rose from her place wiping the dusting of dirt off her hands on the back of her old jeans. She froze as Nathan showed her a CD. Flipping to the inside cover, her face stared back at her. "I've found your doppelgänger."

Nathan laughed oblivious of the lump forming in Issy's throat. "I like this group. Steve gave me the CD, said he knew the lead singer. And this gal is his wife. I read online the guy dropped dead during a worship service. Weird huh." Issy swayed. Mindy had joined her in time to steady her.

Issy found her voice. "Yeah weird." Tears formed.

"It is you." Nathan pulled the CD from view. "Sorry, I didn't mean to..."

"Thanks, Nathan, way to rob a girl of a fun day by bringing up the worst one of her life." Mindy wrapped her arms around Issy. She tried to pull away. "It's ok."

"Is Melinda your stage name?"

Her sister's grip tightened and anger form in her eyes.

"You're a real jerk. Why don't you mind your own business?" Mindy looked around at the others and whispered to Issy. "You want to go home?"

Ming as usual had blown everything out of proportion. Embarrassment and buried shame surfaced. Words cemented to her tongue. She nodded her head and her sister went into action. Mindy collected their purses and directed Issy to the passenger seat of her Prius. "I came with Steve."

Driving back to the apartment Issy wanted to crawl under the seat. "I can't keep avoiding the truth."

"True. But you looked ready to faint and I couldn't let...."

"Stop." Issy struggled to keep her voice even. "Stop trying to protect me." She touched her sister's shoulder.

"Nathan wasn't going to hurt me by asking an innocent question. I was hurting myself by not revealing the truth and owning it."

"Well, now everyone will want to know. If they haven't pieced it together already." Mindy turned the car into their driveway. She faced Issy. "It'd make my relationship easier with Steve. We promised to have no secrets. I've kept yours and it's not fair to him. He and Jeff were close. They went to grade school together. When Jeff moved away their sophomore year, if not for Dan, it would have been a tough year. The three were in a band together." Mindy unsnapped her seatbelt. "It was hard to stay silent when Steve mentioned how bad he felt. He found out Jeff died after the funeral. A friend at church showed him an article about this worship leader who died during the service."

For the first time, Issy realized keeping her past out of her present hurt her healing. "I'm sorry. I never... sorry. I promise to have a conversation with Steve and Dan soon."

"The truth is always good."

"Right." Isabella's chest hurt from the prospect.

~

WHEN DAN RETURNED to the front yard Ming and Issy were gone. Laura was finishing up the flowerbeds and the men were talking among themselves. "What's up?" Dan noticed the sheepish look on Nathan's face. Laura patted the soil around the last petunia. "Nathan upset Issy."

Dan restrained himself from strangling Nathan until he explained. "Hey, how was I to know? The name is different." Nathan handed the CD to Dan. "I've been trying to figure out who Issy reminds me of since I met her. Today I realized. I made a joke. You know, seeing her doppelganger. How was I supposed to know it was her?"

There on the back cover was J-boy and Issy. Except their names were Ron and Melinda Marklin. Her hair braided passed her waist. She wore a jean skirt and a matching jacket. J-Boy looked more country than rap singer. This was his friend's widow. How did he not notice? At some level, he must have. The crazy dream made sense now. "What upset her?"

"After she admitted it was her. I asked if Melinda was her stage name. She began to cry and Ming yelled at me to mind my own business."

"Mindy never mentioned it to me either. Her grief must be deep, man. I think we should respect that and not press her." Steve said.

Dan stood stark still. J-boy was the lousy husband. His jaw tweaked with anger at himself. He'd heard Ron was in Indiana a year before he died. Maybe if he'd visited... I could have... what? Nothing. He knew how good J-Boy had been at fooling his friends. He bragged about his abilities. Buttered up every adult and classmate who could benefit him. The anger melted into sadness for the woman he'd come to care for.

A few hours later the yard was in order. Everyone had left except Steve, who was hauling lawn waste bags to the curb. Dan filled the last bag.

A large truck pulled into the driveway. Brutus bounded out of the passenger window.

The dog yelped at their reunion. Slobbery kisses found his master's face. Dan pushed him down and walked to the truck. "Thanks, Jamal."

"Anytime, man. Brutus wore Rufus out." The two men shook hands through the driver's side window and Jamal pulled away.

Dan patted Brutus. "Glad you're back, boy." As he stroked his friend the earlier revelation about Jeff lingered. Anger and shame still fought for dominance in his thoughts. Brutus leaned close. On his signal, the dog followed at his side into the house.

Steve washes his hands at the sink. "You okay."

Dan fought the tightness in his chest. Brutus hovered close. He signaled for his aid to lay down. Brutus complied.

"I can't believe I didn't figure it out."

Dan plopped on a kitchen chair and ran his fingers through his hair remembering her touch on his forehead. "Steve, I went to Jeff's funeral. I spoke to Isabella. I didn't make the connection."

"Didn't he die while you were in rehab?" Steve pour himself some coffee then warmed it in the microwave. "You were pretty messed up, man."

"Still." Dan watched Steve's cup spin in the microwave. "Before I went on that cross-country ride Jeff sent me an email inviting me to a concert at his church. I should have gone."

"I got the same email." Steve added sugar to his cup and joined Dan on the other end of the sofa. "I had other plans. But honestly, I remember thinking. Wow! After all these years, he sends me an invitation and doesn't even bother to ask how I'm doing. Same J-Boy. All about himself."

Dan's shame confirmed he'd felt the same.

Steve put his cup on the counter and faced his friend. "Maybe it's a God thing."

"How?" Anger resurfaced with his friend's declaration. God wanted Isabella to suffer abuse? Brutus rested his head on Dan's lap.

"If you had known who she was maybe you two wouldn't be friends. Mindy said you've brought her back from some serious depression."

Dan stroked Brutus letting calm overtake him as he considered Steve's words. If it was a God thing that he met Isabella now, then...

"If you're right. Now, what do I do?"

"Wait for her to talk to you. You know she will. Otherwise, it's going to get awkward."

"No kidding."

23

MURAL AND TRUTH REVEALED

Isabella met Mrs. Crawford in the foyer of Community Church. Excitement and anxiety wrestled in her stomach. Excited to see the youths' response and anxious over the interview for the Beacon News.

"Dearie, I am so looking forward to this whole event." Clare patted her arm. "You are an amazing artist. The whole senior group is so pleased with the room. Are your church friends coming?"

"Dan and maybe the pastor." Let her think she announced it at her church this morning. Issy didn't want to lie. But after Saturday's embarrassment, she didn't sleep well and was too tired to even bother to get out of bed. When sleep claimed her, it was restful and deep. But she'd had to hustle to get ready for the one o'clock event. "I know friends from Hobby Life are coming, including Mr. Clayton."

"Excellent." Clare gave her an appraising smile. "I love your outfit. Not too artsy. I think the stereotype of artist dressing in caftans in rainbow colors is absurd." She squeezed Isabella's shoulders. "You look very stylish."

Isabella had purchased the royal blue A-line dress and white sling for the occasion. She'd found the perfect shimmer pumps and borrowed Ming's pearls with matching earrings. She felt elegant but not overdressed. "I'm glad you like it too."

Clare waved at someone, Isabella turned. Dan and Reverend Whitehall headed their way. "There is your friend. And Paul Whitehall came too."

"That's Dan's uncle."

"Really. How fun."

Clare signaled for the men to join them. "Paulie, I haven't seen you since my husband's funeral."

"My, my, that was…"

"Five years. I'm sorry I never made it to Sally's. Pneumonia kept me in the hospital."

"You sent her favorite orchids."

"So, this fine specimen of a man is your nephew."

Dan's faced reddened and an awkward smile formed on his lips. "You know each other?"

"If Clare hadn't turned down my proposal, I would never have met my Sally."

"Sounds like a fascinating love story." Isabella teased Clare.

"Paul and I were six."

The old friends laughed at the joke. Isabella got the feeling they'd told it before.

"Sally and I became best friends in junior high. Then Paul renewed our childhood friendship after taking the I-hate-girls oath a few years earlier." Clare patted Paul's arm.

"It took me until after seminary to convince Sally I was serious."

"You proposed once a week after senior prom." Clare winked.

"You exaggerate. But I did it so often that when I stopped, she thought I'd fallen out of love with her."

"I remember her crying on my shoulder." Clare noticed someone behind his shoulder. "Excuse me, I believe the reporter is here."

"My, my, Uncle Paul, I never pegged you for a romantic." Dan nudged his uncle's shoulder and to Isabella's surprise, the old man nudged back. "Desperate, son, very desperate." Their playful banter was just the medicine to calm her nerves.

"Look. There's a few people from church. I promised we'd sit together. If you will excuse me." Reverend Whitehall left them alone.

Dan and Isabella stood staring at each other. Isabella could think of nothing but her awkward scene yesterday. She pushed the thought to the recesses of her mind when Steve and Mindy arrived with John and Laura. "I see you got your rest." Mindy hugged her sister. "You look fabulous. That is your color, girl."

"Love your shoes." Laura sighed as Isabella moved her foot forward so she could get a better look. "Where did you get those?"

"Famous Footwear."

"I hope they have my size."

"Oh, Dan your shoes are to die for." Steve's mimicking voice caused everyone to laugh.

"You girls love your shoes." John wrapped his arm around Laura. "Honey, you get those and I'll have to wear my cowboy boots."

"Ugh. Men and their egos." Laura gave John a playful slap. "I'm one inch taller than you when I wear heels?"

More laughter as the group entered the sanctuary. Isabella hadn't realized how much she missed nonsensical conversation.

Living with Maureen suffocated her humor. Maureen's grief so deep, so unrelenting she felt the need to lash out at Isabella. Even fashion was a touchy subject.

"Melinda, why on earth do you insist on wearing those red heels? They look ridiculous. Are you trying to dishonor your late husband?"

"Maureen, Ron liked these shoes, the matching purse and the entire outfit he bought for me." Isabella fought a headache that was crawling from the top of her head down her neck into her shoulders. *"It's time to move on, Maureen."*

"Red shoes just aren't proper right now."

"According to who, Maureen? A 19th-century etiquette book." Isabella picked up the matching red purse and moved the content from her black one. *"Mourning black is no longer a thing. Wearing these red shoes gives me happy memories of Ron."* She slipped the red purse onto her arm. *"I'm wearing red with this black dress and tomorrow I'm putting these black dresses in my closet for good."*

"Please, Melinda, you mustn't. I'm not ready." Maureen sobbed. *"I need you to wait, please. Wait a little longer."*

"Maureen, I can't."

"Call me, Mother."

"Only if you call me Isabella and not Melinda. I hate it."

"But you'll always be Melinda to me." Maureen grabbed her arm. Her mournful tone sharpened as her grip tightened. *"You will not disrespect my son or embarrass me by your foolishness. You may wear your wretched red shoes and purse but you will not discard your mourning clothes until I say you can."*

Isabella rubbed her arm.

"You ok?" Dan's concerned look brought her back to the present. She was among friends and the art muse had returned.

"Sorry, my mind wandered for a moment. Come on, I'll show you to your reserved seats. The four of them sat in the front row next to Clare and the senior Sunday school class. The brief program introduced Isabella and the idea behind the room.

Mrs. Crawford gave a brief history of the room before its transformation. "This 100 by 200-foot area once house a nursery and four pre-school class-rooms. During the expansion project, last year, the nursery and preschool were moved to the annex, the pastors' old office, making the children closer to the sanctuary. We have a growing youth department who deserve a place of their own. We tore out the inner walls giving the middle school class more room. Then we added a fresh coat of paint."

Mrs. Crawford avoid mentioning the color.

"Although freshened up. it still seemed barren. We enlisted the help of a wonderful artist, Miss Isabel Wilson. She transformed it into... Well, some-thing magnificent."

Clare placed her hand over her heart and stretched a hand toward the front row. "I'd like to call Isabella forward and present her with a love gift."

Issy blushed as she made her way to the podium while Clare continued speaking.

"She volunteered to do a mural on one wall and we were so impressed our senior class persuaded her to do the other three walls. Then we felt compelled to reward her hard work." Isabella stood with the seniors for photos as they gave her the honorarium. Tears of joy formed, having her work recognized overwhelmed her.

After a few more pictures the guests moved to form a line outside the youth department door. Isabella held her breath waiting for the first reactions. The youth group entered first.

Wow! This is so cool!

"Hey, is that me?"

The last wall Isabella had painted was a modern scene of teens serving the community, praying, and worshiping together. Each member of the youth group exclaimed over the life-like representation of themselves. The wall opposite had young people from Asia and Africa, another had European youth engaged in similar activities to the American kids. The remaining wall illus-trated the verse, "Let your light so shine before all men." A three-dimensional cross appeared to radiate toward the other three walls shedding light on the youth of the world.

Reverend Whitehall grasped Isabella's hand. "Spectacular. God has given you a wonderful gift. I am blessed to see you use it."

Isabella let the happy tears fall and gave the surprised pastor a warm hug. "I am thankful to God for allowing me the opportunity to reignite this gift. Your words... your words confirm what I felt God called me to do while I was still a child."

"God makes all things beautiful in His time." Reverend Whitehall gave her hand a squeeze and turned to look at her work further. Ove the next two hours' people made their way to her side to share their appreciation for her hard work. The Beacon-News reporter had to settle for asking questions between the interruptions of well-wishers.

DAN WATCHED Isabella hug Uncle Paul. His heart filled with pride seeing the accolades received. She glowed. No trace of the sorrow she brought to Aurora. Steve, Mindy, John and Laura soon joined him near the youth wall. "I am amazed." Steve continued to stare at the walls. "The detail is fantastic. Too bad these walls can't be shared with the world."

"Hey, why not asked Mrs. Crawford if I can make a video?" John pulled out his cell phone and took a few pictures.

"John does some pretty amazing films." Laura pointed out a section for John to capture on his phone.

"Since when?" Mindy laughed.

"Since I finished a film production class. I help a guy at church who makes short films for various companies."

"So, you're more than a park cop." Steve shook his head.

"I'm a man of many talents." John turned to Laura and wiggled his eyebrows. "Right, Babe?"

Laura patted his arm. "You just keep thinking that." She gave him a peck on the cheek. "I'd love to see a documentary on this wall."

Dan kept tabs on Isabella with his peripheral vision. "I'd ask Isabella first. But I bet she'd go for the idea." He couldn't wait to hear her take on the day. She'd found her path. Could she make room for him on it?

Mindy squeezed Steve's arm as her excitement for her sister built. "I know she'll jump on the chance to get her name out there." Mindy wrote in the air. "Art by Isabella Wilson."

"What's this?" Isabella appeared beside Mindy.

"We were singing your praises." Mindy shared John's idea and fresh tears formed in Isabella's eyes. Mindy grabbed her sister, dancing as she hugged her. "I am so proud of you."

"Hey, they're getting ready to boot us out of here." Steve took Mindy's hand. "Let's go check out the eats."

"Food is your middle name." Mindy did her best to keep pace in her high heels as he quick-stepped toward the fellowship hall.

As the group moved along Laura slowed to walk beside Isabella leaving John to keep pace next to Dan. "You don't have to wait for me. Go grab Laura, I'll catch up."

"Laura wanted to ask Isabella if she could paint a wall in her new home. She lost her parents in a car accident when she was a freshman in college. They missed so much in her life—graduation, getting her real estate license, me." John said. "She mentioned while we were looking at Issy's amazing work she needed her parents in her new home and Issy was the one to put them there."

"I'm sure she is." Dan and John arrived at the fellowship hall in time to see Laura waving them over to two seats they'd saved for the guys. The girls had gotten a plate of assorted cookies and coffee for all of them. They'd saved Dan a place at the end of the table to stretch his leg.

Dan watched as Isabella became animated discussing the mural possibilities. "Bring me pictures of your folks. Not portraits but activities. Let's create a mural of them doing something they loved."

"Sounds great. Promise you won't put me in the mural."

"I did that for the kids to make them feel a part of God's commission to make their lights shine. Leaving you out of the picture gives me more creative license to capture your parents."

"Work up an estimate so I can add it to my budget. It will be a few months before I'm ready for you to take on that project.

When everyone dispersed after the refreshments, Dan walked Isabella to her car. "Your art talent is breath-taking."

"Wow, no one has paid me a compliment like that since art school."

"I worked hard to be original."

Isabella's smile faded and a serious frown accompanied a sigh.

"Dan, can I come over tomorrow so we can talk. I've asked Mindy and Steve too. It's time I admitted a few things."

"Sure. I've been working with Brutus to behave. But if you prefer I can put him in the backyard."

"I can't believe I'm saying this, but use your best judgment." Isabella took his hand as they walked toward the parking lot. "I need to work on my fear of dogs."

"I promise to make sure he behaves."

"Well, don't expect a miracle. You saw my reaction to the mouse."

~

"Good Boy." Dan plied Brutus with another treat. It had taken the entire week. Steve and John had dropped by with the sole purpose of helping Dan train Brutus. "Bed."

Brutus crept to his doggie bed. He stood refusing to lay down.

"Come on, Buddy. I need you to be well-behaved for Isabella." Brutus complied, a huff filtering through his closed mouth.

"Atta, boy." Dan brought him another treat. Brutus stared at him, then the treat, and back at him. Canine eyes begged for release. At last, he ate the treat.

The doorbell played its patriotic tune. Dan gave Brutus the stay sign. The dog waited as he answered the door. Laura smiled and held out a plastic container. "John asked me to come by to help keep Brutus in line. I brought homemade doggie treats."

"I'm impressed." Dan closed the door behind her. Brutus remained on his bed watching Laura and Dan. "Ignore him." He instructed her. "Wait until I call him."

Laura sat on the couch and Dan called Brutus. "He is not allowed to greet you unless you call him. I want to see if he can be ignored your whole visit. Otherwise, I'll have to put him in the utility closet and that always makes him hyper."

"There's always the back yard."

"After a while, he'll bark to come in. After a while he howls and make a ruckus." Dan patted Brutus. "That's a discipline for another day."

"You care for Issy. But you need Brutus. There isn't any me or the dog in this relationship?"

"Yeah." Dan sat on the other end of the couch and signaled Brutus to laid at his feet.

"Good luck with the training. I need to get going."

"Going someplace special?"

"John talked me into going to the gym. After a few laps around the track, I'm drenched. The gym isn't well ventilated."

Laura stood. Brutus stayed at Dan's side as he walked her to the door. Not once did the dog rush ahead to give her slobbery kisses. When Laura left, Dan placed his hands on his chest the signal to jump up. Brutus rose, careful not to knock Dan over and licked his face with abandon.

"That's enough, your big baby. Great job, Brutus." Dan signaled and Brutus sat at his feet with a happy grin on his face. "Pretty proud of yourself, huh?" Dan opened the plastic container and laughed. The treats were people shaped. "Here you go Brutus." Dan tossed one in the air and Brutus devoured his treat before it hit the ground.

Two hours later the real test came when the doorbell rang again. Brutus took his place on his bed at Dan's signal. Opening the door Steve and Mindy entered. Isabella remained on the porch.

Dan held out his hand. "Brutus is on his best behavior tonight."

Isabella hesitated as she spied Brutus on his bed.

"I promise he'll behave." *Please, God, help Brutus. I can't afford to blow this.* Dan kept his hand extended and after a few long moments, she took it. Dan brought her into the house and Brutus remained docile on his bed. Steve and Mindy sat on the couch so Dan gave Isabella his easy chair and brought in a kitchen chair for himself. The whole time Isabella eyed Brutus who continued to have a disinterested look as his head rested on his paws. "Thank you, Lord."

Steve looked from Brutus to Isabella's pale face. "Dan has been working with Brutus to stay there when he has company. Dan leads a hermit's life and Brutus is a people person so it's been tough on the poor guy. He gets excited when Dan has visitors." Brutus' tale wagged while the rest of him remained quiet. Isabella giggled and seemed to relax. Dan watched Brutus start to rise and signaled him to lay down. The dog obeyed with a groan which caused them all to laugh.

"Hopefully, he will stay there so you can share without fear of dog slobbers." Dan winked at her and watched her face warmed to a deeper brown. He hoped he wasn't being pushy. The conversation she'd come to have was stalled with the focus on Brutus. It would have been more relaxing to have this time at Mindy's apartment. He knew the location was so Dan didn't have to climb those stairs. Her thoughtfulness was both a blessing and a curse. He needed to conquer the stairs. Yet, he appreciated not dealing with them. *Forgive my pride, Lord.*

～

ISABELLA FELT her fear abating as she watched the gentle giant recline on his bed looking forlorn. Strange how she could relate to Brutus' dilemma. He couldn't be himself. The poor thing had to conform to those in control of his life. She remembered how constant compliance grated on her spirit and sent her into depression. Maybe after she told her story, she'd have the nerve to introduce herself to Brutus.

"Anyone want coffee?" Dan interrupted her musing. She watched him hobble toward the coffeepot. He'd worn his prosthetic too long. Why did he insist on pushing himself.? The familiar regret of trying to do just that brought a knot to her chest. Pushing herself into Ron's music mold became painful. If she'd stood her ground. Not let herself be talked into being a part of the worship team. If she'd been less concerned about what others thought. If, if, if... Stop it Issy, stay in the present.

"Coffee would be nice," Mindy said.

"Let me help, bro." Steve grabbed the creamer from the frig and the sugar bowl off the counter and brought them to the coffee table. Dan carried a tray with four large mugs of coffee. "Hey, what's in the plastic container?" Steve opened the lid and picked up one. "Is this a gingerbread man?"

"I wouldn't eat that if I were you." Dan grinned as Brutus rose from his place. He signaled and Brutus laid back down. Another huff and a moan followed the action. Steve looked at Brutus and laughed.

"I almost ate a dog treat." Steve blushed. Laughter filled the room. Steve barked causing Brutus to bark. Dan's stern admonishment for quiet caused Brutus and Steve to cease their duet.

Dan settled back into his chair and mixed sugar in his coffee. "There's some oatmeal raisin cookies in a bag in the pantry."

Steve snagged them and joined the others.

Each fixed their brew and settled in. Isabella took a sip before beginning. "I owe you all an explanation after I bolted from here on Saturday." Ming nodded encouragement. She took a few more sips of coffee debating where to begin.

"Ron and I married right after I graduated from Art school. He worked as a manager of a Walgreens. I stayed home with the intent of starting my own business. Ron lead worship most Sundays at DaySpring Community Church. The first-year things were good, I knew Ron loved me. We had no family there so when he got the call from his mother's church to be the Music Director we jumped at the chance. Ron seldom talked about his childhood and when he did, it was sketchy. I do know his mother and dad divorced when he was young. His dad had custody until he died when Ron was in high school. Ron moved away from his mother's home after college." Isabel absently stirred her coffee.

"I was surprised he wanted to move there because the two weren't close."

She moved her cup to the other hand. "Ron had migraines. They got worse after he took the position. He went to a specialist his mother knew. At first, I went with him then he stopped going. He failed to tell me he changed to a different neurologist. Ron had the notion he needed to keep his illness from me. He'd had a tumor since he was a child. It had been pea size for years. The doctors said to wait and see."

Isabella ran her finger around the edge of her coffee cup. A sigh followed. She stared at her silver sandals for several seconds before continuing. A knot formed in her throat. A few swallows of coffee loosened it.

"Ron's physician said having the surgery early gave him an eighty percent chance of a full recovery. Ron chose to 'live by faith.'" Issy made air quotes. "He never told me about the tumor." Anger tinged her words. "He and his mother fabricated some story that she wasn't well and needed to be taken to the doctor."

"But she was taking him." Mindy shook her head. "Why?"

"The tumor was pressing on the part of the brain that controls rational thought. He became paranoid. Verbally abusive to me." Another sigh escaped her lips. "He was convinced God told him the headaches were his thorn in the flesh. After our son, Ronald Jeffrey Jr. died he got crazier. He scolded me for grieving. He said I should be like King David and accept the Lord's will for our sin."

"What sin." Steve interrupted. "Sorry."

"I had no idea." Isabella said.

"Sis, you do know RJs death was not your fault." Ming knelt in front of her sister. "God doesn't take babies to punish parents for their sins."

"I know. But Ron was persuasive after RJ died. It hurt too much. I wanted to blame myself. Punish myself." Isabella wiped a tear. "Ming, I'm ok."

Her sister nodded and returned to the couch. No one pushed her to continue. She knew she could have stopped at this point. But she needed to finish the story for her own healing.

"Ron played rock music on the radio and heavy metal on his guitar. Creepy melodies filled the apartment. I wasn't allowed to talk about it to anyone. He dictated how I dressed and every other aspect of my life. My love turned to fear. There was a stone in my heart. I'd planned to leave him." Tears fell. Mindy grabbed a tissue from her purse for her sister. Isabella shared the details of the Sunday morning Ron died.

Mindy reached for a tissue to wipe her own tears.

"Did his mom tell you about the tumor?" Dan's gentle tone caressed her heart.

"No. She told me about an aneurysm but I was too upset to read the coroner's report for myself."

"Why didn't you go home to mom and dad after Ron died?" Mindy's question caused Isabella to leave her chair and pace.

"Guilt. I felt responsible for his death and leaving Maureen childless. When she asked me to move in, I did, I hoped if I could bound with her, we would both heal."

"That's messed up." Steve looked at Issy. "Jeff, I mean Ron told me the real reason his mother didn't get custody of him was because she was crazy. She had supervised visits. When she came to town, Jeff would ask me to hang out too. His mom acted normal around strangers."

"I wished I'd known. She and I never got along but I thought it was because she spoiled Ron as her only child. I had no idea she was bi-polar and border-line schizophrenic until after Ron died. His death pushed her over the edge. The verbal abuse and control intensified living with her. By the time, I went to visit the same neurologist Ron had used for my migraines, I felt worthless. When he mentioned Ron's tumor, that was the first I'd heard of it. Ron hadn't given permission. HIPPA laws and all. The doctor and I had a long talk about Ron, his mother and the lawsuits she threatened when Ron died."

"So, you left." Dan stretched out his leg and rub his thigh.

"No, I confronted her." Isabella finished her story of emotional imprisonment.

"That's when you took a taxi to the airport." Mindy stood with her mug. "Anyone want refills." Steve handed her his mug.

"A one-way ticket to Chicago and never looked back."

"A few weeks after she got here, she had her name legally changed back to Wilson and all her paperwork came in the mail last week." Mindy handed Steve his mug and squeezed her sister's shoulder before sitting on the couch again.

"Man, so sorry you went through all that." Steve added three spoons of sugar to his coffee. "That's messed up."

Steve's awkward attempt at sympathy touched Isabella. Dan remained quiet which made him hard to read. She'd grown accustomed to his silences. Today it seemed wrong. Where were his constant words of encouragement? Looking down Isabella gasped. Brutus had sneaked over and rest at her feet. At the sound of her voice, he placed his large head in her lap. His sad eyes seemed to capture her tears. Isabella stroked his head. "Thank you, boy."

"Down, Brutus." Dan's tone gentle but firm. Brutus laid at her feet.

"Oh, me. He is an amazing dog. Somehow he makes me feel safe."

Dan smiled. "Yes."

"He reminds me of a man who came to Ron's funeral. A soldier. I can't recall his name. But he said he knew J-boy. My husband said his rapper name in high school was J-boy."

"Why did Jeff start calling himself Ron?" Steve took the last cookie from the bag. "You need to get more of these."

Dan rolled his eyes at his friend.

"Ron didn't want any connection with his rapper and rock attempts when he went to work as the Music Director. He became obsessed with making it big

in Contemporary Christian music. It was destroying our marriage. Entertaining the congregation robbed me of joy. I stopped listening to Christian
music altogether after he died. Even quit attending church and let Maureen tell
the pastor and anyone else who asked whatever excuse she wanted. Spent
months taking long walks alone. At the library, I could be by myself. Too many
church members found me in in restaurants and stores. I hated hearing— "Did
you know he was sick?" or "That must have been quite a shock." Isabella wiped
her nose. "The worse was that old cliché..." God's ways aren't our ways, He
knows best."

Steve frowned and focused on Isabella. "I know I would have said something lame and traditional. But I'd have meant it. I'd helped if I'd known. His
freaky death made headlines." Steve blushed "I..."

"Freaky is as good a word as any." Isabella felt the burden of guilt and anger
leave. "Thanks for caring Steve. I wish I had known his friends. Things might
have been easier."

"We're here now," Dan said. "Whatever you need we all have your six."

Isabella laughed. "Once a soldier always a soldier. Thanks, the support
means a lot."

"Look at the time." Mindy grabbed her purse. "Steve is taking me to meet
his folks and if we don't leave now we'll be late. Not the first impression I want
to make."

"Good luck, cyber girl," Isabella gave her a hug. "They'll love you as much
as I do."

She watched Steve and Mindy leave in Steve's BMW.

"You drove yourself?" Dan asked.

"No. But I didn't want to make them any later. I think Mindy planned this
so we could be alone."

Dan put his arm around her waist. "I don't mind if you don't."

"I don't."

Brutus squeezed between them. Isabella leaned down and patted Brutus.
"You are one in a million."

"Want to take him for a walk?"

"Are you sure. You're limping."

"I could let Brutus out the back door instead."

"To be honest, I don't want to walk the dog. I just said that to be nice." She
moved to the window. "I'm sorry."

"No worries," Dan admitted to himself his leg ached. "I'll let him out and if
you'll wait here I'll be right back."

Isabella watched Brutus out the window. Some smell had him tracking all over the yard. Soon she heard Dan's bedroom door creak. Dan rolled up to her. Seeing him in his wheelchair brought back the memory of that moment of peace at the funeral. How did she not see it before?

"It was me."

"Wow." She stared at him. The same feeling of peace renewed her heart once more. "I wish you had contacted me."

"I went back to rehab. Focused on healing my broken body. Your grief spoke to mine when you cried. It helped me put my own pain in perspective. I used that perspective to get where I am today. I never recognized you when we meet at the church. You look so different." Dan's eyes lingered on Isabella. "Recently, I was wondering about Jeff's widow, but I couldn't remember her name or where I put the thank you note you'd sent. I remembered your name started with an M."

"Well, Ron liked calling me by my middle name Melinda." Her voice caught. "How did I not recognize you?"

"Well, longer hair, a beard and no uniform."

She knelt in front of his chair and stared into his eyes. There it was. The look of peace mixed with sorrow. It spoke to her soul. She stood up and backed away. Overwhelmed by the wonder of God's goodness.

"I always wished I'd contacted you and thanked you in person for the healing that took place. You understood my loss. It was like being with Ron before he changed." She came forward and pushed hair out of his eyes.

Dan took her hand. "You're the first woman since my therapist I'm comfortable being myself—minus one leg."

"I'm glad to know it." Isabella smiled feeling awkward. "Want to order pizza?"

"Sure."

24

RETRAINING AND REMORSE

Dan smiled as natures alarm woke him, chick-a-dee-dee-dee called outside his bedroom window. Mindy had insisted on adding bird feeders to his landscape design. The one near his window attracted early risers. The barks of squirrels and the neighbor's Chihuahua caused Brutus to woof in response. He raced from the bedroom to yelp out the front window. "So much for obedience training." Dan pulled himself into his wheelchair and headed to the kitchen to make coffee. "Down Brutus. Come." He opened the back door and Brutus flew out. The barking stopped as the dog stood sentry over his domain.

"Crazy mutt." He laughed and rolled to the counter. Scooping coffee into the basket and pouring water he pressed the brew button. Turning toward the window, he saw Brutus stalking a cat who was stalking a squirrel. The cat prepared to pounce. Brutus barked. The squirrel scurried up the tree as the cat arched his back, hissed and shot up and over the fence headed for home.

Dan felt happier than he had since his accident. Isabella had stayed for pizza and they'd talked for hours. Mindy had called to see where she was and Steve and she had swung by to pick her up. Dan hadn't minded. Trying to impress people with his normal function was fatiguing.

"Lord, you've shown me through Isabella my disability doesn't make me less in your eyes. Sorry, I care so much what other people see."

Dan used his chair all morning to allow his leg more rest. He made his bed, picked up the living room, and paid his bills on-line. Brutus tried to hover over him. He sent him to his bed where he stayed under protest. Dan had fewer panic attacks thanks to Brutus. So why the dog insisted on staying close mystified him. Today he felt good, strong and excited with life. He didn't dare think of his feelings as love—but like was safe. Safe until Isabella sorted out her feeling.

They'd talked, held hands, shared funny stories from their childhood. It felt like a date. Without kissing or cuddling. The image of her sweet smile kept him company while he finished his morning tasks. Thoughts of her made him bold. By ten o'clock he'd gotten up his nerve. Dan grabbed his cell and pressed Isabella's number. "Hey, sleepy head. What's on your agenda?"

"Do I sound sleepy? I've been up since six." Isabella's joy radiated through the phone. "I'm doing thrift store shopping with Ming today. Remember, next Saturday is moving day. I am so excited. I can't believe it."

Dan closed his eyes and imagined Isabella's smile. It worked. Her joyful face hovered in his mind. Now he understood why Isabella closed her eyes to capture a memory.

"Could I ask you..." Isabella's next words muffled. "Sorry, Ming asked me something. Dan could you do a favor for me?"

"I guess."

"Could you and your truck be available today to pick up any great furniture finds? I don't want to pay for delivery."

Dan didn't answer right away. He took a moment to swallow his pride. "Can you get Steve to bring his muscles?" Admitting his limitations didn't hurt much.

"Ming said he'd be available after five. So, you bring the truck when I call and the store people can load it. Then when Steve gets off we can unload it at my place."

"Smart plan."

"We'll have dinner after. Ming is making my mother's stroganoff."

"I'll be waiting for your call." Dan shook his head as he envisioned an Asian woman making stroganoff. Did she make Chinese food? Did Isabella prepare food from her native country? He laughed at his own stereotyping. The very thing his disability caused others to do.

"I wonder how good a cook Isabella is?" Dan pulled the full trash bag out of the kitchen can as his mind focused on Isabella. She hadn't cooked for him. Maybe after she got moved she'd invite him over for dinner. Just the two of them. Brutus jumped in his lap taking him away from his daydream of beautiful chocolate eyes.

"Down."

Brutus moved away, taking a piece of the bag with a claw.

"Smooth move." The smell of rotten garbage permeated the room. Dan reached for the lower cabinet and opened the door where he stored trash bags. Before he could adjust his chair to better reach the bags Brutus retrieved the box for him.

"Thanks." Dan removed a bag and placed the box on the counter. "Trying to redeem yourself, hey boy."

Brutus picked up a fallen coffee filter and placed it in the new bag. Dan pulled the new bag over the ripped one.

"I'm heading to the shower. I'll take care of this trash later. Don't you dare eat the banana peels."

Brutus sulked to his bed and made a few circles before he settled in with a mournful sigh.

Dan had gotten dressed, put on his prosthetic and finished taking out the trash when his cell phone rang.

"Are you ready to come help?"

"I'm up for the mission."

"Here is your mission if you chose to accept it." Isabella giggled, the movie reference not lost on him. "You better get paper, I have three addresses for you."

Dan grabbed a grocery receipt and wrote on the back. "Should I memorize the instructions then swallow the paper?"

Another giggle, "You are so weird."

Dan laughed along with her wishing she was standing next to him instead of miles away.

She had found three great deals that filled his truck bed. A dining table and six chairs from a thrift shop, a bookshelf from a garage sale and a new mattress from Sleep Better Bedding Company.

Dan pulled his truck into his garage. He'd taken Brutus. Confined to the truck cab the canine was ready for a walk. Dan grabbed Brutus' leash. The two walked at a leisurely stride. Brutus aware of Dan's need for precise pacing. Two laps around the block and Brutus headed for the door. Dan needed to take him to the dog park so he could have a good run. "Tomorrow boy," Dan rubbed Brutus' head before unlocking the door. His cell phone played a Sousa march on his counter. He'd left it on the charger during the walk.

"Uncle Paul."

"Mr. Sweeney, I am Angela Jones, a nurse at Northwestern Delnor Hospital. Paul Whitehall was in a car accident. He listed you as next of kin and we need you to come and sign permission for surgery."

Dan started toward his truck then remembered it was full of Isabella's furniture. He paced for a moment. Brutus rubbed against him. Dan sat fighting the panic attack trying to overtake him. Brutus laid his paw on Dan's hand. Dan stroked his friend until the attack passed. After a few cleansing breaths, he called Steve. His friend picked him up in record time and drove him the 20 minutes to Saint Charles.

"Dan, you ok?"

"Not really." Dan had left Brutus at home. Another panic attack waited on the fringes of his emotions.

Pulling into the parking lot Steve touched his shoulder. "Let's pray." Together they asked God for help, direction, wisdom and healing. Steve did all the praying as Dan received the peace the Holy Spirit poured into his heart. "Ready."

"Let's do this." Dan clung to the momentary confidence. His parents had died in a car accident. He'd almost joined them back then. Deja vous was not what he needed.

Dan filled out the necessary paperwork, time dragged. He found his uncle being prepped for surgery. "Danny boy, you came. No need to worry I'll be fine." Uncle Paul was getting groggy. His eyes heavy as the meds took effect.

Dan turned to the doctor whose tag said Abernathy. "What happened?"

"It's unclear. The police said your uncle was sideswiped by a truck." Dan's mind filled with visions of semis. His chest tightened. "The driver of the pickup was a sixteen-year-old who just got his license."

Dan relaxed at the word pickup. The doctor continued sharing while Dan wrestled to stay focused.

"The boy got pinned under the wreckage. He's in surgery as we speak." Dr. Abernathy glanced at a chart in his hand. "Your uncle has some internal bleeding and a broken hip." His pager went off. Dan's heart quickened. The doctor touched his shoulder and pointed toward the hall.

"There's a waiting room just past the double door, turn left and follow the signs. You'll find coffee. Your uncle should be in surgery for a few hours."

Dan sat dazed. He half heard Steve say he'd make some calls. Sitting was confining so he paced until his leg ached. Then he sat on the stiff-backed chair and propped his leg on the coffee table. A home decorating show played on the waiting room TV. Another family gathered in a corner praying. Dan assumed it was the teen's. Steve came back and sat beside him. "I called Mindy and told her we'd get Isabella's stuff tomorrow. Pastor Clark will be coming and got the prayer chain started. He's taking care of notifying your uncle's church too. And Mindy and Isabella are coming up to get keys to your house so they can let Brutus out later. Unless you need them to bring him."

"I'm ok" Dan lied as he took slow breaths. He didn't want to ask permission to bring a service dog when he'd come without him. Pride battled with reason. Pride won.

Isabella and Ming appeared at the door. Dan felt better just having Isabella there.

She gave him a warm hug. "Any word?"

"Not yet." Dan reached for Isabella's hand. Her small fingers brought comfort. "Can you stay?" Fear gripped Dan. If Uncle Paul died he'd be an orphan.

"Mindy," His gaze switched from Isabella to her sister. "Steve can handle Brutus better than you. But my uncle has tropical fish that will need food in the morning. If you don't mind, the key to his house is on a hook near the garage door." Dan released Isabella's hand long enough to extract the door key from his key chain. "Can you guys stay? Brutus can handle being alone for a while."

DAN WOKE after dozing throughout the night sitting in a hospital recliner next to his uncle's hospital bed. The others had left right after the surgeon said his uncle did well and arrangements were being made for him to enter a rehab center by the weekend. The pronouncement almost brought on another panic attack. Isabella, Steve, and Mindy had circled him in prayer and stayed until his tears abated. He'd been a big wimp over his uncle's prognosis. God was working overtime to humble him.

"Danny boy." A croaky whisper accompanied Uncle Paul's smile. His face was pasty white. He licked his lips. The tube the nurse had removed from his throat earlier in the morning made words difficult. "Water."

Dan placed the straw from the Styrofoam cup to his uncle's lips. Pushing the cup away with his IV clad right hand he focused on Dan. "I'm sorry to trouble you."

"No trouble." Dan patted his uncle's shoulder.

"You don't understand." Uncle Paul struggled to sit. "They're closing my church."

"What?" Dan tried pressing him back on the pillow but his uncle pushed his hand away. "I got in the accident because I was angry. The board of elders and the church council are closing our church. Move the congregation to Batavia to our sister church. That congregation is larger and growing."

Dan didn't know how to respond. His uncle had mentioned after Aunt Sally died that the church board was considering joining the large group. But it never happened. The church membership was under 100 than and it was even smaller now. "Let's concentrate on getting better. Go back to sleep." Uncle Paul turned his head, not before Dan saw a tear slide down his face. "Did anyone die?"

"What?"

"Did anyone die because of my carelessness?"

"No. A young man was injured."

"The poor child. It's all my fault. God forgive me. I'll pray for him. Can you check on him for me?"

"If you promise to sleep I'll check."

"He's right Reverend Whitehall." A portly nurse with short gray hair added something to his uncle's IV after taking his vitals. "You rest now."

"And you, young man." She eyed Dan, her hands on her hips. "Go home. He'll sleep most of the day. Come back later. He'll be in better shape for visitors."

Dan nodded and started for the door. His leg screamed at him. Remembering he had left his truck at home he reached for his cell phone. "Dead battery, argh."

He headed toward the nurse's station planning to call a taxi when Isabella came up the hall. She looked beautiful even in jeans, lavender T-shirt and sneakers. The words Teen Angel came to mind. "Hey, can I hitch a ride."

"Sure. How's your uncle?" Her quick warm hug gave him the comfort he wasn't aware he needed. Too soon she stepped away. He longed to pull her back into his arms.

"Sleeping. The nurse kicked me out. Told me not to show my face until late afternoon."

The two walked out to her car. Once again, she matched her stride to his, but this time, she took his hand. How he wished fatigue and pain weren't his companions now. Spending more time with Isabella was what his heart wanted. But his body couldn't wait to get home, free his leg and take a long shower before taking an even longer nap.

"You look beat." Isabella smoothed his hair from his forehead. Her touch almost undid his fragile emotions. No way was he crying today.

"More than you know." Dan updated her on his uncle's condition and what he had mentioned.

"While you sleep, I'll make a few calls. I overheard the parents mentioned Mrs. Crawford's pastor. She'll know who to ask."

"I'd appreciate that."

They pulled into Dan's driveway. "I'd invite you in."

"But you look rung out." She patted his hand. "How about I swing by later and take you back to the hospital? Your truck is still a moving van."

"Aren't you working for Mrs. Crawford now?"

"She'll be coming with us." Isabella watched him get out of the car. "I'll bring dinner."

"Sounds good."

Brutus met him at the door. He walked beside Dan sensing his mood. Steve had left a note on the kitchen counter listing the times Brutus had been fed and let out. He opened the back door but Brutus refused to leave his side. "Ok, Boy, it's your call but don't you even think about waking me up before I'm ready."

Dan put in a call into Mom's Massage before drifting off to sleep. The shower had helped but his back and legs burned from overuse. When would he learn? He set his alarm for three thirty in case he didn't wake before his appointment. His phone rest on his nightstand recharging and Brutus rolled up on the rug at the foot of his bed.

25

MASSAGE AND JEALOUSY

Isabella stared at the blond who answered Dan's door. Her hair in a neat ponytail. Tall, willowy, gorgeous green eyes and a creamy complexion. Everything Isabella wasn't. The woman's smile polite and brief.

"Dan asked if you could come back in thirty minutes. She closed the door leaving Isabella holding the reheated stroganoff. Her frown deepened to the point of painful. "What in the world?" Isabella placed her finger on the doorbell. *Stop it, get a grip.* Isabella's head rose as she straightened her back and walked toward her car. Her feet clad in tall heels stumbled on the grass as she crossed through the front yard to avoid the white van parked in the driveway. "I'll just come back later—maybe." *Maybe I'll leave him stranded. Stop acting like a middle schooler.*

Isabella decided to pick up Clare and have her join them for dinner. She would keep the mood light and Isabella's jealousy at bay. Jealousy—where did that…. Isabella pressed the clicker causing the car alarm to sound. Heat rose on her neck as she clicked it off. She glanced around the neighborhood but no one was outside staring. She gave the unlock button a gentle press. They were friends, just friends. Or were they? He never called her Issy like her other friends. Always Isabella. Her name, a caress on his lips. She put the car in reverse. A horn sounded and angry colorful language assailed her ears. Heat returned to her face as the driver sped around her. Shifting into drive, she restrained her foot from accelerating.

"Shake it off, Issy. Life's good now. Don't ruin it. Besides, he has more friends than I realized."

Isabella was still miffed when she arrived at her friend's front door. Clare appeared wearing black slacks with a lavender blouse.

"You're early, Twinny."

"Dan wasn't ready yet. I thought I'd pick you up and take you with me to his house. We can eat dinner together."

"Sounds perfect. I'll get my purse." Clare stared at Issy for a moment. "What's going on? I can see trouble written all over your face."

"A woman answered his door. She said come back in thirty minutes."

"Did you ask why?"

"No, I stood there stunned."

Clare laughed, grabbed her purse and toddled toward Issy's car. "Well, I intend to find out why he couldn't answer the door himself."

Isabella couldn't decide whether to laugh or groan at the prospect of Clare getting to the bottom of things in her no-nonsense way.

By the time, they arrived at Dan's home the woman was loading something into the back of her van. "Look dear." Clare pointed to a magnetic sign on the van. Clare read it out loud "Mom's Massage, Have Table Will Travel. Call for appointment." Clare laughed and Isabella's stomach tightened at her foolish behavior.

"I suppose you were too upset to notice that big ol'sign."

"I came from the other direction. Too stunned to notice anything."

"Stunned you say?" Clare's crocked smile irritated her companion.

"Yes." Isabella stared at the steering wheel. "I made a beeline for my car."

Clare's chuckled as she exited the car. "I will say having you in my life won't be boring."

Dan met the ladies at the door in his wheelchair. "I apologize for putting you off like that. My massage wasn't over. Michelle sets her table up in my living room. I was in my underwear. His face flashed embarrassment. I mean... I overworked my leg yesterday and...."

Isabella smiled, hoping she sounded casual. "I understand. I was early. It's fine. I picked up Clare so after we eat we can leave for the hospital."

"If you'll point me to the ladies' room." Clare followed Dan's finger point . "There's a half bath off the kitchen."

Dan moved his chair closer and looked up at Isabella as she waited in the center of the room, still holding her covered dish. "I am so glad you came. I thought after I had Michelle send you away you'd never come back." Brutus nuzzled her free hand.

"No worries." Isabella hoped her voice sounded light as she moved to put her dish in the microwave before continuing. "But Clare couldn't resist finding out your secret." They both laughed. Brutus ruffed. Clare gave the dog an affectionate pat as she joined the others.

The three enjoyed their dinner. Clare entertaining them with stories of her childhood adventures with Paul. Brutus sat in his bed watching the trio. Isabella stole glances at the dog. He made no move to join them. Dan put on his prosthetic while the ladies cleaned up the meal.

They arrived at his uncle's room just after he'd finished his own liquid dinner. He looked less pale. "Danny, I see you've brought company."

Dan squeezed his hand and Clare and Isabella kissed his cheek. "My, my, ladies. What would my congregants think?" Gentle laughter filled the room.

"How are you feeling." Clare straightened his blanket.

"Like Jacob wrestling with the Angel of the Lord. My hip aches enough to make a sailor swear." He lowered his bed and look out the door. "That servant of Lucifer made me walk the hall." He lowered his bed one more notch. "That's better. Can you fluff my pillow?" Isabella fixed the pillow and added another one behind his back. "Now tell me about the boy."

"His name is Bryan Sanders. He goes to my church." Clare sat beside Paul. Leaning forward, she continued her tale. "His parents told me he admitted he was at fault. He'd been texting and not watching where he was going. When his truck hit your car, it spun into a tree. The impact penned his leg under the dashboard. He will recover but the progress will be slow. His leg broke in three places, he broke a few ribs, has a concussion and a fractured wrist. It's a miracle he survived."

Tears glinted in his uncle's eyes at the news. "Poor, poor boy. Please tell his parents I am so very sorry to be the instrument of their grief."

"Uncle Paul, Clare said the boy admitted to texting while driving."

"But if I were honest, I need to admit I was wishing while driving. Wishing I was dead because my church was being taken away from me. My pity party over forced retirement was in full swing. If I hadn't railed against God's will while driving, I'd been alert and avoided the accident."

Dan knew nothing they could say would convince him otherwise. "Let's pray for Bryan and his family."

"And for you Reverend." Isabella took Clare's hand and reached for Dan's across the bed. They prayed.

Isabella came around to Dan's side and patted the older man's shoulder. "Don't keep blaming yourself. God has forgiven you and Bryan for your carelessness and he will bring you both through to the healing side."

"Isabella, you are a wise woman." Uncle Paul smiled through teary eyes.

"No, my grandma was the wise one. She always reminded me in tough times God would take me to the healing side." *I wish I'd remembered her wise words a year ago.*

～

"DON'T BOTHER SPENDING the night, Danny Boy." That lounger will cause your leg hurt. I'll rest better knowing you're comfortable in your own bed. Arguing with his uncle was not an option. "But I expect you here bright and early in the morning to hear what the doctor has to say."

The three stopped at Bryan's room. They found him asleep. In the hallway, they prayed with his parents and assured them his uncle wasn't planning on suing anyone.

"When Bryan can get out of bed he wants to visit Rev. Whitehall and ask forgiveness." Mrs. Sanders said.

"My uncle has the same intention. He had upsetting news he feels distracted him. He blames himself for your son's injuries."

"Sounds like they both need a lot of prayers to forgive themselves. Thank you so much for checking on Bryan. Please, tell your uncle he's in our prayers." Mr. Sanders took his wife's hand, and they went back into their son's room.

26

MOVING DAY

The last curlicue on the last vine on the last window frame on Isabella's sun porch took shape. She'd spent her free time painting a floral motif throughout her art studio A satisfied sigh followed the click of the paint can lid. This room reflected her feeling of freedom. The wall with no windows bloomed with a floral arrangement reminiscent of Georgia O'Keefe. The rest of the house less dramatic. She didn't want to cause Mrs. Crawford's kin to have a lot of repainting when she moved out.

"Thank you, Jesus, for this blessing."

The smell of turpentine, as she cleaned her brushes, brought back college memories. Late-night discussions on art and politics. Spending time on the Lake Michigan Beach and visiting the various art and craft shows on Navy Peer and other Chicago venues.

"I am so grateful for this job. Mrs. Crawford isn't too needy, and she allows me lots of time to paint. Father, only you could arrange such a blessing."

This last month dedicated to decorating the carriage house had been the happiest of her life. Renewed purpose a balm to her soul. Each room a unique inspiration. Her creative juices infused her with joy. Steve and John had moved the furniture from Dan's truck into Clare's garage temporarily. Isabella's mind played with furniture placement.

She missed a few special pieces she'd purchased in Indiana. Resurrection had provided a furnished apartment as part of Ron's salary. She'd added a Thomas Kinkaid painting and some vases from Pottery Barn. After Ron's death,

Maureen had moved Isabella's things in her storage locker. A pain throbbed in her chest recalling that huge mistake. Maureen sold the content to a collectibles dealer with no warning. She donated to the church and spent the rest to take a cruise with her church friends. After she left on her cruise Isabella had opened the door to a stranger. He handed her a large box of photos. The unit had been in Maureen's name. Her wedding dress, her grand-mother's brooch—gone. The anger she once harbored melted to sadness as she recalled her mother-in-law's smug expression when confronted.

"Lay not up for yourself treasures on earth, Melinda. God told me to sell those things and give the money to the building fund." Maureen's word framed in hypocrisy as she pulled out expensive jewelry she'd purchased on her get-away.

"My things weren't yours to sell."

"Oh well, what's done is done." Maureen took her luggage to her bedroom and refused to talk to her for the rest of the day.

The whole incident triggered a severe migraine. The headaches sent her to the neurologist which lead to the whole awful truth. The revelation brought her to Aurora.

"Other than my grandmother's brooch I don't regret the loss. Father, you have worked things out for my good. In my weakness, your grace kept me and your wisdom guided me."

"Twinny, you ready to take me to visit Paul?" Clare, dressed in plum colored blouse and white slacks, stood in the doorway.

"Is it that time already?"

"This room is amazing. So, warm and inviting. I'm sure you will create wonderful masterpieces in here," Clare's eyes brightened as she scanned the room. "I love, love love it."

Isabella wiped her hands on a rag soaked with paint thinner, removing the specks of oil paint. "Let me get cleaned up and then we'll go."

"Excellent. Let's go to lunch at Ari's Place after we check on Paul. I've been wanting to take you there." Clare clapped her hands in delight. "I'll wait for you to come for me when you're ready. I can catch the rest of the *Price is Right*."

~

ISABELLA AND CLARE found Rev. Whitehall seated in a chair near the windows watching birds flit around the bird bath. "Ladies, I am so pleased you've come."

"I brought you more books. Another Louis Lamour and *Pride and Prejudice* —Jane Austin is one of my favorites." Clare continued to draw books from her tote bag placing them on his nightstand. "Let's see, *A Man Call Peter* and *Beyond the Horizon* are two biographies Dan thought you might enjoy."

"Has Dan been in today?" Isabella hoped her question appeared nonchalant. Since she'd begun working for Clare and painting the carriage house, she'd seen little of Dan. He offered to help paint. But she wanted, no needed to do it herself. Every inch of the place had her seal of approval. She missed Dan now that the project was behind her.

"No, he comes after class. Thanks for the books. I don't care for TV other than the news. TVs blaring at all hours. It makes me work harder in rehab so I can get back to the quiet of my home." He sighed and turned toward the window again. "If I have a home to return to."

"The church is closing for sure?" Clare sat in the chair left of her friend and squeezed his hand.

"Frank, the board president, came in yesterday to tell me the news. He didn't want me reading it in the paper or hearing from a member. My home is going on the market. They are giving me time to recover and pack my things."

"What are you going to do?" Clare's eyes misted. She dug in her purse for a tissue.

"Retire. I suppose. The last bout of flu knocked the wind out of my preaching. And the accident confirmed I need a less stressful life. It's heartbreaking to see my church die and now I lacked the fortitude to help revive it."

"Dan told me once you always reminded him that when God closes one door, he flings open another. You don't have to go turning doorknobs." Isabella fluffed the pillows on Rev. Whitehall's bed and smoothed the sheets.

"Yes, knock and the door shall be open to you." Paul smiled. "You are a gift to my nephew and I thank God for you."

Her face flamed. It appeared everyone saw more in their friendship then she was willing to accept. Clare must have sensed her discomfort because she redirected the conversation.

"I heard they are looking for a chaplain at Heritage Woods Assisted Living Center. I can make a call and see if they've filled the position."

"Thank you, but I'll call myself. After I've sought the Lord. If you hear of anything else, I'd be happy to inquire. I might as well seek God's exit plan for me. After 40 years at the same church, I've forgotten how to job hunt. My denomination won't be giving me a new church. I'm too old." Paul sighed in resignation. "Pastors my age don't have a retirement package in place." A resolute smile formed on his lips. "I appreciate your visits. At first, my congregants came but after three weeks it's Dan and you ladies."

"When will you be released." Clare threw the wadded tissue in the trash.

"Hopefully, by the end of next week."

"Good. There is plenty of time to hear God's direction." Clare's confident tone brought a nod from the pastor.

"True." Paul reached for his walker. "Shall we take a walk up the hall and get ice cream. My treat."

~

ISABELLA AND CLARE walked through the packed parking lot of the small strip mall toward Ari's. Isabella steadied Clare as she stepped on the curb with her cane.

Ari's bright smile greeted them at the door. "Ah, Clare, it's good to see you again. Come, sit wherever you like. I'll be right there."

The restaurant was tiny, tasteful. The red checked cloths homey. Each place had a homemade printed menu. A TV screen ran the specials. Ari returned, iPhone in hand to get their orders.

Clare never even opened the menu. "You know I love your homemade soup."

"We have chicken noodle and French onion, today."

"I'll take the chicken noodle with a small Cobb salad, please. And iced tea, no lemon."

"Very good."

"I'll have the chicken salad wrap and the French onion soup," Isabella said.

"I'll bring them right away." Ari pressed the send button on his phone. "Are you a friend or family?"

His Greek accent added to the restaurant's charm.

"Isabella is my companion and a wonderful artist."

"I would like to see this art of yours." Ari smiled and leaned toward Clare. "We have coconut cream pie, I think. Let me check."

"I hope so." Clare grinned and patted his hand before he left to check.

"Ari dreamed of owning a restaurant. He was my favorite waiter at Mom's Table. When Ari opened, most of his old customers came here. Do you know he shops every afternoon for the food for the next day? Nothing frozen. See that cute sign? We don't have a microwave."

Soon their food arrived. It was every bit as delicious as her friend claimed. Ari stopped by to check on them. Clare and he teased one another. His laughter was genuine. Here was a man who loved and took pride in his business. Another person to inspire her not to give up on her artist dream.

"Come again, ladies. Don't wait so long next time. You make me sad when you are not here."

Clare laughed and waved as they left. "Don't worry. My ladies group will come for breakfast soon."

Issy made sure Clare was napping before pulling out her sketch pad. Her hands flew over the page. Every detail vivid in her mind. Joy filled her as the creative juices flowed again. Soon a stately Greek waiter laughing with Clare formed under her charcoal pencils.

⁓

DAN DROVE toward Mindy's apartment. A truck overflowing with household items and furniture sat on the curve. Dan pulled into the driveway. Isabella stood hugging a black man. Then she kissed his cheek. He lifted her up in the air swinging her around. She giggled and squealed with delight. Dan felt his heart turn to stone. He stayed in his truck too mindful of his disability to move. The façade of normal surrounded him as he sat in the driver's seat. Mindy ran down the stairs and leaped into the guy's arms. He swung her around as well.

Steve walked up to the truck and tapped on the window. "You getting out or what?"

"Who is that guy?"

"It's Henri."

Steve didn't appear disturbed, Dan loosen his grip on the steering wheel. "Where's your car?"

I parked around the corner. There's no parking on this side of the street. Figured you'd want to park in the driveway. I'll ride with you or Mindy. What Isabella has left should fit in your truck."

Isabella tapped on the passenger window. Dan pushed the window button.

"Come out and meet my brother. He came to help and brought stuff from my parents."

Dan let out a breath, a smile of relief formed on his lips. "I'll be right there."

Steve waited for him and they walked over together.

Mindy introduced the men. "Henri, my boyfriend Steve and our friend Dan." They shook hands.

"My sister can't stop speaking about you, Steven." A slight French accent colored Henri speech. "And you, Dan, I have heard nothing." He shrugged his shoulders. "But then I had heard nothing from Isabella since her husband's funeral. I've been out of the country. When Isabella called Momma last week I was there visiting. She made me promise to bring this truckload of things for my sister's new home."

Isabella wrapped her arm around Henri waist and laid her head on his shoulder. "Mindy kept his visit a surprise for me. "Henri was adopted three years after me, but we are the same age."

"He still has some of his Haitian accent. Girl's love it." Mindy teased.

"You are so amusing. But no. There is no girl that fascinated with my accent." Henri reached around Isabella and ruffled Mindy's hair.

"I have a few boxes we can put in Dan's truck and then we're off to my house." Isabella started for the stairs then turned. "I have coffee and pastries at my house." Her arms did a fist bump. "I love it—my house."

Dan unlatched the tailgate of his truck while the others carried boxes down the stairs. He hefted himself into the bed and arranged the boxes as the others passed them to him. He slid carefully off the tailgate and latched it back.

"You handle yourself well with your injury. I am impressed." Henri placed a last-minute box in the truck bed.

"I have a prosthetic leg." Dan surprised himself with the admission.

"I know. I was kidding about not knowing who you were. Mindy has told me many things and Isabella thinks you are special." Henri winked then headed to his truck.

Special. He wondered how she meant that. Hey, he'd put a positive spin on it. It gave him hope.

27

NEW BEGINNINGS

Dan carried his uncle's small bag into the empty parsonage. The elderly man's shoulders drooped while his eyes scanned the interior.

Uncle Paul sat in his favorite recliner. "The end of an era." His sigh resolute. "I should have retired a few years ago, while I still had my health. Sally and I discussed buying an RV and visiting every state. We imagined holding a church service in every camper park we stayed at." Paul turned to his nephew and shook his head. "Don't say it." Paul held his palm toward Dan and frowned. "I have no wish to travel the country. That was Sally's dream. I'm a homebody."

"Is that why you took Aunt Sally on a cruise and then a trip to Canada?"

"Yes, they were two of the many trips on her bucket list. If I hadn't been such a frugal fool, she could have enjoyed a trip every year."

Dan stared at the floor. Awkwardness fought with compassion. It was odd to hear the man's intimate thoughts. His uncle held his personal life close not sharing even when his wife became so sick. He buried his pain deep. When Aunt Sally died, the congregation lost the zealous man of faith. Dan never saw old Uncle Paul resurface until he returned from his second tour in Afghanistan. Then he'd poured the love he'd hidden away after his aunt's passing onto Dan. The action had revived his smile and sense of humor. Joy and renewed faith had returned, but not in time to save his dying congregation. Dan had no words of encouragement so he remained silent. He took the chair opposite his uncle. Brutus curled at his feet.

"These two chairs are mine. Sally and I purchased them. The other furniture belongs to the church." Paul stepped to the fish tank and reached for the container of fish food. An array of colorful fish headed to the surface. "These were Sally's pride and joy. They'll need a new home."

"You don't need to think about it now."

"Yes, I do. The realtor is coming this weekend and by month's end the church will have its last service." His words were matter-of-fact. The former tears replaced with acceptance.

"Come stay with me while you figure things out, Uncle Paul." Dan watched Brutus go to his uncle and nuzzle his hand. The old man stroked the dog's head.

"I think I will. If you have time, come by tomorrow and we can start packing. Right now, I need a nap."

"I'm off this weekend."

"I'll see you at nine sharp on Saturday. This afternoon I want to put my sermon together for Sunday." Uncle Paul headed for his bedroom. Dan signaled for Brutus, his mind making a list of what he'd need to do to prepare for his uncle's arrival.

~

DAN PULLED his truck into Isabella's driveway. It had been over a week since he'd spent any time with her. Her brother, Henri stayed on to visit and help her get settled in her new home. He hadn't seen his sister in years. Dan envied the three siblings closeness.

He and Katie had never been close. She was ten years his senior and had kids in college now. He always spent his holiday leave with her family. Katie and her husband, Trevor and her two girls. They did what they could to help after Dan's accident. Things on a personal level, awkward. His nieces didn't know how to behave around him after he lost his leg.

Now a quick trip for Thanksgiving would fulfill family duty. He'd travel to California in the summer to see Kayla graduate from UCLA. It'd be nice to have someone go with him besides Brutus. He envisioned a certain dark-haired beauty on his arm making things less awkward for him.

Isabella came to the door in over-sized T-shirt and capris. Her curvy form made the ratty shirt look good. "Come on in. I needed a break. You're the perfect excuse."

Dan liked the sound of that. Brutus sat on the step. "He's waiting for an invitation."

Isabella patted Brutus' head. He extended his paw and Isabella shook it. "Welcome to my home." Brutus wagged his tail in greeting and followed them into the house. Dan signaled for Brutus to stay at his side.

The carriage house make-over transformed it. An eclectic blend of furnishing graced the open living/dining room area. The kitchen had a fifty's feel with a red metal kitchen table. The thrift store chairs had been reupholstered in a red vinyl.

"Your place is different."

"Hey, I'm an artist, not an interior decorator. I like what I like. And I figured I'd have fun discovering my true self."

"The Felix the cat clock is pretty cool."

"It's so fun, makes me smile every time I check the time." Isabella pointed up the stairs situated toward the back of the kitchen.

"I have a Victorian look in my bedroom and a modern flare in the second bedroom, my office." Isabella opened the fridge and pulled out lettuce and deli meat. Depositing her finds on the kitchen counter, she nodded her head toward the door behind her. "Walk through that door and see my art studio."

Dan stepped into a room of faces staring back at him. There were canvases covered with smaller versions of the youth group mural but new canvases full of familiar faces. A man bowed in prayer. His uncle's hand wrinkled and veined as Dan always remembered them. His left hand displayed the unique three cord wedding band his aunt had a jeweler make for them. Their only extravagance in their over forty years of marriage. The painting so lifelike he expected his uncle to raise his head and greet him.

On another canvass, Mrs. Crawford and her friends sat around a card table. Dan could hear their laughter in his mind. He turned a canvas leaning against the wall. The Swimming Stones from downtown Aurora undulated before his eyes. Water appeared to flow onto the studio floor.

Dan explored more paintings, Henri passing out food at the mission and Mindy dancing with a group of international children. Isabella's easel held an incomplete painting of Clare chatting with a waiter. Once completed, Dan was sure he'd want to step into that painting too.

"Wow! These are amazing. You've been a busy beaver."

Her laughter carried from the kitchen. "Clare has posed for me a few times which allows me to paint and watch over her at the same time. Her bridge club was happy to let me take their picture and sketch them while they played. I work 20 hours and I'm still not sleeping well. But I feel more alive when I'm creating something."

Dan sat at the kitchen table and waited for Isabella to join him. "Does that include reupholstering these chairs?"

"No, Henri did that. He is a little OCD. He drove me to distraction getting everything in order. There's not one box left to unpack. He even took the things I didn't want back with him to sell on e-bay."

"What does he do for a living? I don't think he mentioned it."

She laughed again. "He is an e-bay entrepreneur, a garage sale guru, and a thrift shop devotee."

"What does that mean?"

"He finds treasures and buys them for small amounts and then resells them to collectors for lots more. He is hired to hunt for specific items and he travels the country, sometimes the world to check out possibilities. Henri loves what he does. When my folks found him on a mission trip to Haiti, he was picking through garbage and reselling anything that had value. After he came to live with us he kept bringing home things to repair and resell. My father suggested Henri go to business school."

"Did he?"

"He took a few courses. My brother is too ADD to sit through unrelated classes to get a degree. But he makes a six-figure income, so he's accomplished his goal. Dad always insisted we all learn business skills. That's why Ming has a successful salon."

"Looks like you could open an art gallery."

"I might." Isabella's face lit up as she placed two square cobalt blue plates on the table. "Last week I got a call from an art dealer who wanted to negotiate terms for producing portions of the youth room into lithographs. He'd seen the article from the Beacon on their web page."

"Fantastic."

Isabella poured iced tea into matching tumblers. "Mr. Stanford is coming next week; I plan to show him my other stuff."

"I can't believe you went years without painting." Dan watched her place the finished sandwiches on the plates along with pickle slices.

"I can't believe I accepted the lie that my training was not something God could use. Ron didn't appreciate it and Maureen felt my time could be better spent."

"Did you know Ron's paternal grandmother painted landscapes and did ceramics? I guess Maureen had no use for anything that reminded her of her ex."

"I had no idea." Isabella shook her head. A few strains of brown hair fell loose from the clip holding them. Dan resisted the urge to tuck them back.

"Your paintings draw people into the moment, they inspire."

Isabella dashed a tear from her face. "You think so? I can see so many imperfections. But the joy I get from creating makes up for my lack of talent."

Dan took her hand. "If you lack talent, then I can't wait to see what you create when you get some." No more was said as they blessed the food. "Tell me why didn't you paint for yourself? As a hobby."

"Our finances were always tight. After paying bills Ron took any extra and bought some new instrument or electronics or put money on studio time. We couldn't even afford a box of crayons."

Dan couldn't believe his old friend had been so self-centered. Sharing his growing aggravation would accomplished nothing. "I brought my uncle home from rehab today."

"You should have brought him with you."

"He wanted to nap. I think he needed time alone to get used to the idea of moving."

"So, it's true. Stone Church is closing."

"And my uncle's home goes up for sale this weekend."

"That's not much time to find something else"

"He's agreed to move in with Brutus and me."

"Good. That reminds me." Isabella went to the fridge and brought out a zip lock bag. She removed a large ham bone and grabbed the throw rug. She placed the rug and bone in front of Brutus. Patting his head, she smiled. "Enjoy."

Brutus looked at Dan for permission before digging into the treat. Brutus dived for the bone. She backed up watching him gnaw away. "Wow. He is one amazing dog. Can any dog be trained to do what he does?"

"Any dog with the right temperament. But all dogs can learn obedience. The trick is to train the owner to be consistent. I'd gotten lax about Brutus greeting strangers and staying until released. It was just me and Brutus the first month at the house. When you freaked out, I had to retrain both of us to exercise better manners."

They finished their lunch and Dan helped clear the table. "Can I get your opinion on something?"

Isabella nodded as she poured dish soap in the sink. "My uncle is pretty depressed about his church closing. I have an idea. A service to commemorate the legacy of Stone Church. Reminding every one of God's call on our lives and sending everyone out to fulfill the great commission."

"Makes sense. Just because the church is closing doesn't mean God is closing shop. He scattered the early church for the greater good."

Dan dried the dishes as Isabella drained the sink and wiped off the table.

"The plates go in the left cabinet." Isabella placed the damp rag over the faucet to dry. "How do you envision the service?"

"Nothing now—just a feeling it's the right thing to do."

"Well, that's a good start. Steve is one of the worship leaders at his church, and I think Laura is on a committee for historic preservation. Maybe they can come up with a music program and presentation of the church's history."

"Sounds like a plan. If we keep it simple, we can pull it off."

"And if we stay prayerful." Dan reached for her hand. "Thanks."

"No problem." Isabella squeezed his hand. "I love your uncle and am happy to make his last service special."

"I'm glad to hear it."

28

OUTSIDE COMFORT ZONE

"No way. Ask someone else." Isabella walked away from the meeting table and stared out the window. *I knew it would come to this. Oh God, help me.* The view from the conference room at Steve's law office suited her mood. An alley with litter strewn from an overturned recycling bin and an overflowing dumpster describe her pain. Tears burned her eyes.

Dan came up behind her. His gentle touch on her shoulder reassuring. "No one is forcing you to do what you're not comfortable doing."

She turned to face her friends at the table. "I'm sorry." She grabbed a tissue from the box on the counter and dabbed her eyes. Glad she put on water-resistant mascara. She pasted a smile in place. "I'll be glad to work with the choir but no solo."

Laura spoke first. "That's perfect. You'll do a wonderful job." A few of the choir members know you sang professionally and wanted you to do a solo."

"A reluctant backup singer is more accurate." She let Dan lead her back to her seat. Brutus moved before she tripped over his paw. Once she was in the chair, he laid his head in her lap. She rubbed between his ears, the action a comfort.

"Steve, can you get Amy to do a duet?" Laura moved the meeting along without further discussion.

"I guess. Can I choose the song?" Steve wrote a note on his iPhone.

"If it speaks to the theme." Laura took notes on her laptop.

"The theme is servants of Christ going forth," Dan said.

"You're going to accompany me, Dan." Steve wiggled his brows. "Don't tell me no. I've seen you practicing on my guitar. You can take it home and learn the song."

Dan glared at Steve. His sigh signaled his indecision.

"I'm still rusty. I mean mega rusty."

He took a sip from his coffee cup. She watched the group give him smiles of encouragement.

"You'll regret this." Dan crossed his arms. "It's been years and back then I had all my appendages."

Steve patted his friend on the back. "Hey, I've seen you use finger picks to play. Sounds great. You'll be fine."

"I guess, if it's only one song."

The group nodded. Steve slapped Dan on the back as he struggled to write on the notepad before him. "Which song did you have in mind?"

"God's Bond Servant." Steve tapped the title into his phone as she spoke.

"Which one?" Bile formed in Isabella's throat.

"I found a copy of Ron's song on YouTube. The words speak to the theme."

Isabella felt her skin get clammy.

"Sorry, I wasn't thinking." Steve shook his head. "I love the lyrics. I forgot— I'll find something else." Steve's awkward apology touched Isabella. She needed to work through this. No more running from her past.

"You're right, the words are perfect." She felt the comfort of her friends. No pressure, just encouragement. "If I don't have to sing its fine." She hoped. Watching a live performance of the song connected with her husband's death presented a chest tightening challenge.

"Great." The relief in Steve's voice switched to concern. "Are you sure, no doubts?"

"Yes." The one-word answer masked her anxiety.

"Dan, I'm sending the link to your email." Steve hit a few keys on his cell.

ISABELLA HAD RIDDEN with Dan and the ride home was quiet. Brutus stuck his head between the front bucket seats. She stroked his head. "It's ok, boy. No worries."

"I think you're brave for allowing Steve to sing Ron's last song. Maybe when he doesn't keel over you can move on." Dan's neck reddened when she didn't laugh at his joke.

"Moving on sounds wonderful. Listening to the song without remembering every detail of his death even better. The few times I've played the CD I end up in a puddle of tears on the floor. But maybe different voices singing will make it less traumatic. I have the rest of the month to build up my courage."

She watched the tree-lined streets go by as they neared her home. "The words are powerful. It's the most anointed song he ever wrote."

"I can't wait to hear it." Dan pulled in her driveway. "Dinner after church?"

"Don't you need to help your uncle pack?"

"All that's left are the books in his library. I need to get more boxes. Uncle Paul said Clare and Louise were stopping by to help him finish.

"Then I'll see you tomorrow. I hope the service we're planning brings him joy. I can't believe how fast you got everyone together." She reached for her door handle as the truck stopped.

"Hey, back in the day, Stone Church had the best youth group around. Lots of people who attend Community and Living River were once part of Stone's youth group. Laura reminded me she was the skinny kid with braces."

Isabella's foot shifted on the floorboard. A burger wrapper crumpled beneath her heel.

She flicked a French fry off her shoe. "Yuck."

"I need to run this truck through the car wash."

"Are you planning on vacuuming the interior too?" Her eyes scanned the collection of fast food wrappers and paper cups on the floor and the dog hair clinging to the seats.

Dan shrugged, flashing a sheepish grin her way.

"I'll take Brutus home first. He barks at the water spraying on the car and tries to bite the vacuum hose."

"Why not leave him with me?" She couldn't stop the thought from trooping out of her mouth.

"Seriously?"

"I have another bone Clare gave me for Brutus. I think she's on Brutus' side of this love/ hate relationship."

"If you keep him I can drive up the street and be back in thirty minutes." Dan placed his hands on her face and stared into her eyes. "Are you sure?" His hands felt so different from her late husband. Ron's touch meant he wanted to be sure she wasn't planning on disagreeing with him. Dan's gentle touch on her cheeks reassured her, courage flowed through his fingers to her heart.

"I think we can manage for thirty minutes." She smiled in response to Dan's ever-widening grin. The boyish sparkle in his eyes warmed her.

"I'll take him in so he knows you're in charge. If I go to the car wash with attendances, it will go faster. I promise unless the line is long I can get the truck in and the guys can even get the interior cleaned in less than thirty minutes."

Dan leashed Brutus, and the two followed her inside. She watched as Dan went over a few hand signals. "Ok. Let me see you try." Brutus followed her commands until she signal heel. Brutus cocked his head to the side. "Your hand needs to be at your side. Straighten your fingers. Perfect. Remember you're in charge. No matter how adorable his face becomes he must obey."

"What if he won't?"

"He will." Dan knelt beside Brutus. "Isabella's in charge. You mind her and keep her safe." Brutus enjoyed Dan's head rub and gave a soft wolf of consent. "I'll be back real soon." Dan rose from his position on the floor with little effort and headed for the door. "You should have zero trouble. Call my cell if he gets sassy and I'll deal with him."

"You'll tell him to mind over the phone." Isabella crossed her arms. "You're serious?"

"As a heart attack."

"OK then."

Brutus watched Dan leave. Once the truck pulled out of the driveway, he turned his full attention to Isabella. She sensed the same boyish excitement she'd seen in Dan. How weird. "Well, boy, it's you and me." Staring into the dog's gentle eyes she spoke with conviction. "I'm in charge."

Brutus wolfed in response causing Isabella to jump then giggle.

Isabella slid out of her heels and slipped into her fuzzy slippers. "Come along, I have a treat for you. She extracted the bone from the refrigerator and placed it on the kitchen floor. Brutus waited. Oh right." She gave the signal to eat and Brutus picked up the bone and found a spot near the wall out of her way to enjoy his prize. Isabella changed into sweats and started cleaning her much-neglected bathroom. The task distracted her from Brutus' presence.

The doorbell rang as she wiped the shower. Removing her rubber gloves, she laid them on the sink. Brutus waited for her outside the bathroom door, alert and watching her. She signaled stay. Then went to the door. Two men in suits waited outside. "Are you Melinda Macklin?"

Alarms went off in her head. No one in Aurora knew her by that name. "Ye-e-s-s."

"We're from the FBI." The shorter of the two flashed his badge too fast to read it. "We need to ask you some questions."

Panic engulfed her stomach and burned toward her throat. Brutus was beside her before the acid reached its destination.

"What's this about?"

"Can we come in?" The younger agent had a small scar on his cheek. His eyes hidden behind sunglasses. Brutus' low growl caused him to step back from the door.

"No." She locked the screen. If Brutus didn't like them, she knew her instincts were right.

The younger agent reached for the knob. Brutus growl and pressed closer to the screen door. "You need to put your dog away."

"You need to get away from my door."

Brutus' presence emboldened her.

The short agent smiled. "I apologize for my partner. He doesn't like dogs." He shifted his weight from foot to foot before continuing. "It's imperative you speak with us."

"It's imperative I call my lawyer."

Dread began to overtake her. Brutus stood watch at the door. She picked up her cell phone, the wisdom of her father echoing in her mind. "It's always better to consult a lawyer even if you're innocent. Too much identity theft to not watch your back." Isabella called Steve. Hoping the men would leave before Steve arrived. They remained outside. She watched the shorter one make a phone call but couldn't hear what was said. The younger one appeared to be texting.

Steve, dressed in jeans and a Cubs jersey, arrived in a few minutes. He greeted the men with a nod and signaled for her to unlock the screen. Brutus backed up but kept himself between her and the two agents. She heard Dan's truck pull in the driveway. He let himself in and sat next to her on the couch. Brutus issued low growls as the men sat on dining room chairs Steve had arranged for the three of them.

"Mrs. Macklin."

"My name is Wilson. Isabella Wilson. I had my name legally changed back to my maiden name. Melinda is my middle name." Fear caused her to babble.

"Very well" The short balding man took notes while the taller dark-haired agent asked the questions. He never removed his sunglasses, putting her more on guard.

"When was the last time you were in contact with Maureen Macklin?"

"Six months ago."

"We believe you were living in her home as recent as last week."

"My mother-in-law is not well. She is bi-polar or something. You have to take what she says with a grain of salt."

"She didn't tell us anything. We found her dead yesterday."

Isabella gasped at the agent's declaration. This couldn't be possible.

Isabella fought the need to faint or scream. Dan's firm grip on her hand steadied her. Maureen was dead. Tears sprang to her eyes. Dan handed her the tissue box from the end table and rubbed a circle of comfort into her back.

Steve spoke for her as she fought for control. "What makes you think she still lives there? I can vouch for her whereabouts and so can Dan."

"We found a closet full of clothes and this note on her bed." The agent handed her a paper in an evidence bag.

Isabella found her voice. "This is a page from my diary. The note I wrote the day I left said I needed to move on, nothing more. I left most of the clothes she bought for me and took a cab to the airport."

"Did you empty her bank accounts before leaving."

"I transferred *my* bank account to a bank in Missouri."

"Why not here?"

"I hadn't changed my name yet. That was still in my married name. It was easier and safer to transfer the funds to an existing account until I got established here. I left our joint account. There was ten thousand dollars in it."

"And you say that was six months ago?"

"Her sister can verify it. Ms. Wilson lived with her before she moved here." Steve's confident tone and Dan's presence made this nightmare easier to bear.

"If you can give contact information for her sister and anyone else who can verify her statement, that would be helpful." The balding guy took over the questions. "Are you sure of the amount remaining in the joint account?"

"I have receipts and bank statements to prove it. What's this all about?"

"It's an ongoing investigation. So, we're not at liberty to elaborate. You are her only next of kin?"

"I guess." The revelation startled her. She needed to return to Indiana and bury Maureen. Then smile at the church ladies and explain her absence. "I don't know why the FBI is involved. Was she murdered?"

"Her death is not our concern." The young man's tone off-putting.

"What is your concern?" Dan spoke for the first time. "I think it's strange the first contact Isabella receives is the FBI at her door. And you claim you're not here to talk about Maureen's death."

The younger agents jaw tightened and his fist clenched and unclenched triggering another low growl from Brutus.

The older agent answered. "All we can say is we think Mrs. Marklin was involved in money laundering."

"What?" Isabella jaw gape open for a nano second. "That's impossible."

"Oh, it's very possible." The younger agent's voice tinted with anger.

"Excuse me..." Steve interrupted. "I didn't catch your name or your partners."

A long pause rested between them before the shorter one said. "Farnsworth. I'm agent Farnsworth and this is Agent Benton."

"Well, Agents Farnsworth and Benton if you could leave us your card, I'll see you get everything you need." Steve rose and folded his arms staring at the men.

Agent Benton fumbled around in his jacket pockets. The whole time eyeing Brutus. Dan held the dog's collar keeping him from any sudden moves. "Sorry, forgot mine."

"I left mine at the office." Officer Farnsworth took out a piece of paper and jotted a number. "Call me when you have what we need. We appreciate your cooperation." Turning to Isabella "Sorry for disturbing you."

The two left to the sound of Brutus' ever-increasing growl.

Steve stood at the window with his cell. He snapped a picture then typed a note.

"What's up. Bro?" Dan and Brutus came to his side.

"Got the plate number. Bet it's bogus."

"You thought they were phony too."

"As a wooden nickel."

"They're not FBI agents?" Isabella joined them at the window. The street lights had come on and a boy was skateboarding down his porch steps and up a homemade ramp.

"If your mother-in-law was dead, the police have a protocol for tracking down next of kin. The Aurora Police or the Indiana cops would have contacted you." Dan took her hand.

"They didn't have business cards." Steve crossed his arms as he put the facts together. "And did you get their names?"

"What about their names?" A shiver cascade through Isabella.

"Farnsworth and Benton are main streets here in town." Dan shook his head. "Not too bright."

"Well, they fooled me. I haven't lived her long enough to remember street names." She knelt and snuggled Brutus. "If it wasn't for you...well, I don't know what might have happened." Isabella held her hand up to keep Brutus wet kisses at bay. "I would have told them everything and believed I was guilty of something." She rose from the floor. "Thanks for coming, too, Steve. I didn't know any other lawyers."

"I'm not a criminal lawyer but you won't need one." Steve dialed 911. "I'm reporting those guys"

"Is there anyone you can call to check on your mother-in-law?" Dan's practical question calmed her.

"I don't have any numbers for the neighbors on my phone. Isabella opened the laptop she'd left on the dining room table. It took a few moments to find the church's website and the pastor's number. While she dialed, panic rose in her chest. Brutus nuzzled close guiding her to the couch. She sat and Dan joined her, placing his arm around her shoulder.

"Pastor Reid this is Melinda Marklin." After a few moments of niceties explaining she lived in Illinois now and had reclaimed her maiden name, she put the phone on speaker and got to the point. "Can you do me a favor and check on Maureen? I heard she was dead."

The pastor sucked in his breath before answering. "Where did you hear that?"

"Let's just say an unreliable source. If you could check for me, it would save Maureen the embarrassment of having the police knock on her door."

"What if she doesn't answer? It's a little late to go calling." The pastor's tone reluctant.

"She's always up until 2AM. If she doesn't answer, there is a key under the puppy statue near the evergreen bush at the corner of the porch."

Isabella left her number. After she hung up, she realized Pastor Reid hadn't mentioned having Maureen return the call. Did he fear she was dead or did he know the truth about Maureen's mental state? As much as that woman put her through, Isabella never once wished her dead. Every night she'd pray God would provide the help Maureen needed to get better.

"Are you OK?" Dan's voice startled her out of her musings.

"Not really." Isabella leaned into his shoulder. "Keep me close."

DAN STROKED HER HAIR. Grateful God had answered prayer otherwise Brutus would not have been with Isabella. "I'm not going anywhere, sweetheart." Her tears wet his shirt as he held her tight. Her heart beat against his chest. A floral scent lingered on her skin. The closeness filled a longing in his heart. Please, God, let her see how much I care for her.

The doorbell rang. Dan released Isabella and leashed Brutus, signaling him to stay. He obeyed and Steve opened the door ushering in two Aurora police officers. Brutus eyed them but remained still.

The female officer spoke first. "I'm officer Hadley and this is my partner Officer Collins."

"We're here to take your statements." Officer Collins placed his clipboard on the dining table.

Isabella joined them to give her statement. Steve and Dan took their turns next.

"We'll run the plates." Officer Hadley gave Isabella her card.

"We'll check out the phone number and send our information to the FBI tomorrow." Officer Collins rose from his place. "Hopefully, we'll have some leads."

"Don't you call in a sketch artist or give us mug shots to look at?" Dan knew he could identify the guys.

"We'll contact you for the next step." Officer Collins turned to leave.

"Isabella is an artist. She could make some sketches." Dan pressed. No way was this thing getting swept under the rug.

"Sure. Bring them by tomorrow and leave them at the front desk." Officer Hadley said.

"If you recall anything else, give us a call."

Before the officers left, Isabella's cell phone rang. She noted the number. "This is the pastor checking on my mother-in-law." Everyone waited as she answered the call.

"Yes." Isabella's face unreadable as she listened to the caller.

Thank you for that." She kept nodding but made no response. "Yes, thank you so much."

Ending the call, she looked at the group. "She's not dead. They found her confused with a large bump on her head. A pool of blood on the carpet. An ambulance took her to the hospital."

"We'll call the Mooresville Police to follow up." Officer Hadley trailed her partner to the door. "Again, call if you remember anything else. We'll let the front desk know you're bringing sketches."

The officers left and Steve rose and gave Isabella a hug. "Why don't we meet tomorrow before you go over to the police station. I want to see the drawings first. Say nine."

"Sounds like a plan." Isabella held her hand on her chest.

Dan placed a protective arm around her shoulder.

"I'll drive you."

"Good. I'll meet you guys there" Steve headed out the door dialing his cell as he left. "Mindy, honey...."

Dan watched his friend leave. "Are you going be OK?"

"No." Isabella shook.

He wrapped her in his arms. Pulling her close. Her tears flowed with

abandon once again as Brutus squeezed in close offering comfort, licking the
hand that hung at her side. "I can't believe this...," More sobs. Dan remained
silent as he guided her back to the sofa. She grabbed more tissue and dabbed
her tears and blew her nose. "I guess I need to go back and help Maureen. She
has no one else. It's my fault she's hurt." Her wounded eyes fixed on him before
she moved out of his arms leaving space between them on the couch.

"How is this your fault?" Dan's sharp tone reflected his irritation at her
accusation. He understood how guilt played tricks on rational thought.

"I wasn't there to prevent this." Isabella shredded the tissue in her hand.

"How self-righteous of you." Dan crossed his arms.

"What is that supposed to mean?" Isabella clenched her fists at her side.

"You really think you could have kept her from being hurt? Did it ever think
maybe God brought you here to kept you from being injured or killed?" Dan
kept his arms crossed resisting the urge to shake sense into her. Brutus brush
up against him.

Isabella sniffled and stared at the floor. "Maybe I could have prevented her
from doing whatever she did to get herself hurt."

"Think. All the stuff she hid from you. Maybe this thing she's involved in
started before you left."

"Maybe you're right." Isabella flopped backward on the couch. "I need to do
something"

Dan grabbed a chair and sat it in front of her. Lowering himself into it, he
took her hand. "What do you want to do?"

"Hide in a hole." She dabbed her eyes, giving a frustrated smile.

"I get that."

"Perhaps I should go back and check on her."

"Move back?" Dan held his breath waiting for the answer.

"No." The one word came out sharp. "I've found myself here. I don't want to
go back. But..."

"You need to face your past."

"Yeah."

"I'll go with you."

"You can't. You've got school, a job, your uncle."

"Semester ends next week. I can take a few days off work and Uncle Paul
doesn't need me to babysit him."

Isabella's gentle smile tugged at his heart. "You'd do that for me."

"Baby, whatever you need, I have your six."

She chuckled at his declaration and planted a kiss on his cheek. "You are so
good for me."

29

FACING FEARS

Dan held Isabella's hand as they walked into the mental health wing of Community Memorial. Dan's limp pronounced after hours in the car. A throbbing pain matched the rhythm of his stride. Isabella's grip tightened when they reached the service desk.

"I'm Isabella Wilson. We're here to see Maureen Macklin." She pushed her hair behind her ears causing the hoop earrings to dance for a second.

The clerk, a middle-aged black woman in neat business attire check her computer. Her name tag read Denise. Dan's skin became clammy. He'd spent time in the Psyche ward when he returned from his first tour. A few weeks learning how to deal with PTSD. Dan caught himself beginning the breathing techniques for his panic attacks. *Hold it together, Sweeney.* Brutus was keeping his uncle company. *You can do this.*

"Mrs. Macklin is in room 419. There is a note here that Dr. Prentiss wants to meet with you before you visit her." Denise reached for the phone. "Take a seat while I let him know you're here. It might be awhile if he's in session."

Dan watched Isabella shrink as they walked toward a sofa near the windows. He sat next to her. "You can do this."

Isabella shook her head.

He stroked her cheek. "Talk to me." His hand moved to guide her face to look at him.

"After Ron died, I came here three times a week for counseling. Maureen tried to persuade the doctor to admit me." A sigh escaped her lips. Her eyes gloss over with unshed tears. "Now, she's the one admitted." A small smile formed on her lips then disappeared. "It'd be laughable if it wasn't so sad."

"Ms. Wilson?" Denise rose from her seat, leaned over and pointed. "Dr. Prentiss is waiting for you. Third door on your right."

Isabella rose and helped Dan rise from the too soft chair. He held his shame in check. Together they walked down the hall to the designated door. Her grip on his hand painful. Dan pulled his hand free and placed his arm around her shoulder. "Relax. It's not about you."

Her eyes sparkled. "How do you read my mind?"

"I was reading my own mind. I was in a place like this once too" Dan squeezed her shoulder. "Relax, you are not the patient."

They reached the doctor's office and stood for a moment. He opened the door waiting for her to enter first.

A man with salt and pepper hair with welcoming blue eyes rose from behind his desk. "Ms. Wilson, I'm Brad Prentiss. Please, please sit." He indicated the chairs in front of the desk.

"This is my... boyfriend Dan Sweeney. He's here for moral support." Dan schooled his face at her declaration as he shook Dr. Prentiss hand.

"I wanted to talk with you before you saw Maureen. She's been asking for you. Her severe head injury has complicated her mental state. Coherent conversation can be difficult. Are you aware of her bi-polar disorder?"

"Sort of. I lived with her for a year after my husband died. Although she didn't talk about her mental health, I googled her medications. Her erratic behavior was alarming."

"We have done a thorough physical and mental evaluation. We've discovered early onset Alzheimer's. The head injury magnified her mental issues. As I said, she has been asking for you but may not know you. Her sister visits every day. Sometimes Maureen recognizes Ann. Some days not. Be prepared for the latter. She's had a bad day."

"Is Ann here?"

"She was here this morning."

"Can someone give her my cell number?"

"." Dr. Prentiss passed a pad of paper across the desk. Isabella jotted her number. "We'll be in town a few days."

Dr. Prentiss led them down the hall. "This is an observation room." He opened a door and ushered them in. "There's cameras in here. We can watch her reaction."

"Is that necessary?"

"The police requested we pass on any information that might relate to their ongoing investigation. Technically, your mother-in-law is under house arrest."

"Why?" Isabella paled and stared at the camera in the corner.

"Information regarding a gambling ring or something. The police have been informed you are here. Together we will be watching Maureen' responses from the adjoining room."

Dan's jaw twitched. "You're joking? What happened to doctor-patient confidentiality?"

"Before she was attacked, she was cooperating with the police. After the attack during a lucid moment, she signed a release form. I'm not privy to all the details. But she wants to help the police."

"Can we speak to the officers?" Isabella found her voice.

"I'll send them in before I have Maureen brought in."

Dan watched the doctor leave. "This is surreal."

"No kidding." Isabella paced the small room. "I can't believe I was so self-absorbed not to see her needs. I even forgot she had a sister. What kind of daughter-in-law acts like that?"

"One grieving her own loss. Let it go, Babe."

"It's so hard."

"I know." Dan reached to comforted her when the door flew open.

A tall black man in a gray suit entered followed by a short Asian man in a sports coat. They both showed their credentials. Allowing Isabella ample time to see the IDs.

The Asian officer spoke first. "I'm Detective Ho. This is Detective Simons. He signaled for them to sit at the table near the observation window. He opened his file.

"Mrs. Marklin came to us with a confession last month. She has been working with us to get information on an illegal gambling and identity theft ring."

Detective Simons stood near the counter and removed the lid from his Starbuck's cup then reached for the coffee carafe. "It seems her conscious bothered her after she attended a religious women's conference." He replaced the cup lid and joined his partner at the table before continuing. "Were you aware she has a gambling problem?"

"No—yes, I suspected maybe." She hugged herself, eyes glistening.

Detective Ho added. "When she got in so deep she couldn't pay, they asked her to steal credit information from her friends."

"This is unbelievable." Isabella sat opened mouth for a moment shaking her head. Dan sensed her confusion and stepped into the interview.

"How was she supposed to do that?"

"The men gave her a phone that cloned credit cards and bank account numbers on smartphones." Ho referred to his file. "Maureen was attacked before she could give us the names of the men."

"She texted us for a meetup and never showed." Simons took a sip from his Starbucks' cup and frowned before continuing. "She didn't respond to any texts or calls for several hours. The 911 call from her home helped us find her again."

Dan stared at the officers. *What kind of knucklehead doesn't protect a witness?* "Why didn't you go to her house when she didn't answer?"

"We did. There was no one home." Detective Ho's irritation with Dan's interference showed on his face. "We had no reason to enter her home uninvited."

"We speculate the men found out she was cooperating with the police and abducted her." Simons read from his file.

"Then they returned her to her home to fake a suicide."

"How is hitting her in the head a suicide?" Isabella's angry tone surprised Dan.

"She hit her head fighting off the men trying to shove her prescription drugs down her throat. She put up quite a fight. During the struggle, she banged her head on the corner of the coffee table. It's a miracle she didn't die."

"Per the medical report the head injury accelerated the Alzheimer's. We are hoping you might get her to mention the names of her attackers."

"I can try." Isabella looked to Dan. He nodded.

SHE WATCHED THE DETECTIVES LEAVE. Dan squeezed her hand sending confidence into her fearful heart. A desperate prayer for strength and wisdom shot heavenward waiting for Maureen to enter. Her palms were damp and she loosens her grip on Dan's hand to wipe them on her beige slacks. The toe of her brown slingback tapped a nervous rhythm and her purple scarf felt like a noose around her neck.

"I'm going to sit over here, out of the way." Dan rose, pushed in the chair and moved to the one at the farthest end of the table. Loneliness and vulnerability seeped back into her heart with each action. She wanted his hand in hers. She needed him close. The six-foot distance, miles.

"Why move?"

"Maureen might be intimidated by a strange."

Isabella drank in the compassion in his eyes.

"If you need...," Dan's unfinished statement said more than a thousand encouraging words. He had her six. The phrased made her smile. Dan would protect her. Her self-esteem had grown under his sincere encouragement. Fear had less control in his presence.

Maureen entered, accompanied by a female aid whose name tag read Zoe. The thirty-something CNA appeared stout next to her charge's thin frame. Isabella kept a gasp in check at her mother-in-law, disheveled and wrinkled appearance. A sharp contrast to her former self. Maureen never left the house unless every hair was in place and her makeup perfect. Bare-faced she looked twenty years older. Her black hair streaked with gray and in need of styling.

"Maureen, how are you?" Isabella smiled and reached for her.

Recoiling toward the aid Maureen shrieked. "Stay away." Her hands flayed the air. "Stay away."

"Now, now, Maureen." Zoe gave her a hug until she calmed. "This is your daughter-in- law Isabella."

"Who?"

"I'm Melinda."

Maureen stared at her. "Melinda? You've changed? What happened to your long hair?" She reached toward her than recoiled back. "I hated that hair. This style is no better. Guess it won't matter how you look. I hate you."

The words stung Isabella. She fought back tears. Maureen's face transformed from fearful to hateful in a nanosecond. Her eyes ablaze.

"Don't take her words to heart, ma'am." Zoe escorted Maureen to the table. "Sit over there. I'll bring coffee. Sometimes she's in a more congenial mood when she thinks she's entertaining. The woman filled paper cups from the coffee carafe. She signaled for Dan to join them. After placing a plate of Oreos on the table along with cream and sugar, she knelt to Maureen's eye-level and took her hand. Miss Maureen, you have company. They've traveled a long way to visit you today."

Maureen's eyes softened. She reached into the neckline of her three layers of blouses to retrieve her pearl necklace. Touching the family heirloom changed her demeanor. She stroked it, a smile brightening her sad, confused face.

"I am delighted to see you, Melinda. My, my, how you have changed. It's been years since we've had coffee together." She extended the plate of cookies. Isabella took one. "Who is this shaggy lady killer you have with you?" Maureen winked at Dan.

Isabella watched Dan's eyes laugh as he shook her hand.

"Dan Sweeney, ma'am."

How could he be so calm when her skin crawled in this place.

Maureen's smile transformed her face.

"A man with manners. How delightful." She held the plate out to him. "Dan Sweeney." She stretched out the name on her tongue. "Dan Sweeney. My son Jeffery's best friend was a Dan Sweeney."

"In the flesh."

"My, my, what a wonderful treat. Have you seen Jeffrey?"

"No ma'am."

"I miss him so much." She swiped a tear and smiled. "He's singing with the angels now." Sipping her coffee, she added. "Did you know he's releasing a new CD next month? He promised to send me a copy."

Isabella's heart ached. How sad. This once vibrant woman reduced to a confused state. "How have you been?"

"I am blessed and highly favored of the Lord. He has taught me whatever state I'm in to be content."

The words were ones Isabella heard Maureen recite often. This time, they lacked the haughty sting.

"Tell me, Melinda, what brings you here. I know we did not part on the best of terms. I am so sorry for that."

Tears formed in Isabella's eyes. "I am too." She cherished the sincere apology knowing any moment anger could take its place.

Everyone sipped coffee in silence for a moment.

"Maureen, can you tell me about the night those men attacked you?"

Her mother-in-law frowned and her lips twitched before she took another sip of her coffee. "This isn't the worst coffee I've ever drank. I remember a lady's luncheon I attended once. Sadie Worley made the coffee." A chuckle interrupted her tale. "Now that was terrible coffee." Maureen rose from her seat and went to the window. She stared out at the parking lot for several minutes.

"I remember that night. It terrifies my dreams." She turned to face Isabella. "You sent them, didn't you?" A snarl arose from her throat.

The aid jumped to her side. "Now, now, let's finish our coffee." Maureen allowed herself to be seated again. Her chin quivered. "There were three men. The first one was tall and always wore sunglasses. They called him Jerry. The second was short and bald, they called him Bill."

Isabella pulled the sketches from her purse. "Are these the men?"

Maureen flattenened out the centerfold, examining the images before her. "That's them. Except their eyes were full of evil. They told me if I didn't get them what they needed, they'd send me straight to hell."

"The men threatened you?" Dan's question caused another chin quiver from Maureen.

"Yes." Her voice took on strength again. "But I went to the police and confessed my sin. God was faithful to forgive my sin and cleanse me from all unrighteousness. Being a righteous woman, I wanted to help the police catch the devil himself." She crossed her arms and nodded.

"Did you catch the devil?" Dan continued to probe while Isabella fought tears. The roller coaster of emotions played out by Maureen, a woman she no longer knew, scared her. Her fingers sought Dan's. He leaned closer, covering her hand with his.

Maureen gave her full attention to Dan. She nodded. "I got his name. He was big and scary. He knew I was going to tell the police. The three of them stopped my car and pulled me out. They threw me in a dark place. Then I was home fighting for my life. I cried out to God. I screamed for help. Then everything went black. When I woke up Kasper Bolton, and the others were gone." Maureen dipped an Oreo in her coffee. "Jeff always loved these. He'd dipped them in milk. That boy could eat a whole box."

"Are you sure his name was Kasper Bolton?" Isabella had found her voice.

"Who?" Maureen smiled. "Melinda, you say the oddest things. I thought your friend said his name was Dan."

Isabella and Dan finished their coffee as Maureen continued to flit from topic to topic with no more signs of aggression. "I'm ready for my nap." Maureen reached for her aid who escorted her out of the room.

As the door closed Isabella burst into tears. Dan pulled her into his arms as the detectives entered the room. The men stood in awkward silence giving her time to compose herself.

"Thank you, Ms. Wilson. Your presence helped confirm the name she'd repeated to her sister yesterday." Detective Simons waited for Isabella to respond.

Dan handed her a tissue from a box on the table. She wiped her eyes and blew her nose. "That was the hardest thing I've ever done."

"You did a fine job." Detective Ho held passed them papers. "These are release forms. We need your signatures. You are giving us permission to use this recorded statement."

"Who is Kasper Bolton?" Dan asked as he signed the paper.

"He's wanted by the FBI for identity theft, illegal gambling. money laundering, extortion to name a few." Detective Ho placed their release forms in the folder. "Thank you for your help." He shook their hands as did his partner and left before Dan or she could ask another question.

Isabella clung to Dan for several minutes before she took his hand, collected her purse, and headed for the truck. Not until they'd exited the hospital did she speak. "I wished you'd brought Brutus."

"Brutus gets car sick."

"Oh."

"I know he has a calming effect on you, too."

Isabella's phone chimed inside her purse. Dan unlocked the truck doors just as she found her phone. She pressed the answer button as she climbed in the truck.

"Hello."

"Melinda, this is Aunt Ann."

30

RESTORATION

Isabella directed Dan to Maureen's house.

"You Ok, Babe?" Dan wondered if Isabella even noticed his term of endearment. He'd watched their relationship change with this crisis. His military training made him good in a crisis. Would her feeling toward him change when this was over? His peripheral vision watched her as they neared Maureen's home. She'd not closed her eyes. He flicked his vision toward the road, the rear-view mirror and back to her for a moment. "Isabella." Dan nudged her with his three fingers "Honey, you, all right?"

"What? Yes, no. I'll be ok."

"Breath, Babe. Maureen isn't in that house. You've got nothing to fear. You can do this."

She squeezed his right hand. "Sorry for bringing you into this. But you help me be strong." Isabella released his fingers and watched the road. "Three more blocks than a left." Her hand signaled. "The Maureen I knew is gone. Her hateful words didn't sting as much as they used to, knowing she is ill. I wish I'd been stronger. Maybe I could have gotten her help earlier."

"Woulda, shoulda, couldas never makes the present better. It was what it was, Isabella. Let it go."

She nodded, her jaw tense. Maureen's spacious home loomed before them as his truck pulled into the driveway.

"Take your time. We'll get out whenever you're ready." He watched her close her eyes and take a cleansing breath.

"I'm ready." She squeezed his fingers again. "Thanks."

Before they could knock on the door a short woman with salt and pepper hair wearing jeans and a red boat neck top greeted them. "Melinda." Her eyes sparkled. "You look wonderful. Come in, come in."

Closing the door behind them, she smiled again giving Dan the once over. "I'm Ann Rogers, Maureen's baby sister."

"Dan Sweeney, ma'am." He shook her hand.

"Manners. A military man?"

"Yes, ma'am. Army."

"Thank you for your service and being here for Melinda." Her thank you didn't evoke unworthiness from Dan but rather confidence in his ability to help the woman he loved.

"Aunt Ann, if you don't mind, I prefer Isabella." Her voice matter-of -fact.

"Isabella suits you better." Ann pointed to a floral couch. "Sit, sit, let me get coffee and we can have a chat."

Dan noticed myriads of pictures covering the walls and table tops. It was obvious Maureen loved her son. Only the wedding photo, declared Isabella's existence. The furnishing spoke of better days, worn and faded. Stale cigarette scent lingered in the air. Dan's nose wrinkled.

"You noticed it too," Isabella whispered. "She was a closet smoker. Never wanted to admit it. The bathroom and the den got bad when she was stressed. She wore strong cologne and gargled with mouthwash often to cover up her habit."

Ann balanced a tray with a coffee carafe, three cups and a plate of banana bread slices. She placed it on the coffee table. "Help yourself. There's cream, sugar and sugar substitute."

Ann took a cup and sat in the chair opposite them. "Thank you so much for coming. After the way she treated you, it must be difficult to be here. More than anyone I know how she can be. I apologize for not coming to visit while you lived here." Ann sipped her coffee.

"It was fine." Isabella's smile didn't reach her eyes.

"No, it wasn't. I dumped her on you. After caring for Maureen, I wanted to get on with my own life. I'd visited every week, twice a week for years. Once you and Jeff moved to town, I came less often." Ann placed her cup on the end table and held her hand over her heart. "My sister wasn't always like this. After our mother died, she raised me."

Ann pulled out a photo album and showed them pictures from childhood. Pointing to a soldier's picture she sighed.

"Dad went over the edge into mental illness when our older brother died in Vietnam."

Ann stroked the picture and closed the album.

"He took his own life when I was 15. Maureen was away at college. She came home for me. Maureen was a strong woman. When I went off to college, she finished her nursing degree. Then she married Ron senior and had Angela."

"Ron had a sister?"

"Angela died of crib death at 6 months. That's when my sister changed. After Jeff was born, her postpartum depression made things worse. A few years later she surrendered her nursing license rather than go to prison for stealing prescription drugs" Sorrow itched her face as she shared her sister's secrets.

"Her paranoia got worse. Ron senior divorced her the next year when she kept Jeff locked in the house. She refused to see a doctor. The courts awarded Ron custody. That's when she tried to take her life."

Isabella paled at the revelation. Dan placed his arm around her.

"My husband and I moved in for a while. I took her to a psychiatrist. When he wanted to commit her, she refused to go back. "Ann took up her cup.

. It was years before Maureen admitted she needed help. By then she'd gambled away every dime she made at every job she couldn't hold. I bought this house after my husband died and put Maureen in it. I pay the utilities and taxes. She collects disability social security and I give her an allowance."

"She said she received an annuity from her father's estate." Isabella's face unreadable.

"Well, she was always more comfortable with her illusion."

"Ron seldom talked about you." This time, Isabella's voice a whisper. The emotional roller coast this visit evoked worried Dan. Who would Isabella be at the end of the day?

"We saw little of each other once he left for college." Aunt Ann said.

"Maureen insisted I not visit if Jeff was home. She was afraid I'd tell tales out of school and upset her delusion of wellness. She was a great actress around her son." Ann offered the plate of banana bread. Dan took a slice, Isabella shook her head.

"Jeff and I were very close once. After his dad died...did you know he had the same kind of tumor?" Isabella shook her head, Dan sensed her distress and squeezed her shoulder. She leaned into him. Ann took another sip of her coffee. "Ronnie put off surgery, he was afraid. Afraid he wouldn't be able to care for Jeff. Afraid Maureen would file for custody if she knew. He kept putting it off. His excuses, a busy work schedule and Jeff activities left him no time. The surgery had a 95% success rate. But if he were in the 5% he'd lose custody of his son."

"I had no idea." Isabella looked at the floor in front of her. Dan knew she was hiding tears.

"We were all surprised by the heart attack. Jeff never knew about his dad's prognosis. He asked me not to tell him. I had no idea he had a tumor because Maureen didn't mention it." Ann said. "The one thing Ronnie and Maureen had in common—they kept their secrets, even from Jeff."

Isabella found her voice. "Did you know he and Maureen kept his tumor a secret from me?"

"Doesn't surprise me. Maureen called me to complain about you. During her rant, it slipped out about the tumor and how you'd found out."

All this new information danced through Dan's mind like the dust bunnies in the sunlight streaming on the worn carpet. *Father, help Isabella be strong.* His mind came back to the conversation.

"I'm so very sorry you had to live with her deceptions. If I'd not moved to Florida, I'd have stepped in even if it made my sister angry." Tears formed in Ann's eyes. "Can you forgive me?"

Isabella leaped from her seat and hugged Ann. "I don't blame you. You're braver than me. A year with Maureen was suffocating. I don't know how you stayed sane all those years."

"For one I wasn't grieving a loss. I had the support of a good husband and I know my sister as well as I know myself. I've watched her struggle with her mental illness for years." Ann patted Isabella before releasing the hug. "Why did you stay?"

"Guilt."

"Jeff's death wasn't your fault."

"I know. But a part of me felt if I'd been a better wife...I'd packed my bags to leave him the Sunday he died."

"Oh, sweetie." Ann hugged her again.

Isabella wept and Ann whispered assurances. Dan's heart ached over how much Jeff had wounded her. How paralyzed she had become with guilt. Ann's words seemed to be getting through.

"Dearest child, on behalf of my sister I ask your forgiveness. Maureen told me in her more lucid moments, how sorry she was. She cried bitter tears for driving you away with her deception. You were her last connection to Jeff."

Ann handed a tissue to Isabella.

"After you left, she went back to the doctor. I flew up and went with her.

She was afraid to go alone. When we heard the early onset Alzheimer's diagnosis, we made plans for her to move to Florida."

Ann took her seat again and sipped her coffee before continuing.

"I should have taken her with me right then. Instead, we decided I should find a place first. That's when, her gambling addiction got the best of her. She confessed the whole sorted mess at a women's retreat. Her pastor promised to watch over her while I made arrangements. We both knew I needed to move fast."

"I should have..." Isabella stopped when Ann held up her hand.

"I believe God gave you the strength to leave so Maureen would face her sin. If you had stayed, it would have over time destroyed both of you. It's God's mercy Maureen wasn't murdered by those evil men."

Ann and Isabella shuddered in tandem. Dan stroked Isabella's back. Silence held them captive for a moment. Ann found her voice again fixing her eyes on Isabella.

"God has this whole matter in His hands. Don't you even try to pull responsibility out of the Almighty's hands and take it on yourself. All is forgiven. Maureen is getting the care she needs."

Isabella wiped her tears.

When Isabella returned to sit beside him, Dan sensed her change. Her touch tender and relaxed. "You ok, hon?"

"Yes. Now I am." She smiled and rested her head on his shoulder for a moment. "Aunt Ann, how are you going to get Maureen to Florida. Do you need help?"

"Maureen always said she'd love to live in a hotel with room service. I've told her I was flying her to her dream hotel. She is looking forward to it. As far as this place, the ladies from her Bible Study are packing up most of the stuff for their garage sale. I'll pack photos and things that belonged to our family and ship them home. Ralph Sparks will be the realtor for the sale."

"He attends Resurrection. He was always kind to me." Isabella gathered up the cups. "I'll wash these." She took the dishes to the sink.

Busy hands were Isabella's way of processing all she'd learned. In the months since they'd met, he'd learned so much about her. Not so much in words. Their connection in the spirit was strong. If soul mates are real, he'd found his. There wasn't anything he wouldn't do for this woman washing dishes in the house where so much pain surrounded her.

"Isabella, take anything you'd like." Ann put the dishes away.

"I might take a picture or two." Isabella placed the last cup in the drying rack. "The thing I would love to have is my wedding dress. It had been my Mom's. And there was my Grandmother's brooch. But Maureen sold them."

"Come with me." Ann took Isabella's hand. "I want to show you something."

~

DAN NODDED ENCOURAGEMENT but remained on the couch. She took his courage with her.

Ann showed her into Maureen's bedroom. A place off -limits to her. Maureen had kept it locked. The walls filled with pictures of Ron's father and Maureen in their younger years. Pictures of a tiny baby in pink sat on the dresser. Boxes cluttered the floor. Ann maneuvered around the mess to open the closet door. Isabella followed her. A once spacious walk-in closet burst with clothes, shoes, and Rubbermaid containers. Ann pulled out a container marked Melinda's dress. She placed it on the bed and removed the lid.

"Oh, my." Tears form as she extracted the wedding dress from the container. "It's a little wrinkled but..."

"That can be remedied, child." Ann hugged her shoulder. "Maureen did love you. She knew this dress was special. These containers are the few things she kept from the storage unit." Ann retrieved a small box from another container.

"Grandma's brooch." Isabella stroked the delicate pattern. "Why didn't she give these to me?"

"To ask is to answer."

"Right, that control thing." Isabella sighed as she pressed the dress to her. Closing her eyes, she took a moment to remember the joy of marrying Ron. Happy memories of his affection and care flooded her heart. *Thank you, Maureen, for not selling this.* Isabella placed the dress and brooch back in the container and sealed the lid. "My sister will be thrilled. She'll want to wear this too someday."

"Well, before you head home please take whatever you want. Most of the stuff belongs to me. That's why Maureen never sold any of it to pay her gambling debts. There's no place for this stuff in my condo. I found a few photo albums of Jeff and some of his awards." Ann reached over and patted her hand. "You don't have to take anything. I won't be offended."

"Thank you for stepping in to care for Maureen. I don't think I could have managed."

"Sweetie, this is my responsibility. She is my sister. I owe her this for all she's done for me." Ann lead the way from the room leaving the door standing open. "You go on with your life. Marry your new young man and have babies. Put the past behind you."

"He's not my young man. We're just friends." Hadn't she told the clerk at the hospital he was her boyfriend. What was wrong with her? She refocused her thoughts. "Maureen was my mother-in-law. That makes her family."

"True, but soon Maureen won't remember you. She'll be in a world from her past. Her caregivers will be the only family she remembers. The most helpful, loving thing you can do is pray for her."

"I will. But isn't there something ..."

"Nothing. Give your guilt to Jesus. Receive his cleansing grace and move on. You'll see her again in eternity and she'll be the delightful woman she once was."

Isabella joined Dan in the living room. She hoped he hadn't heard Ann's declaration for her future. *Lord, I receive your grace. I will continue to move forward. Tell me, Lord, is this wonderful man a part of my future? Can I trust him? Is he on the inside what he appears on the surface?* Isabella sat the container on the floor, no mention of its content.

THREE HOURS later the container and a few boxes were loaded into the truck bed. Isabella couldn't get Ann's comment out of her head. Had God given her a new young man? Dan's handsome profile drew her. She resisted the urge to stroke his bearded chin. *Lord, no matter our future together. Thank you for bringing Dan into my life when I needed a friend.*

31

NEW DUET

I sabella entered Stone Church sanctuary two hours before the special closing service began. Reverend Whitehall had given her his key. She savored the quiet solemnity as she made her way up the aisle to sit in the front row. Her eyes went to the stained-glass window behind the pulpit, admiring its intricate patterns of colored glass. Individually the pieces appeared useless. When a master craftsman joined each piece in a careful framework, sunlight reflected the magnificent colors around the room. A reminder of God's ability to take broken things and make them beautiful.

"Father, I'm amazed at the journey you've taken me on these last months. You've delivered me from fear and evil intent. Brought me wonderful friends, restored my love of art." Isabella almost pinched herself from the sizable check for her paintings. And a commission to create at least a dozen more. Teaching painting was the frosting on the cake of God's design. She bowed her head listening to the quiet.

"Today. Jesus, I am surrendering my musical gift. You know I never appreciated it because Ron was so critical. I've forgiven him. Thank you for helping me remember joyful times we had together. Helping Dan learn Ron's song has given me a new appreciation for the talent you gave him. Continue to help me forgive myself. I release those things that were out of my control. Ron made his choices. I forgive Maureen for thinking less of me. After all, I thought less of myself. Thank you for getting her the help she needs. Keep her safe in your care."

Isabella lifted her gaze once again to the prism of light. This church had been her sanctuary. Helping her heal. Today she'd encourage these sweet people to go forth and continue serving Jesus.

Footsteps echoed behind her. The familiar gait made her smile. She closed her eyes allowing her other senses to register memories. He smelled of musk, and the rustle of khaki pants against his titanium leg added to the rhythm of his pace. His rough palm touched her shoulder sending a delicious shiver down her spine.

"Hey." Dan's baritone whisper tickled her neck. Opening her eyes, she turned to gaze into the ocean blue of his eyes. "How are you feeling today?"

"Better, at peace." She patted the place beside her and Dan sat resting his arm on her shoulder. "I wanted to spend time with Jesus preparing my heart for today."

Together they sat in silence.

"It's hard to believe this is the last service." Dan squeezed her shoulder pulling her closer. "My uncle lead me to Jesus in this church."

Dan's voice choked as he continued. "If Dad hadn't taken Uncle Pauls' advice moving here when things got bad, he'd have never joined AA. Aunt Sally and Uncle Paul were a God- send. Mom knelt right there at the altar and let me lead her in the sinner's prayer. Together we prayed Dad back to church. He'd returned to Jesus a month before the car accident that took their lives."

Dan cleared his throat. "The ironic part—they were killed by a drunk driver." Dan shook his head and squeezed her hand. "Wow, I never realized how many things I recall based on the accident."

"It was a significant event." Isabella leaned on his shoulder. "Finding this church reconnected me with the church body and helped me heal. I have that as a focal point for great memories."

"There you are." Reverend Whitehall limped toward them. "No spooning in the sanctuary." Isabella felt her face warm matching the blush on Dan's cheeks.

Dan rose and gave his uncle a bear hug. "Are you ready to say goodbye?"

"Yes. I believe I am." Rev. Whitehall let his eyes roam the sanctuary. "Lots of wonderful memories I can hold in my heart forever."

"I was looking for you because I received a call from Amy. I assume you both have your cell phones off. Which is wonderful in the house of the Lord."

"Don't tell me she's sick." Panic grabbed Isabella. She stood looking at the elderly man.

"I'm afraid she had to leave town. Her grandmother died yesterday."

The panic gained momentum. "Oh, I wasn't planning—I can't sing today."

"You'll do fine." Dan squeezed her hand. "We could change the song."

"No, it's the perfect ending." Isabella knew she had to do this. Another step toward wholeness. "We've worked too hard to put this program together. Singing with Steve will be fine."

"Are you sure?" Dan moved his arm around her shoulder again.

"Well, he sings in an uncomfortable key for me. Other than that, I'm good." Isabella gave a teasing smile. "You're my Brutus, you know. You keep me from going off the deep end."

"Happy to serve." Dan kissed her forehead.

"Where is Brutus?"

"At home, I never bring him to church."

"Son, you know he is welcome. I know he keeps you grounded during stress. Feel free to go home and get him." Uncle Paul turned at the sound of others arriving to set things up for the service. "Excuse me."

"You have time to get him." Isabella said.

"Not a chance. Brutus loves to sing along."

Isabella giggled realizing why Dan never brought Brutus when he came to get help for Ron's song. "I'd like to see that sometime."

"If you think Steve's key is hard, try singing over Brutus."

DAN SAT in the front row tuning his guitar. He had a few minutes to warm up his fingers before people arrived. Wearing finger picks had made it possible for him to strum with his right hand. Although he was nervous, he looked forward to accompanying Isabella. He'd watched her guide the senior citizen choir through its paces. They'd never sounded better. Rather than sitting in his uncle's office to run through the song a few extra times he'd been drawn by the music. Her arrangements of familiar old hymns and an introduction of *Amazing Grace my Chains Are Gone* by Chris Tomlin blended together in a marvelous offering of praise to God. Isabella glowed as she applauded the choir when the practice was over.

"Are you ready?" Steve had left the piano and sat beside him. "She is in her element."

"For sure." Dan smiled at her transformation. "Would you believe she has never conducted a choir?"

"No way." Steve coughed so hard Dan reached over and patted his back.

"Where did that come from?"

Steve caught his breath after the cough subsided. "I've been fighting this since last night."

"Your plate's been too full."

"Yep. Brings it on every time."

"You ok doing the duet?"

"We'll see." Steve popped a cough drop in his mouth and took a swig from his water bottle.

The two joined Isabella on the platform to run through the song. She knew her part as if she'd practiced it a hundred times. Dan noted Isabella was right the key was too low for her. But she still sounded wonderful. It all fell apart when Steve modulated during the chorus. The hacking cough grabbed hold causing Steve to gasp for air when it ceased. "Danny, you got my six right." Steve's request came between gasps for air.

"You know it." Dan put down his guitar and went to find Steve's bag. "You brought your inhaler?"

After several sips of water Steve found his voice. "Won't help this. I have an antihistamine in there. It'll take too long to kick in. You gotta step up and do this."

Dan looked to Isabella for confirmation. "We've gone over sections together. You have a wonderful voice."

"Go for it. I can still accompany on piano." Steve said.

"Maybe you should play the guitar. Trade places?"

"No way. If I start to cough it won't be pretty. If I have throat issues at the piano Claudia can stop turning pages and play. I'm well supplied with cough drops."

Nervousness attacked him at the prospect of singing and playing the guitar, but for Isabella he'd give it a shot. "Please, father don't let me mess it up."

The service moved smoothly through choir selections, special readings by members of the church, a slide show capturing the history of Stone Church and a video of testimonies of former members of the youth group. Dan watched his uncle dab his eyes with the handkerchief he always kept handy. When it was time for the message, his uncle hobbled to the podium. His gray hair seemed grayer, his body more fragile but when he reached the microphone, his back straightened and the confident voice Dan had missed of late captured the audience.

"Today is not the end. It may be the end of worship in this wonderful old building. But it is not the end of worshiping our Lord. As in the time of the first century church, God scattered his people to spread the gospel. We have gotten too comfortable sitting here Sunday by Sunday following the same order of service, singing the same songs and praying the same prayers. We've not grown as a body in numbers or, I believe, in the spirit realm because we've hidden our gifts under a bushel called Stone Church traditions. Now God is calling us forth to use our gifts in new places. Wherever God is sending you in the coming months and years, find your place of service. Open your ears to learn and your heart to grow and let your light shine to all the world for his glory."

Tears formed in Dan's eyes as his uncle's voice broke with the declaration. Paul cleared his throat and sipped from the water glass he kept beneath the podium.

"Once I surrendered to God's will, he has filled me with peace. I am excited to discover God's next avenue of service for me. Whether it's sharing his love over a cup of coffee with an old friend or traveling around to RV camps to preach, I know God will continue to work his will in my life." Reverend White-hall raised his hand in blessing.

"Go and serve Jesus in greater measure."

Isabella and Dan made their way to the stage. Dan strummed the opening line. Isabella smiled at the key change. Together their voices blended as they declared they were bondservants of the Lord. Each verse intensified as the word brought conviction to his own heart. Dan knew he'd spent too much time trying to prove to the world he was whole. God had made him whole the moment he knelt at this very altar and surrendered his heart to Jesus. His voice captured the spirit behind the words, His heart held to the soul grasping melody.

∼

ISABELLA CLOSED her eyes as the opening notes lead to the first stanza. Her heart confessed as she sang that she'd been afraid—not so much of reliving the tragedy behind the song but her lack of faith in following Jesus after Ron's death. The two years leading up to his death had been wrought with frustration and anger toward all things Christian. Now as she sang her confession of being a bondservant for Christ, she once again felt the intimate moment when God's presence surrounded her. This time, more intense, more precious. Tears formed behind her closed lids but her voice remained strong. As the cleansing tears escaped to her cheeks, a vision of heaven came to rest in her mind. A reward for a life lived for Him. She knew despite Ron's illness God saw a heart of a bondservant. The truths of the lyrics moved through the auditorium as Dan sang the final line.

Isabella opened her eyes and stared at Dan whose face was wet with tears. The room erupted in hallelujahs and applause. Something Stone Church had never experienced. The crowd dismissed to the fellowship hall where

Reuland's Catering had provided a buffet. The young people helped put away the sound equipment. Steve and the others headed toward the fellowship hall. Dan and Isabella remained together at the front of the church. Dan took her hands in his. "Ron's lyrics got to me. I haven't felt this close to my savior since before my parents died."

"God's lyrics made Ron's melody a glorious thing. Ron wrote that melody as a new believer. But he never felt it was anything until God gave him those words. They need to be shared with the world."

"Are you going to record it?"

"Of course, not." Isabella shook her head. "I'm going to sell it to Hallelujah Press. They approached me after Ron died. But I wasn't in a good place then. Now it feels right. I have you to thank for that."

Dan's questioning eyes made her smile.

"You've been there as my rock and encourager."

"You're easy to encourage." Dan's hand stroked her cheek.

"I was wrong." Isabella placed her hand on Dan's causing his sweet caressing of her cheek to cease. "When I said I wanted nothing more than friendship, I was afraid, too wounded to be more. And you'd been wounded enough without taking on my baggage." Isabella moved his hand from her face and kissed his palm. "The truth. Fear covered my heart."

"You were afraid of me?"

"Afraid you would turn into the demanding self-centered man Ron became. Knowing he'd been ill didn't lessen my fear."

Dan pulled her to him. "I was afraid too. Afraid my disability marred me in your eyes. Afraid you'd run when you saw my struggles. Afraid you wouldn't be interested in half a man."

"We were both wrong." Isabella pulled Dan's face toward her. "You're not half a man. You're the man God has given me."

He responded with a kiss that confirmed his love. It spoke of the promise of protection and care. His tenderness made her feel worthy. The kiss deepened, and when Isabella thought she would dissolve into joyful particles on the floor Dan's kiss became feather light as he pulled away.

"Wonder what people will think of our first kiss being in the sanctuary?" Dan hugged her close and placed a second quick kiss on her lips.

"I think God is smiling. We sang a duet that honored Him. Now we want to move toward a life together that honors Him." Isabella adjusted her position to consider Dan's eyes. There she saw the love she'd felt in his kiss.

"Isabella Melinda Wilson I'd get down on my knee if I thought I could do it gracefully."

Isabella's hand covered a tiny gasp.

"Marry me." Dan pulled a ring from his pocket.

"How long have you been carrying that around?"

"Answer me first."

Silence reigned as his heart beat a frantic rhythm.

"Could we have a long engagement."

"I know you felt you married Ron too soon." Dan stroked her hand. "Let's not make it too long."

"This time next year?"

He placed the ring on her finger. "My uncle gave me Aunt Sally's engagement ring before we went to Indiana. It was my grandmother's." Dan kissed her again sealing the promise. "He was confident you were the one."

"Oh Dan, God has brought me full circle. You are my new duet."

Hand in hand they walked down the aisle, leaving at the altar the pain of the past to embrace a new future.

LOVING THE DOG GROOMER IS
COMING SOON

Keep reading for a free preview of the next book in this series of standalones.

LOVING THE DOG GROOMER
CHAPTER 1

Sugar Hill, Illinois

Chapter 1

"Man, you are in so much trouble." Marc Graham tugged the leash of the giant brown matted-haired dog. "Brownie, out of the car." The door to the Puppy Pamper Palace loomed ahead. "Come on." Marc's shoulders slumped. "What is it with you?"

Brownie leaped over the backseat into the back of the SUV, jerking the leash out of Marc's hands.

"Do you have radar or something?" He slammed the back door shut, stepped to the rear of the car, and raised the hatch. Brownie jumped into the back seat again and squeezed over the console into the front seat.

"Fine, be that way." Marc got back in the driver's seat, forcing the huge dog to scramble over the console again. Brownie settled himself on his blanket in the backseat. His lop-sided grin of satisfaction in the rearview mirror added to Marc's irritation.

"Lord, what am I going to do? You led me to this stupid mutt." This was the third time in a week he'd tried to get Brownie to a groomer. "If I had my way." His jaw tightened with frustration. "You'd still be at the pound." He slammed the car door, then clicked his seatbelt.

He wrinkled his nose and glanced back at Brownie, whose innocent eyes didn't acknowledge his contribution to the air pollution. "Really?" Marc gagged and cracked his window. "You just had to get into the garbage at home." The odor of dietary dilemma mixed with the unwashed pooch canceled the car deodorizer. "I could use a little help here." He raised his face heavenward for a moment before starting the car and moving on.

Turning left on Main Street, his eye caught a storefront with a large sign proclaiming Doggie Designer Duo and depicting a dog sitting happily under a hairdryer. Where had he heard of this place? The Sunday paper. Recalling the article's picture of a guy with a mustache and a tattooed forearm posing with a well-groomed poodle brought a chuckle. He'd won some award for grooming.

"Maybe that guy can deal with you." Marc smiled at the canine through the rearview mirror. Brownie sat up and stared out the window.

He parked in front of the shop. "Grammie said don't bring you home without a bath." He turned, making eye contact. "If not for me, do it for her. Do it for Tyler." Would his grandmother turn out his son's therapy dog? Maybe not, but Brownie didn't need to know that. Good grief he was giving the dog more credit for intelligence than the mutt deserved.

Marc opened the back door, sweeping his hand in a downward motion. Brownie came out without a fuss.

"Now you comply." He grabbed the leash, then squatted to get on the dog's level. "Tyler needs you, I get that. You're the only reason he sleeps at night. But I need you to cooperate." Brownie slapped his face with a soggy tongue. Marc grimaced and wiped his cheek. "I hope that's a yes."

He tugged on the leash, and the two headed toward the door.

***

Bria Willis opened the back door of Doggie Designer Duo Salon. She'd spent the morning grooming the newest arrivals at BowWow Rescue. The two Cocker Spaniel mixes had hot spots, infected areas that needed a vet's care, Both dogs had damaged paw pads from neglect. They'd been rescued from a puppy mill where the dogs spent their days in cages.

Making the two more comfortable by bathing and grooming them brought her more joy than any charity event she'd held in her former life. And now that she was President of BowWow Rescue's board, she hoped to make a bigger impact.

Bria noted the hair around a dog grooming station as she passed through the shop. The barks of dogs waiting in crates for their parents echoed in the room. She smiled at her burley brother and partner in the front lobby.

"How's the schedule look, Aaron?" She removed the scrunchie from her ponytail and pulled it tighter, refastening it as she entered the front of the grooming shop.

At the counter, her brother leaned toward the computer screen while standing with the phone to his ear. "Can you bring Bucky in at ten tomorrow?"

His nose wrinkled, and his brows arched as he listened to his client. "Yes, I have the pink dye. He'll look fantastic, I promise."

Bria grinned and shook her head, visualizing Bucky's new do. Shelves full of trophies decorated the wall behind the counter, declaring Aaron a master groomer. She admired his creative talent but found her niche as Doggie Designer Duo's more conservative groomer. Bria picked up the picture of the grand opening of the shop off the top shelf behind the counter. She'd returned to her hometown five years ago, emotionally broken. Her brother had taken her on as his assistant, and now they were equal partners. If not for his loving support, she'd have never survived. Life surrounded by canines who loved and needed her was fulfilling.

Aaron nodded and uh-hummed a few times before he laid the phone in the cradle. "Poor Bucky."

"Mrs. Archer wants her labradoodle pink?" Bria came around the counter and tried to peek over his broad shoulders at the schedule on the screen. She nudged him, and he moved.

"Yeah, something about looking his best for her daughter's princess party." Aaron laughed and scrolled down the screen. "Yep, that was my last appointment. Pick-up for the last three dogs should be within the hour. All I have left is cleaning my station."

"I appreciate having Mondays at the rescue, it revives my spirit to know I'm helping those dogs find a forever home. I'll throw a load of dirty towels in the washer." Bria stretched her back.

"How are things going at the rescue? You know you can always bring the dogs here. We have a better setup."

"It was only two cocker mixes. Poor dogs need a loving home." Bria patted his brother's arm. "This week's schedule is full. What's next week's look like?"

"Monster big." Aaron flexed his shoulders as he stood straighter. "We can handle it. Remember, January slows way down, and we'll be begging for a schedule like this." Aaron patted her arm as the doorbell rang. The distinctive odor of skunk permeated the space as a black standard poodle walked beside his owner, who had a hanky to his nose.

Bria pinched her nose while Aaron waved a hand in front of his face. "Woo wee, Royal, where have you been?"

A middle-aged man signaled for Royal to sit. "His friendliness wasn't well received. My wife said you could fix this." Mr. Wright's mournful expression relaxed with Aaron's thumbs up.

"Sure thing." Aaron took the leash and held it away from his body. "Royal, come on back." He led him to the bathing area as his owner left.

Bria threw the towels in the washer before pulling her high stool up to the counter and clicking on the accounting program. She was behind on balancing the books for last month. The bell rang before she could even look at the spreadsheet.

A tall man entered, attempting to drag a large dog into the room. *Possibly a lab, collie, and... I don't know what. What a tangled mess. This'll be a challenge.* Bria covered her smile as she noticed how the owner's mussy blonde hair fell across his forehead. *Thirtyish, not a gym rat like Aaron. So cute. Stop it, Bria.*

The brown mass stumbled partway inside, then froze. His owner grabbed the dog around its middle and tugged. A whine split the air as the dog planted his feet and sniffed the air.

Bria approached the pair and addressed the dog in a gentle voice. "Hello, fella, look what I have for you?" She held the dog treat near his nose, then stepped back a few feet, and the canine followed. Once inside, she gave him the treat and held her hand out for him to smell. After he sniffed it, she rubbed between his hair-covered eyes.

"How are you doing, boy? You look familiar." Her hands moved under his chin. The speckled-brown dog snuggled close, and his tongue hung out in contentment.

Bria looked up at the owner as she gave the dog a final pat on the head. "How can I help you today?"

"You already have." His eyes held a smile. "Brownie needs a bath and a haircut."

Bria went behind the counter, Brownie followed. "Hey, boy, I need to get your daddy's name." The big dog reclined on the floor at her feet as she found the new client form on the computer.

"Marc Graham, and I'm not his daddy. No way. I doubt he considers me his friend. My son, Tyler, is his owner. They're best buds."

"I'm Bria, I'll need some basic information." She caught him staring at her before he glanced at Brownie. A warmth rather than a shiver spread over her from his gaze. *Let it go, Bria.*

"And what have you done with the monster?" he said. "I have never seen him this calm."

"Well, I'm no dog-whisperer. He may revert to terror once I take him back to groom him." She wiggled the computer's mouse. After gathering the basics from him, she stared at the screen for a moment.

"Claremont Street." Bria glanced up to find his sapphire eyes looking back.

Butterflies did aerobics in her stomach. Directing her gaze at the computer again, she said, "I'm your neighbor. My house is up the block from you. Doesn't Delores Carter live there?"

"You know my grandmother?" He pushed stray hairs off his forehead and grinned at her.

"She brought me cookies when I moved in a few years ago. My house used to belong to her best friend. When I'm out running, I stop and talk with her if she's out in the yard tending her flowers. Tyler must be the little red-headed boy I saw walking with her to the ice cream truck last night."

"Yeah, I wish that truck wouldn't come by at all. Sugary treats make him hyper. Too much makes him throw up."

"My mom felt the same way about ice cream trucks. My siblings and I suspect that's why my parents moved to the family farm when my grandparents passed." They shared a grin. Then she typed in his cell number and email. "Now, is he allergic to anything?"

"Have no idea." Marc's embarrassed smile was endearing. She scrolled to the next screen.

"Has he ever been groomed before?"

Marc looked down at his charge. "It's a good possibility. I've tried three other groomers, and he's never gotten past the door. He's a rescue, they shaved him down before we got him."

"I volunteer as a groomer at Bowwow rescue. I love giving them an extra advantage to find a forever home. Did you get Brownie there?" Bria made notes in the comment section, then leaned down and patted Brownie's head. The sweet, trusting look that glimmered in his brown eyes reminded her of her prize-winning collie, Clarence.

"Maybe, Grammie and Tyler picked him out together. I don't recall where. His hair grew out so thick and tangly in a matter of weeks."

"Let's take him back and see how he does." She opened the half-door separating the front waiting room from the rest of the shop. "Let's go, boy." He stood to follow. She gave a professional smile to Marc. "We give new clients a tour. Helps them feel more comfortable leaving their babies with us."

Marc followed Bria to the grooming area. Brownie stood like a stone. Marc tugged and coaxed until he'd pulled the canine skidding on his paws a few steps. Then Brownie plopped on the floor and refused to move.

"I'm so sorry." Embarrassment colored his neck. He tugged the leash, and the dog stretched his head over his paws and moaned. She held her laugh in check. The poor guy was trying too hard to be in control.

"It's fine." Bria took the leash and nodded. She sat on the floor and petted the giant dog. "Come on, Brownie, you can do this."

"Want to bet?" Marc crossed his arms and scowled at his dog.

"I learned a few tricks from my brother that always calm the most terrified beasts."

A few extra treats didn't hurt.

"I hate to use a muzzle or ask owners to sedate their pets." She stroked Brownie between the eyes. "The extra time loving on them beforehand often works wonders."

She looked up at Marc and caught him staring again. She pointed. "See the tattooed muscle man in the bathing room? That's my brother, Aaron. We own the shop." Usually, the sight of Aaron kept the interested guys at bay. Dating was way off her life radar.

After a few minutes more of Bria's loving attention, Brownie rose and walked beside her. Marc flanked his dog.

Bria stroked Brownie's fur. "I'll take him back to the bathing room. Once he's clean we'll have to shave him down again. Then his nails need clipping. Let's make his first visit positive and simple. Combing out these tangles would be a nightmare for him."

***

Marc tried to keep his mouth from falling open. The confidence in her voice as she chatted with the troublemaker impressed him. The dog stood transfixed, staring up at Bria. Brunette tendrils framed her face as she patted the dog. When Brownie leaped onto her grooming table, Marc shook his head.

Bria fastened the safety collar for the table around his neck. "You're getting ahead of me, boy." She laughed and pressed a button that lowered the table.

"Now that you've test-driven the table, let's get to that bath." She unhooked the safety collar and Brownie came to her side.

"This might take a while." She ran her fingers over the dog, then pointed toward the door. "I'm estimating about three hours. Most people pick their pets up later."

"Three hours?"

"Takes time to make him beautiful." Bria stroked Brownie's head.

"Okay, that'll give me time to get Scooter, I mean Tyler, from school and get a few groceries. Since it's just me and Tyler Brownie has really helped calm him. And he won't want to be away from his friend for very long.." Marc opened the half-door and closed it. From his vantage point, he could take in her tall curvy form and pert nose. When her eyes caught his, he grinned.

Bria frowned for a nanosecond, then gave a bright smile and made a shooing gesture. "Go on. I promise to take good care of him."

Marc nodded and walked out of the grooming shop, his mind fixated on her green eyes. Two blocks away he halted. "Oh, man. My car's back there." He walked nonchalantly back to Doggie Designer Duo and slid into his car. *Hope no one saw that.* He stared at the sign before backing out of his space. *She's beautiful and a dog lover.*

Marc shook his head. Beautiful on the outside didn't mean beautiful on the inside. His late wife's image haunted him as he pulled out of the parking space. Her looks had drawn him in and ruined his life. Marc glanced at the dash clock and headed to Tyler's school.

Brownie's presence helped his son cope and rest at night. But the mongrel's misbehavior added to Marc's anxiety. *Maybe Bria'll be the one to tame that monster.* He smiled as he pulled up in front of Tyler's school.

ACKNOWLEDGMENTS

I am thankful for those who were my Beta Readers in the first and second edition of this novel. I'm especially grateful to Paige Jenkins, who has taken this leap with me into self-publishing. Without your expertise in all things techy, this would not be possible. Thank you, Pegg Thomas, for encouraging me to re-release this book. Thank you, Charley, my patient husband who is so supportive when I'm in the writing zone. Most importantly, I thank my Jesus for giving me the gift of words and comforting me when I'm not sure I want to do this anymore.

ABOUT THE AUTHOR

Cindy Ervin Huff is an Award-winning author of Historical and Contemporary Romance. She loves infusing hope into her stories of broken people. She's addicted to reading and chocolate. Her idea of a vacation is visiting historical sites and an ideal date with her hubby of almost fifty years would be the theater. Visit her website www.cindyervinhuff.com

Or on social media:
https://www.facebook.com/author.huff11
https://www.instagram.com/cindyervinhuff/
https://twitter.com/Cindyhuff11Huff
https://www.tiktok.com/@cindyehuff

Made in the USA
Monee, IL
21 June 2023

36018784R00142